ROOTS
OF
MY FEARS

Edited by
GEMMA AMOR

Also available from Titan Books

FANTASY
Rogues
Wonderland: An Anthology
Hex Life: Wicked New Tales of Witchery
Cursed: An Anthology
Vampires Never Get Old: Tales With Fresh Bite
A Universe of Wishes: A We Need Diverse Books Anthology
At Midnight: 15 Beloved Fairy Tales Reimagined
Twice Cursed: An Anthology
The Other Side of Never: Dark Tales from the World of Peter & Wendy
Mermaids Never Drown: Tales to Dive For
The Secret Romantic's Book of Magic

CRIME
Dark Detectives: An Anthology of Supernatural Mysteries
Exit Wounds
Invisible Blood
Daggers Drawn
Black is the Night
Ink and Daggers
Death Comes at Christmas: Tales of Seasonal Malice

SCIENCE FICTION
Dead Man's Hand: An Anthology of the Weird West
Wastelands: Stories of the Apocalypse
Wastelands 2: More Stories of the Apocalypse
Infinite Stars
Infinite Stars: Dark Frontiers
Out of the Ruins
Multiverses: An Anthology of Alternate Realities
Reports from the Deep End: Stories Inspired by J. G. Ballard
Revolution in the Heart

HORROR
Dark Cities
New Fears: New Horror Stories by Masters of the Genre
New Fears 2: Brand New Horror Stories by Masters of the Macabre
Phantoms: Haunting Tales from the Masters of the Genre
When Things Get Dark
Dark Stars
Isolation: The Horror Anthology
Christmas and Other Horrors
Bound in Blood

THRILLER
In These Hallowed Halls: A Dark Academia Anthology
These Dreaming Spires: A Dark Academia Anthology

ROOTS
OF
MY FEARS

Edited by
GEMMA AMOR

TITAN BOOKS

Roots of My Fears
Print edition ISBN: 9781803369365
E-book edition ISBN: 9781803369372

Published by Titan Books
A division of Titan Publishing Group Ltd
144 Southwark Street, London SE1 0UP
www.titanbooks.com

First edition: September 2025
10 9 8 7 6 5 4 3 2 1

This is a work of fiction. All of the characters, organizations, and events portrayed in this novel are either products of the author's imagination or are used fictitiously. Any resemblance to actual persons, living or dead (except for satirical purposes), is entirely coincidental.

FOREWORD © Gemma Amor 2025
LAMB HAD A LITTLE MARY © Elena Sichrovsky 2025
THE HOUSE THAT GABRIEL BUILT © Nuzo Onoh 2025
THE FACES AT PINE DUNES © Ramsey Campbell 1980. Originally published in *New Tales of the Cthulhu Mythos*, 1980. Reprinted by permission of the author.
IN SILENCE, IN DYING, IN DARK © Caleb Weinhardt 2025
ONE OF THOSE GIRLS © Premee Mohammed 2025
JURACÁN © Gabino Iglesias 2025
THE SAINT IN THE MOUNTAIN © Nadia El-Fassi 2025
CREPUSCULAR © Hailey Piper 2021. Originally published in *Far From Home: An Anthology of Adventure Horror*, 2021. Reprinted by permission of the author
LAAL ANDHI © Usman T. Malik 2014. Originally published in *Truth or Dare*, 2014. Reprinted by permission of the author.
UNSEWN © Ai Jiang 2025
TO FORGET AND BE FORGOTTEN © Adam Nevill 2009. Originally published in *Exotic Gothic 3: Strange Visitations*, 2009. Reprinted by permission of the author.
THE WOODS © Erika T. Wurth 2025
THE VETERAN © V. Castro 2025
CHALK BONES © Sarah Deacon 2025

The authors assert the moral right to be identified as the author of this work.

No part of this publication may be reproduced, stored in a retrieval system, or transmitted, in any form or by any means without the prior written permission of the publisher, nor be otherwise circulated in any form of binding or cover other than that in which it is published and without a similar condition being imposed on the subsequent purchaser.

A CIP catalogue record for this title is available from the British Library.

EU RP (for authorities only)
eucomply OÜ, Pärnu mnt. 139b-14, 11317 Tallinn, Estonia
hello@eucompliancepartner.com, +3375690241

Designed and typeset in Adobe Caslon Pro by Richard Mason.

Printed and bound by CPI (UK) Ltd, Croydon, CR0 4YY.

CONTENTS

Foreword *Gemma Amor* 7

Lamb had a Little Mary *Elena Sichrovsky* 11

The House that Gabriel Built *Nuzo Onoh* 21

The Faces at Pine Dunes *Ramsey Campbell* 45

In Silence, in Dying, in Dark
    Caleb Weinhardt 93

One Of Those Girls *Premee Mohamed* 101

Juracán *Gabino Iglesias* 125

The Saint in the Mountain *Nadia El-Fassi* 133

Crepuscular *Hailey Piper* 153

Laal Andhi *Usman T. Malik* 175

The Woods *Erika T. Wurth* 205

UNSEWN *Ai Jiang*	225
TO FORGET AND BE FORGOTTEN *Adam Nevill*	241
THE VETERAN *V. Castro*	273
CHALK BONES *Sarah Deacon*	293
Acknowledgements	311
About the authors	313
About the editor	319

FOREWORD

"Root" is a powerful word, and an even more powerful natural phenomenon. Charles and Francis Darwin theorised that roots, in a botanical sense, act like a brain, dictating how plants grow, move and behave and how their cells communicate with each other. Their theory was seen as revolutionary biology and is wonderfully applicable as a human allegory. My own roots determined the current version of me; how I act, think, move and grow, like some strange, organic, time-travelling magic based on consequence, for roots also ignore the traditional constraints of time. They stretch into the past and weave through the present and the future.

When I think of roots now, I mostly think of reasons to stay.

Those reasons anchor me to this earth with hopeful tendrils and fibres spreading out through the soil of lived experiences. Or maybe the roots are the memories of those experiences, each one stubbornly tied to this

life. Without them, we are unmoored, drifting, lost. My roots kept me here when I no longer wished to slog through the daily struggles. When my brain told me I wanted to die, my roots nourished me and helped me to grow stronger, fitter, more present. I have these little tubers of obligation, and purpose, and love, and duty, affection, and history, causes that snake through and around everything I do and all who live in my world.

They aren't all healthy, these connective ties. Some of them have withered and rotted in the ground, but I remain attached, even though I do not live where I was planted. Like so many of us who hated where they grew up, I got out of that dying market town at eighteen and never looked back. The sky feels larger and heavier there, the land too flat. The town decays and shops in the centre around the once busy marketplace are empty, metal sheets fixed across the windows to prevent break-ins. I sometimes wonder what my life would look like if I had stayed. Would I be writing or editing books?

The connective family root has not fully shrivelled. Every now and then, there is this little tug on my soul, and I find myself 'home'. It is always as depressing and exhausting as I imagined it would be, even though some good memories remain.

These are also my roots: a pair of headstones in a cemetery, carved with my grandparents' names, who raised me. My mother, who refuses to move from our

hometown. The bus back takes me past my old school before it drops me near my childhood house. Primary roots, without which, I would not exist. I both love and loathe them.

Which got me thinking about ancestry, about a sense of place, about what it feels like to be rooted in a culture, a tradition, a family, chosen or inherited; prejudice, love. Or, what it feels like to be uprooted, transitory, confused. Horror is the perfect playground for such explorations: it is a genre highly bound in identity, in existential explorations, in matters of belonging, or of being alone. The stories in this anthology, *Roots of My Fears*, portray some of those ideas in masterful fashion, from writers you've heard of and a few you perhaps have not. The roots pushing insistently through these pages tell of family dynamics, meaningful places, journeys of identity, death, birth, loss, pain, gain, shame. Customs and lore, traditions and superstitions. Bones, blood, scales, fur and teeth. Hauntings of an intimate and highly personal nature. Monstrous things made of grief, of hate, of regret, of hunger. I am extraordinarily proud of what we've created here, and the breadth of stories we've been able to tell. I hope you enjoy this assortment of magical, and at times, devastatingly beautiful, horror fiction as much as I enjoyed putting it together. I hope that during a time where many of us are searching for meaning in a life that seems fraught and frightening and

overwhelming, a reminder of where we've come from, for better or for worse, can provide some comfort as we try to grow towards the light, no matter how scant. The roots will keep us firm and steady. The roots will provide.

GEMMA AMOR
March, 2025

LAMB HAD A LITTLE MARY

ELENA SICHROVSKY

Lamb had a little Mary, with cheeks as white as snow.

And everywhere that Lamb went, Mary was sure to go.

Lamb never roamed far into the forest, but wherever she walked on her long legs Mary had to run to keep up. Lamb told Mary that one day her body would sprout legs just as long and spindly. Someday, she would be taller than the berry bushes; someday, she would look just like Lamb, with those big, shadow-rimmed eyes and sour breath.

The only place Mary was not allowed to follow was the cellar. Some nights Lamb would go down there and open a spigot of rage and let it rush into her mouth, like a flaming red colony of ants. Mary would sit on the edge of her bed and wait and wait until Lamb came back up the stairs, wobbling on those long, bendy legs.

Mary always knew when Lamb had been to the cellar because she felt fire from Lamb's tummy when she laid her head there to rest. She felt warm droplets hit her dress when Lamb pissed herself while tucking Mary in bed. She felt heat from Lamb's snores when she fell asleep beside her, heavy arms splayed across Mary's thin bones.

The one thing that still felt cold was the light from the window. Lamb always forgot to put the paper-cut stars on the glass pane, so the night became one giant black eye that never cried or even blinked. Even when Mary closed her eyes, she could feel the chill creeping through her eyelids.

The next morning Lamb opened her mouth and last night's dinner came pouring out for breakfast.

Mary was still hungry, so she went out into the forest and plucked black pearls off the throat of a chokeberry bush. Chokeberries had magic because of their ruby-midnight color. She whispered a secret to each berry before pushing it between her teeth. She told the first one that sometimes, in her dreams, Lamb acted more like Wolf, except Wolf wasn't real; it only lived inside storybook spines. She told the last berry that she wished for another Mary. They could be little together; they could push Lamb's sleeping body off the bed and watch the paper stars shine forever.

The last chokeberry must have had the most powerful magic, because it listened to her. By winter Lamb's legs grew much fatter and Mary heard knocking from inside when she put an ear to her swollen tummy. Lamb slept longer, read fewer stories at bedtime, and sometimes didn't return from the cellar until morning.

One day the tummy-knocking stopped and the crying started.

Then Mary met Tiny.

Tiny was wrinklier and pinker than Mary. Tiny cried at the sun when it set and cried when it rose. Tiny even cried at the moon. Sometimes, when Mary told Tiny about the chokeberry that had granted her wish, Tiny stopped crying.

Lamb looked strange now. Parts of her chest looked longer, like bells with pink ends that Tiny would grab and suck at. Mary was hungry too, but Lamb said only Tiny could drink from the bells of white cream and sweet smell. Mary wanted to go out and find more chokeberries, but now the ground wore ice dresses and glass shoes and Mary was afraid to slip into their dizzying dance, so she sat by the window and licked wet mist off the shivering glass instead.

Then Lamb's pink bells stopped ringing.

Tiny cried and cried until her little mouth grew cherry red, but there was nothing left to drink. Lamb went back to the cellar and Mary waited and watched Tiny thrashing in her cradle. After some time, when Lamb did not return, Mary put a spot of spit on her finger and laid it between

Tiny's lips. There were no teeth, just soft elastic gums sucking at her fingertip.

One night, Lamb came back from the cellar and her legs were dancing so hard and fast that when she spun, she flung Mary across the room. Mary hit her head and rolled out the open door, landing in the ballroom of dark ice dresses. Snowflakes spun her into a dream that was silver at the edges and howling in the center.

Mary didn't get up for some time. She just laid there, drinking up the cold beauty like poison. Her fingers and toes disappeared and then returned, again and again like the wooden seat of a swing.

When Mary finally crawled back into the house, shivering and shaking, there was no one in the bedroom.

Mary ran around inside and outside, calling for Tiny. She wondered if the magic had run out and the chokeberries had taken Tiny back. She determined then and there that she would dig through the snow and find more chokeberries; she would tell them every secret she had, about the family of dead snails under the flowerpots and the headless monsters under her pillowcase. Anything they wanted to know, she would give them, if only they would let her have Tiny again.

Then Mary smelled a whiff of piss from below. She wasn't supposed to enter the cellar, but Tiny didn't know that. Mary had to warn her. She climbed down the staircase, one hand covering her eyes, two fingers spread far apart enough to see through the crack.

When she arrived at the cellar door it was open. Lamb was holding Tiny and pressing her little lips to the rage spigot. Mary ran over and snatched Tiny away. The fire that Lamb drank was bitter and angry, and Tiny should only have sweet things in her mouth, things laughing and white and soft-smelling.

But Lamb was angry that Mary had come to the cellar. She rose, loud and red, moving fast and dark, and she scratched Mary.

So it turned out that Lamb was part Wolf after all.

Mary took Tiny to the bed and laid down to sleep beside her. The scratch on Mary's arm burned against the blankets, so she told the scratch a story. The paper-cut stars on the dresser got up and sat around her in a glowing circle to listen, too. Mary talked about the powerful family of chokeberries that wandered the forest beyond the house, and how the magic that had given her Tiny would surely keep them safe.

But then the paper stars heard footsteps coming, got scared and ran away.

Mary saw Lamb-Wolf looming on crooked legs—a tall, faceless shadow—until she moved forward and collapsed

to sleep at their side, her unhappy mouth wide and wet with drool.

The sheets were damp when they woke up. Lamb-Wolf said that Mary had wet the bed. Mary saw the dark stain on the front of Lamb-Wolf's clothes, but didn't say anything. She washed the sheets like she was told and boiled them in the sun until they bubbled to the surface like drowned clouds.

Mary's arm still hurt where Lamb-Wolf had scratched her, so she showed her wound to the icicles hanging from the rooftop. The icicles poured little rivers onto the patch of skin, now rippling in hues of purple and green. Mary explained that the scratch had transformed into a spiral of dream-dust, just like the Northern Lights, and the icicles melted into applause, one at a time.

Lamb-Wolf was different now. Her eyes were even darker than before. Mary followed her to the bed and then down to the cellar and back to the bed, but Lamb-Wolf didn't talk to her anymore. Mary was too afraid to get scratched again, so she just watched Lamb-Wolf hold Tiny up to the spigot, watched Tiny cry all night, watched Tiny reaching in vain for Lamb-Wolf's chest bells.

Days and nights passed. The icy ballgowns of the forest went away, and the earth took out green skirts and thin brown scarves. Mary taught Tiny how to count

Lamb-Wolf's crusty yellow toes and crawl up the long bridges of Lamb-Wolf's legs. She told Tiny that soon the chokeberries would bloom again and they would know how to help. They might even fix Lamb-Wolf so that she would just be Lamb again.

༺༻

The chokeberries didn't come back in time.

They didn't stop Lamb-Wolf from dropping Tiny under a soapy tongue of bathwater. Lamb-Wolf was closing her eyes on the edge of the tub, and Tiny's mouth opened under the water, with no sound coming out. Mary got the sleeves of her dress wet when she reached in to rescue Tiny.

Then Lamb-Wolf woke up and pulled at Mary's wrist, but Mary pushed her away. She didn't want her to sleep in their bed tonight. She wanted to dream with Tiny and the paper-cut stars. So she pushed Lamb-Wolf's head into the warm bubbles of the bath, making her hair all wet and shiny. And Mary kept pushing and pushing and pushing—

—until the water stopped moving.

Tiny sat on the floor, sucking an acorn while Mary dragged Lamb-Wolf out of the bathtub and wrapped her in the bed sheets, turning her into a white log. It took a long time to pull the white log across the floor. When Mary got to the door, she shoved hard and the white log bounced down the stairs in little bunny hops.

one

two

three

Touching the back of Lamb-Wolf's head, Mary felt something wet. She tasted it, hoping for the white sweetness of the chest bells, but it smelled awful and hot and red. It didn't make her any less hungry. Lamb-Wolf didn't move. There was only the sun shining on bright grass, and swarms of black mosquitoes flying around her head, and Tiny started crying from inside the house, screechy and forever.

Mary turned around and screamed right back.

The forest stared at her, wide-eyed. Then it opened its arms and beckoned slowly.

The forest took care of Mary and Tiny. Mary ate flowers and some of her own hair and washed Tiny's dirty bottom in the river. The forest gave them a soft bed to sleep on each night. Sometimes it smelled of beetle earth, and sometimes it reeked of decaying deer, but it never smelled like Lamb-Wolf's piss.

There were huge paper-cut stars in the sky, bigger than any she'd ever seen. Mary told Tiny how the forest cut those shapes out just for them, how the trees had climbed on top of each other to make it all the way up to the sky and then used dried leaves as scissors.

The day the chokeberries finally returned, Tiny was sleeping. Mary didn't want to wake her and hear the loud crying again, so she went to talk to the berries alone. She knelt by the bush and plucked nine dark pearls off, cupping them safely in her hand.

Mary told the first berry that Tiny had learned to stand up. Tiny was getting heavier to carry, too. The noises in their tummies had become quieter but Mary could feel the bones around her chest growing hard. She talked about how they had left Lamb-Wolf behind and how she taught Tiny not to miss her.

When her voice got tired Mary whispered about the scratch on her arm that still hadn't faded; about the nights when Mary was too cold to get up and piss outside the bed; about when Tiny cried so loud that Mary stuffed crumpled leaves in her mouth to silence her.

Mary saved her most important secret for the last chokeberry.

She told it that she might be part Wolf, too.

THE HOUSE THAT GABRIEL BUILT

NUZO ONOH

I

Gabriel was the only son of an only son of an only son. That was his identity in their small close-knit village, the first thing that people thought of whenever they heard his name mentioned—*Poor man! His bloodline is cursed with the only-son hex. Who knows what demons have cursed that unfortunate family!*

These were the thoughts the villagers shared among themselves whenever they saw Gabriel in his familiar worn wrapper and granite face. Nobody could ever remember seeing the young man smile, and at just sixteen, he already had the inscrutable mien of a man three times his age. Despite his short stature and lean frame, Gabriel exuded a menacing aura that intimidated his larger-built peers.

His eyes were icy flints of suppressed rage, his chiselled features unyielding and harsh. He rarely spoke and when he did, his deep voice was as hard as his face.

Everybody knew the reason behind Gabriel's cold personae and the rage that dogged his every step. Despite his mother birthing nine children, Gabriel was the only one to have survived the notorious malignancy of their clansmen, the Onovo clan. Their fabulous wealth had always attracted the envious hearts and evil-eye of their relatives, resulting in many inexplicable and untimely deaths in their family line. The Onovo clan was known to favour poisoning as their favourite tool of elimination, closely followed by vanishings and lunacy. It no longer surprised the villagers to learn that another son of the doomed Agu family of Onovo clan had vanished overnight, stolen by the evil winds or malevolent witches. The murderous kinsmen always kept one son from the Agu family alive, to ensure the ancestors and gods wouldn't curse their own families with total annihilation and an end to their own bloodlines.

After Gabriel's father had died from a sudden blood-vomiting sickness, Gabriel had found himself at the mercy of his male relatives at the tender age of ten years. With the rest of his siblings dead, he became a helpless kitten exposed to the relentless brutality of the vicious hounds that posed as his guardians. Like ravaging vultures, his murderous kinsmen fell on his father's wealth and in little time, devoured his entire inheritance, from countless yam barns, farmlands, mud-huts, and domestic animals, to the last kennel-nut.

Consigned to a life of unremitting drudgery and savage beatings, Gabriel learned to survive by staying invisible and mute. And today was no different. From his secret place behind his mother's hut, he watched as one of his clansmen forced his lecherous way into his mother's hut just as the night fell silent, with both humans and animals deep in dream-slumber. He covered his ears with his hands to shut away his mother's anguished cries and the hoarse grunts of the man's lust. His breathing was harsh, his heart enraged and burning with hate—*Patience, Ike-wa-Agu; patience. Your time will come. It's just a matter of time… soon… soon…*

Ike-wa-Agu; that was the name his late father had given him at birth, the name by which Gabriel was known in the days of his helplessness. That was the name the kinfolk cursed as they rained vicious blows on his wiry body, leaving him so bloodied and battered that bathing and sleeping became agonising rituals. It was the name he used when he shrieked his rage at his father's grave and begged his ancestors for freedom and vengeance.

Finally, on the night of his seventeenth birthday, his late father visited his sleep with a potent message: *"Our good son, your father and forefathers have heard your cries and we will surely wipe your tears. Arise! Find your way to the shrine of the powerful medicine-man at Ukehe, he that goes by the name of Aja. Tell Aja that you're the only living son of Agu*

of Onovo clan and he will show you the way to freedom and revenge."

Gabriel awoke from the dream shivering violently and fighting the hot tears dampening his face. He was not one prone to tears, and the wetness on his cheeks stunned his body into relentless shudders. In that instant, he knew without a doubt in his heart that he had received a potent vision from his ancestors, a message from the dead. And the next day, before the rooster crowed in the dawn, Gabriel left their hamlet for the distant village of Ukehe, armed with a white chicken he stole from one of his relative's coop. By noonday, he had arrived at the famous shrine and presented the medicine-man, Aja, with his gift of the clucking white bird.

"What do you want from the shrine and the spirits it serves?" Aja asked after sacrificing the chicken and completing his divination with the oracles.

"I want to end 'the-only-son' curse in our bloodline," Gabriel said, his voice harsh with rage. "I want to regain our family wealth; I want power beyond that held by any other chief in all the villages; I want unassailable authority to annihilate my enemies with total impunity. Last but not the least, I want fame; that my name may never be forgotten in our village and across the lands. That is my wish, great medicine-man. That is my prayer to the shrine, the spirits, and the ancestors."

For several tense minutes, Aja observed Gabriel in

heavy silence from under hooded lids. Finally, he took a deep breath and exhaled heavily.

"Are you willing to make the sacrifice for your wishes?" the medicine-man finally asked, his voice quiet, yet hard. "A great favour from the spirits requires a powerful sacrifice, one beyond the blood of animals and birds. So, I ask you again, Ike-wa-Agu, only living son of Agu of Onovo clan; are you ready to make the sacrifice required for your wishes?"

Gabriel fixed the medicine-man with his icy gaze and nodded.

"I am ready, great Dibia," he said, his voice hard, his face a granite rock as he stared unflinchingly at the sharp blade in the medicine-man's hand. His body was rigid, yet, his breathing was steady, devoid of fear and uncertainty.

"Spirits, entities, ancestors, and deities, gather and bear witness to this secret gathering before your powerful presence. Let the deal be sealed in blood and your mysterious wills be done," Aja intoned in a stentorian voice.

When he was done, he leaned over and sliced Gabriel's outstretched arm with his knife.

As the blood dripped into the divination bowl, a thick fog instantly covered the room, as if several heaps of smouldering, damp wood had been stoked inside the shrine. Gabriel started to cough violently, his eyes, stung by gritty tears. And in the white fog, he saw a sight that caused him to gasp.

Three men materialised before him, three spirits whose stern faces and burning gazes left no doubt in his mind as to their identities, even before he recognised his late father among their midst—*Papa! Grandfather Agu, and Great-grandfather Agu! Amadioha have mercy! What miracle is this?*

As the thoughts fled his mind, another figure materialised next to the ghosts of his ancestors. This time, Gabriel couldn't stop the loud scream that escaped his mouth. Terror stretched his features into frozen immobility as he stared at the glowing skeletal entity whose claws flexed with rattling menace. The bone-entity was so tall that its skull touched the roof of the shrine. Its ghastly presence suddenly drenched the air with ice, freezing Gabriel's flesh right through to his bones.

He started to shiver violently as Aja fell to his knees, bowing low to the supernatural visitors. Gabriel quickly imitated the medicine-man, prostrating himself on the floor as he called out garbled greetings to the spectres in a quivery voice.

"Ike-wa-Agu, arise before your ancestors and the great deity we serve, the fearsome Ogbunabali, The Death-Lord himself." Gabriel felt goosebumps drench his skin as he heard the familiar voice of his father speak—*Ogbunabali! Ancestors have mercy! What have I gone and invoked now?*

As he stumbled to his trembling feet, bowing effusively over and over, a new voice pierced through his panicked thoughts.

"For countless moons, our family has fallen victim to the wicked machinations of our envious clan," Gabriel's grandfather now said. His voice was raspy, and Gabriel struggled to overcome his awe as he heard his grandfather's voice for the very first time—*Ancestors! So, this is what Grandfather looks like; this is what my grandfather's voice sounds like, this my ancestor I never met in the living flesh!* Once again, a delicate sliver of goosebumps doused his clammy skin. "Thanks to their evil, the Agu family has failed to multiply in great numbers to battle them effectively. As our people say, 'Igwebuike'—there is strength in numbers. They are determined to decimate our numbers and alas, you are the only one to lose your father at a very tender age," his grandfather paused and bowed his head till his jaw almost touched his chest. A heavy air of melancholy hung over him and Gabriel felt the unfamiliar tears sting his eyelids again.

"To protect our last bloodline, your precious self, we convened in the realm of the ancestors and decided to yoke our souls to the powerful deity of death, the fearsome Ogbunabali, He in whose mighty presence you now stand," Gabriel's great-grandfather took over and once again, his body shivered in awe as he listened. "With the mighty death deity on our side, we can conquer and decimate our enemies. You will live to break the hex of the only son that has afflicted our family through countless moons. I already pledged my soul and the soul of every first daughter of the Agu family to the goddess of wealth, the mighty Njoku.

This pact was sealed a long time ago, before the birth of your grandfather. Therefore, no matter what those viper-kinsmen do, wealth will always flow in our bloodline as the beneficiaries of Njoku's benevolence. So, have no fears, good son. With The Death-Lord now on our side, you have a battalion before you to fight your battles. I will give you the secret to our wealth, but first, pledge your soul and the souls of your sons to the great Ogbunabali, right to the eighth generation. With your pledge, The Death-Lord will ensure that our hamlet will never die and our bloodline will live to expand through the endless moons. Now, pledge your allegiance to the great Ogbunabali."

Gabriel's head expanded and contracted as tiny dots of terror layered his skin. He fell to his knees once again and bowed his head even lower, breathing hard and fast. An icy wind burnt his skin and he sensed the close presence of the hulking skeleton. Something reached into his chest, a freezing claw, searing him in icy agony. He screamed as his knees buckled, sending him sprawling on the hard, red-mud floor of the shrine. He was sure he was dying, that the death deity had ripped out his heart in its bloody entirety. But when he reached his hand to his exposed chest, he felt nothing but the clean hard surface of his muscled chest, devoid of the wet warmth of blood.

A squelching sound drew his attention. He looked up and saw The Death-Lord chomping the raw flesh of his bloodied, pulsating heart—*Ancestors! Oh, my ancestors!*

I'm dying... dying. Even as the thoughts left his mind, Ogbunabali vanished, swallowed in a blink by the thick swirl of smoky air. Once again, Gabriel was left kneeling before his ancestors, his breathing harsh and loud like a person fleeing a pride of lions.

"Return and fulfil your destiny, good son," his father spoke to him in his hollow-sounding voice. Gabriel wondered if his father's voice had always sounded this empty, just like an echo. But it had been so long since he last heard his father speak that he could no longer remember how his voice had sounded in his lifetime. "Remember the numbers eight and four. Those are the destiny-numbers of our bloodline. Eight is our ultimate destiny-number but must be reached in rituals of fours. Teach your children the sacred numbers, that they too will share them with their children to the eighth generation when our contracts with both the wealth and death deities come to an end. We leave you now to carve out your destiny, our good son. This is your time. Live it well."

And his ancestors vanished, just as Ogbunabali had done, and once again, Gabriel found himself with the medicine-man in the now smokeless shrine, fighting the warm tears that flowed involuntarily down his face—*Finally! Oh great ancestors! My time has finally come! Vengeance, I call to you now! Come swiftly to me! Bring with you black coffins filled with corpse flies, grave worms, and bone-beetles, so that nothing, not a single hair, will be left of our*

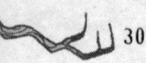

enemies by the time I'm done with them! Great Ogbunabali, your eager servant will be your tool in this earthly realm and will feed you enough souls to satisfy your appetite for eternity.

By the time Gabriel arrived back at his village later that evening, the sun was already down and his relatives were brimming with anger at his unusual absence. As they approached him with menace, Gabriel felt a rage as he had never felt in his entire life—*Enough! Today, your reign of terror ends, you vile bastards!*

From his enraged mind, Gabriel cursed them with the insanity of self-immolation and the dishonour of self-degradation. Even as the thoughts fled his mind, his four kinsmen started to tear the robes from their bodies with maddened hands, exposing themselves to the stunned gazes of the women and children. As the villagers quickly gathered in response to the panicked shrieks coming from the Onovo hamlets, two of the naked men started to slice off their own penises with sharp blades, their agonised screams as deafening as those of their gawking families.

Gabriel stared at them in silent rage, his body as still as a statue. He was filled with the fearsome new powers of the death deity, and his thirst for blood was great—*Spill your evil, you disgusting bastards! Confess your wickedness before the people, then end your vile lives with your own hands.* With each thought that left Gabriel's mind, his four clansmen obeyed his commands with catatonic savagery.

"I poisoned Gabriel's two younger brothers with the tainted peanuts I gave them on their way to the stream," the first man shrieked in a pain-filled voice as he started to hack his torso with his knife. "I squashed Gabriel's widowed mother in lust on too many nights to recall and confiscated her clothes for my wives' use."

Even as the gathered villagers gasped in horror, the man fell to the ground, bleeding his life away into the sandy soil, his severed penis lying limp by his side. Soon, the other three kinsmen began to confess their own abominations before annihilating themselves as Gabriel's silent thoughts ordered. One doused himself in kerosene and set himself on fire; the other poured the entire contents of his hidden jar of poison down his throat, the same poison with which he had killed Gabriel's father all those years gone. The final kinsman, the leader of the band of thieving relatives, started eating his own severed penis before the horrified gazes of the villagers. Those that tried to stop him were shoved away with brutal force, even as tears continued to roll down the man's face as he ate his unholy dinner, his mouth coated in blood and snot, his body trembling violently in feverish anguish.

Just before he collapsed into unconsciousness, his petrified gaze met Gabriel's fiery glare. In that instance, he knew that Gabriel would never offer him the escape of death. He was now an Ọdindu-Ọwu-Kamma, the living that is better off dead.

In the chaos and terror engulfing the hamlet, nobody noticed Gabriel in his silent immobility—save his stunned mother and his younger cousin, Dozie, the last son of the unconscious lead kinsman lying on the ground in his naked mutilation. Dozie was known in the village to spread juicy and unsavoury stories filled with half-truths, and when he later claimed that Gabriel's eyes had glowed a brilliant blue hue as the kinfolk were annihilated, his story was received as truth by half of the villagers. The other half cursed his wild imagination with robust derision.

But not for long.

By the time Gabriel's imposing mansion sprung up overnight on the vast hamlet where the numerous huts of his late ancestors and relatives had once stood, they too became believers. But by then, it was too late. Like a colossal monster with an endless appetite, the house that Gabriel built began to demand its unholy feast and soon, it dawned on the villagers that they were no longer humans, but helpless prey to an invisible evil that now hulked over them in its majestic and terrifying beauty.

II

Magdalene stared at the imposing stone-brick mansion belonging to her new husband's family with awe-widened eyes—Ulọ-Gabriel! *Holy Mother! I can't believe that I'm actually looking at* Ulọ-Gabriel, *the house that Gabriel built!*

Once again, she pinched herself, wincing softly as her fingers pierced the pale skin of her exposed arm. Her wide eyes took in the gargantuan structure that had been one of the wonders of creation in the country for over five decades since it was first built by her late father-in-law, Gabriel, a man rumoured to have sold his soul to the devil. Even at the catholic secondary school she had attended, the reverend sisters used Gabriel and his incredible house as an example of the diabolical works of Satan and his evil minions.

Now, as she studied the high turrets, pointed arches, spires, stained-glass windows, gables, and decorated stone masonry, Magdalene knew that there must have been some truths in the stories she had heard about the infamous building—*Surely, no mortal hands could have built this house in this country, not even the magical hands of the colonial masters! No wonder the villagers couldn't burn it down during the famed* Day of Disturbance.

Again, Magdalene shuddered as her mind frantically tried to retrieve every tiny bit of gossip that she'd heard about *Ulọ-Gabriel* in her nineteen years of existence. Rumour had it that the mysterious villager, Gabriel, had annihilated his entire kinsmen in a single day before confiscating their properties and lands for himself. They said that due to some hex, Gabriel was an only son of an only son of an only son. Yet, by the time he died, he had eight living sons and one daughter, who had died a mysterious death in her sleep.

Incredibly, all the sons were twin births, an unheard-of occurrence in the village. In just four pregnancies, Gabriel's late wife had succeeded in birthing eight living sons. Another strange thing was that each of the eight sons was named Gabriel. Magdalene's new husband was Gabriel-8, and she was the eighth and final bride to be brought into the notorious mansion said to have been built by demons. But more fantastical was the fact that all the Gabriels were born with deformed eyes, a black right eye and a blue left eye. Magdalene always struggled to hide an involuntary shudder each time she met the unsettling gaze of her new groom.

Village lore had it that nobody ever saw the stonemasons that built Gabriel's imposing house. The villagers would go to sleep every night, only to wake up to a new addition to the huge structure. Until *Ulọ-Gabriel* came into existence, nobody ever knew that a hut could grow like a tree, reaching so high into the sky that it dwarfed a palm-tree. But that was exactly what Gabriel's four-storey house did. Even when the villagers tried to stay awake and catch the invisible builders, they claimed a strange lethargy overtook them at the stroke of midnight, as if they were drugged by the invisible mist that always shrouded their village at that unholy hour. And in the morning, when they staggered from their huts, bleary-eyed like people suffering a Palmwine hangover, they would behold yet another major addition to the house, which continued to grow and rise till it reached its towering four-storey height.

Magdalene had heard from her classmates that *Ulọ-Gabriel* was built by the entire members of the occupying colonial forces, whose bodies were possessed by the ghosts of all the murdered sons of the Agu clan. They said that the hexed white colonists were stolen from their beds every night and transported by fearsome beasts on great wings to build the stupendous stone-brick house. They were later returned to their houses at the crack of dawn, tired, bruised, filthy, and dazed, unable to recount where they had been or what they had done.

And when the house was almost completed, villagers claimed to see it ablaze at exactly eight o'clock every night, with dazzling lights and wild drumming, even though there was no electricity in their remote village and the unfinished building was unoccupied. Rumour had it that the blazing electricity and drumming lasted for the final eight nights before the completion of the house and in those eight nights, eight villagers vanished, never again to be seen. Their families claimed to have seen them walking into *Ulọ-Gabriel* like hexed goats, drawn by an invisible and malignant force they could neither ignore nor resist. They never came out of the house once they entered, and yet, every search of the property failed to reveal the missing men.

The villagers concluded that their blood had been used to mix their flesh into the cement that glued the monstrously glorious house together. In their rage over their missing relatives, the villagers staged the famous riot known as *The*

Day of Disturbance. On that fateful day, the entire population rose as one and marched with their torched woods and kerosene jars to burn down *Ulọ-Gabriel* and put an end to the deadly menace lurking inside the cursed house.

They say that Gabriel had stood in front of his gate watching their approach, an inscrutable smile on his granite face. He even opened the gates for the chanting villagers and waved them in. And when they finally doused the house in kerosene and set it aflame, the heavy stones used in its construction swallowed the flames, glowed an unearthly blood-hue, before spitting the fire straight back at its attackers.

Magdalene heard that a countless number of villagers died in front of the gleeful house on that fateful day, writhing on the floor as their burning bodies roasted underneath the blazing sun. And inside the house, the sound of manic drumming could be heard, invisible hands beating a macabre rhythm unknown to the villagers, a sound that filled them with terror as they abandoned the compound and scattered to every corner of the village. By the time the dead were buried, the entire population were finally cowered. Nobody ever went near the building again, not even when it was finally completed in its majestic glory.

As Magdalene gawked at the eight clock-like mouldings sculptured onto each of the eight spires atop *Ulọ-Gabriel*, it suddenly dawned on her that she was seeing a distinct pattern in the formidable structure, something that would elude a less discerning gaze. What she had thought were random decors were actually built in a distinctive order. Everything in the house was constructed in double sets of fours, from the arched stained-glass windows to the triangular gables on each floor of the four-storey mansion. Even the numbers on the clock-like decorations on the pinnacles ended at eight.

Suddenly, something, an inexplicable knowing, told her that when she finally stepped foot inside the building, she would find that the rooms were equally in sets of fours, all equalling the number eight she now saw on the incomplete clocks—*Sweet Mary! What is the meaning of these signs? Are they occultic signs, some demonic numbers perhaps? Holy Mary have mercy on my soul!*

Magdalene shuddered, as once again, she allowed her mind to recall the final bit of lore she had heard about the infamous building. They said that Gabriel died on the very day he completed his stupendous mansion and the only time he entered the house he built was on the day he died—as a corpse. His body was laid out inside one of the eight massive living rooms at his wake, which was only attended by his immediate family members and a handful of brave villagers whose curiosity overwhelmed their terror of the cursed house and its fearsome owner. Even more astonishing, a singular white man, said to have owned the reddest hair and bluest eyes on any human, attended the burial. Nobody knew who the white man was; nobody knew how Gabriel had forged a relationship with a white person, not even the white man himself, who had stared at Gabriel's corpse in silence with a dazed expression on his face. He left as soon as he saw Gabriel's body and was never seen again.

That was also the last time Gabriel was ever seen. By morning, his corpse had vanished, supposedly taken away by the demons he had sold his soul to. There was no grave hosting his body even though his family had constructed a huge white mausoleum inscribed with his name to convince the world that his corpse still existed. The plaque bore the famed epitaph:

"Here lies Gabriel, only surviving son of Agu of Onovo clan.
Father of eight sons and a proud son of Ukari village.
He departed the world at the unready age of 35 years.
May the ancestors welcome his soul with pride."

Some villagers wondered why his family failed to use his known name of Ike-wa-Agu instead of the foreign name of Gabriel, a name nobody knew how, where, or why it was acquired. Even Gabriel's death was shrouded in mystery. All the villagers knew was that they saw him strong and hearty the day before he died. In fact, they would recall that it was the first time they had seen the usually stone-faced enigma laugh out loud, although the sound of his unfamiliar laughter set chills of dread in them rather than cheer. It sounded more like a sinister cackle than genuine mirth, a mocking crow filled with icy malignancy and menace.

Gabriel had walked around every corner of the village greeting the stunned villagers, smiling and laughing and even shaking hands with those brave enough to make physical contact with him. Yet, by the next day, he was dead, and with his death came the sudden deaths of eight villagers, eight strong young men who had retired to bed the previous night in perfect health but failed to come out of their rooms the next day.

Once again, tongues wagged, yet nothing was done. Even in death, Gabriel continued to rule the village with the same icy grip of terror that had been his trademark in life. The villagers never forgot that all it took was a look from Gabriel's icy eyes to send an enemy to a self-inflicted death. And now, Gabriel's eight sons occupied the infamous house he built with their wives and children. The villagers prayed fervently that none of them had yoked themselves to the same diabolical powers that had possessed their father's soul, despite the cursed hue of their eyes.

As Magdalene recalled all the unsavoury stories about her new husband's infamous family, she felt a sudden shudder overwhelm her body—*Sweet Mother Mary! I've now joined the damned fraternity of this accursed house! But, why? Why me? Why did Reverend Mother Elizabeth Rose accept Gabriel-8's proposal and send me into this very house she had deemed as the devil's handiwork? Is it because of the stupendous money the family paid to the school or is it because I'm a tainted orphan whom nobody will ever marry, unless it's somebody like Gabriel-8, whose name is as cursed as mine?*

Magdalene had always been aware of her unsavoury antecedent, the fact that her mother was a witchdoctor who had been seduced by the white priest that had come to convert her to the foreign Christian religion. Their villagers had lynched her mother when Magdalene was born with the fair skin and silky hair of the white people. They would have killed the infant if they didn't fear the repercussions from the gunpowder of the colonists. Instead, they had dumped her at the small, white-washed church-bungalow inhabited by her real father. The priest in turn had abandoned her with the nuns who raised her in the convent until she became an assistant teacher in the convent school. It was no secret that no decent man would marry this bastard of a traitorous witchdoctor and a white priest, save a man like Gabriel-8, the last son of the fearsome hermit who built the most infamous house in the entire country, if not the world.

"Good wife, why do you tarry? Hurry and enter your new house," Gabriel-8 called out to Magdalene, motioning her inside with a nod. His mismatched blue-black eyes seemed to see right through her thoughts and Magdalene gave a nervous smile as she started to comply.

A figure materialised before her, a towering woman with the darkest skin and fiercest face littered with carved

Nsibidi inscriptions. The suddenness of her appearance, coupled with a sizzling, unearthly energy in her fiery gaze told Magdalene that she was in the presence of a powerful spectre. The ghost barred her entrance, its arms wide, eyes glowing. Magdalene stumbled back, her heart pounding so hard she thought she would faint—*Mother Mary! Oh, Mother Mary…*

"Daughter, listen to your blood-mother and obey," the ghost said in a booming voice that reverberated inside her head like drums. "Do not enter into this house without first seeking the permission of the owner. Otherwise, you do so at your own risk. Pledge your soul right now to Gabriel that he may let you into his house without malice."

The spectre vanished before Magdalene could catch her breath. When next she heard her husband call her name, she almost collapsed from shock. Then, sudden rage overtook her—*Pledge my soul to a pagan? Never! Ha! My mother indeed! Just another savage pagan entity doing the bidding of her kind.* She quickly raised her hand to the rosaries she wore around her neck, stroking the beads with frantic fingers—*Oh, sweet Mother Mary, I call on you to come to the aid of your daughter and save me from whatever satanic and pagan forces that reside inside this accursed house. I ask this in the holy name of your beloved son, Jesus Christ, Amen!*

With a strong resolve, Magdalene took a deep breath, squared her shoulders, and stepped into the house that Gabriel built.

A fury-wind like nothing she had ever experienced came at her with such force that it knocked her out. The wind seemed to wear a shadowy human form, and as darkness stole her consciousness, she thought she saw a smirking face carved of cold granite. It leered at her with black icy eyes and before she could scream, a new visage superimposed itself over it, a white face with the reddest hair and terrified blue eyes that wept endless tears of sorrow.

A savage battle ensued as each face sought dominance over the other in a whirring match of overlapping features—black-white, white-black, black-white, on and on and on. In a blink, the two faces quickly merged and Magdalene saw a brutal cold mask that bore an eerie resemblance to her husband superimpose itself over the other pale and tragic face.

Before the terror-gasp left her mouth, unholy hands started to tear at her clothes, exposing her secret parts. Even as she fought her attackers, she felt her body violated, ravaged by an entity she could neither fight nor resist—*G-- Gabriel! Oh, sweet Mother Mary, save thy handmaiden from Satan's hold...*

III

The next time Magdalene awoke, she was lying on a plush sofa, surrounded by her anxious husband and her new family, a family of great numbers, with several sets of twins among the children she saw—*Thank you, Mother Mary! It was just a horrible nightmare brought on by the heat and everything else!* She heaved a sigh of relief as she made to get up.

A sudden swoon toppled her back to the sofa as she felt a painful throbbing in her groin, a searing pain that resembled a knife-cut in her vagina. And in that instant, Magdalene knew the terrifying truth—*Oh, Holy Mother! Oh, my accursed soul! I am truly damned!*

Exactly nine months after she first stepped into *Ulọ-Gabriel*, Magdalene gave birth to a set of twins, all boys. Except they weren't the normal twins seen in the family, but octuplets; the first of such births ever witnessed in all the region. Unlike all the other children in the Agu family, the numerous twin nephews and nieces of her husband, Gabriel-8, all the octuplets bore the same mismatched eyes of Gabriel's eight sons.

Magdalene did not survive the birth. She took one look into the black-blue eyes of her sons as they wailed their first plaintive cries to announce their humanity and gasped herself into eternal silence.

THE FACES AT PINE DUNES

RAMSEY CAMPBELL

I

When his parents began arguing Michael went outside. He could still hear them through the thin wall of the caravan. "We needn't stop yet," his mother was pleading.

"We're stopping," his father said. "It's time to stop wandering."

But why should she want to leave here? Michael gazed about the caravan park – the Pine Dunes Caravanserai. The metal village of caravans surrounded him, cold and bright in the November afternoon. Beyond the dunes ahead he heard the dozing of the sea. On the three remaining sides a forest stood: remnants of autumn, ghosts of colour, were scattered over the trees; distant branches displayed a last golden mist of leaves. He inhaled the calm. Already he felt at home.

His mother was persisting. "You're still young," she told his father.

She's kidding! Michael thought. Perhaps she was trying flattery. "There are places we haven't seen," she said wistfully.

"We don't need to. We need to be here."

The slowness of the argument, the voices muffled by the metal wall, frustrated Michael; he wanted to be sure that he was staying here. He hurried into the caravan. "I want to stay here. Why do we have to keep moving all the time?"

"Don't come in here talking to your mother like that," his father shouted.

He should have stayed out. The argument seemed to cramp the already crowded space within the caravan; it made his father's presence yet more overwhelming. The man's enormous wheezing body sat plumped on the settee, which sagged beneath his weight; his small frail wife was perched on what little of the settee was unoccupied, as though she'd been squeezed tiny to fit. Gazing at them, Michael felt suffocated. "I'm going out," he said.

"Don't go out," his mother said anxiously; he couldn't see why. "We won't argue any more. You stay in and do something. Study."

"Let him be. The sooner he meets people here, the better."

Michael resented the implication that by going out he was obeying his father. "I'm just going out for a walk," he said. The reassurance might help her; he knew how it felt to be overborne by the man.

At the door he glanced back. His mother had opened her mouth, but his father said "We're staying. I've made my decision." And he'd lie in it, Michael thought, still resentful. All the man could do was lie there, he thought spitefully; that was all he was fat for. He went out, sniggering. The way his father had gained weight during the past year, his coming to rest in this caravan park reminded Michael of an elephant's arrival at its graveyard.

It was colder now. Michael turned up the hood of his anorak. Curtains were closing and glowing. Trees stood, intricately precise, against a sky like translucent papery jade. He began to climb the dunes towards the sea. But over there the sky was blackened; a sea dark as mud tossed nervously and flopped across the bleak beach. He turned towards the forest. Behind him sand hissed through grass.

The forest shifted in the wind. Shoals of leaves swam in the air, at the tips of webs of twigs. He followed a path which led from the Caravanserai's approach road. Shortly the diversity of trees gave way to thousands of pines. Pine cones lay like wattled eggs on beds of fallen needles. The spread of needles glowed deep orange in the early evening, an orange tapestry displaying rank upon rank of slender pines, dwindling into twilight.

The path led him on. The pines were shouldered out by stouter trees, which reached overhead, tangling. Beyond the tangle the blue of the sky grew deeper; a crescent moon slid from branch to branch. Bushes massed among the trunks; they grew higher and closer as he pushed through. The curve of the path would take him back towards the road.

The ground was turning softer underfoot. It sucked his feet in the dark. The shrubs had closed over him now; he could hardly see. He struggled between them, pursuing the curve. Leaves rubbed together rustling at his ear, like desiccated lips; their dry dead tongues rattled. All at once the roof of the wooden tunnel dropped sharply. To go further he would have to crawl.

He turned with difficulty. On both sides thorns caught his sleeves; his dark was hemmed in by two ranks of dim captors. It was as though midnight had already fallen here, beneath the tangled arches; but the dark was solid and clawed. Overhead, netted fragments of night sky illuminated the tunnel hardly at all.

He managed to extricate himself, and hurried back. But he had taken only a few steps when his way was blocked by hulking spiky darkness. He dodged to the left of the shrub, then to the right, trying irritably to calm his heart. But there was no path. He had lost his way in the dark. Around him dimness rustled, chattering.

He began to curse himself. What had possessed him to come in here? Why on earth had he chosen to explore so late in the day? How could the woods be so interminable? He groped for openings between masses of thorns.

Sometimes he found them, though often they would not admit his body. The darkness was a maze of false paths.

Eventually he had to return to the mouth of the tunnel and crawl. Unseen moisture welled up from the ground, between his fingers. Shrubs leaned closer as he advanced, poking him with thorns. His skin felt fragile, and nervously unstable; he burned, but his heat often seemed to break, flooding him with the chill of the night.

There was something even less pleasant. As he crawled, the leaning darkness – or part of it – seemed to move beside him. It was as though someone were pacing him, perhaps on all fours, outside the tunnel. When he halted, so did the pacing. It would reach the end of the tunnel just as he did.

Nothing but imagination, helped by the closely looming tree trunks beyond the shrubs. Apart from the creaking of wood and the rattling sway of leaves, there was no sound beyond the tunnel – certainly none of pacing. He crawled. The cumbersome moist sounds that accompanied the pacing were those of his own progress. But he crawled more slowly, and the darkness imitated him. Wasn't the thorny tunnel dwindling ahead? It would trap him. Suddenly panicking, he began to scrabble backwards.

The thorns hardly hindered his retreat. He must have broken them down. He emerged gasping, glad of the tiny gain in light. Around him shrubs pressed close as ever. He stamped his way back along what he'd thought was his original path. When he reached the hindrance he smashed his way between the shrubs, struggling and snarling, savage with panic, determined not to yield. His hands were torn; he heard cloth rip. Well, the thorns could have that.

When at last he reached an open space his panic sighed loudly out of him. He began to walk as rapidly as seemed safe, towards where he remembered the road to be. Overhead black nets of branches turned, momentarily catching stars. Once, amid the enormous threshing of the woods, he thought he heard a heavy body shoving through the nearby bushes. Good luck to whoever it was. Ahead, in the barred dark, hung little lighted windows. He had found the caravan park, but only by losing his way.

He was home. He hurried into the light, smiling. In the metal alleys pegged shirts hung neck down, dripping; they flapped desperately on the wind. The caravan was dark. In the main room, lying on the settee like someone's abandoned reading, was a note: OUT, BACK LATER. His mother had added DON'T GO TO BED TOO LATE.

He'd been looking forward to companionship. Now the caravan seemed too brightly lit, and false: a furnished tin can. He made himself coffee, leafed desultorily through his floppy paperbacks, opened and closed a pocket chess set. He poked through his box of souvenirs: shells, smooth stones; a minute Bible; a globe of synthetic snow within which a huge vague figure, presumably meant to be a snowman, loomed outside a house; a dead torch fitted with a set of clip-on Halloween faces; a dull grey ring whose metal swelled into a bulge over which colours crawled slowly, changing. The cardboard box was full of memories: the Severn valley, the Welsh hills, the garishly glittering mile of Blackpool: he couldn't remember where the ring had come from. But the memories were dim tonight, uninvolving.

He wandered into his parents' room. It looked to him like a second-hand store for clothes and toiletries. He found his father's large metal box, but it was locked as usual. Well, Michael didn't want to read his old books anyway. He searched for contraceptives, but as he'd expected, there were none. If he wasn't mistaken, his parents had no need for them. Poor buggers. He'd never been able to imagine how, out of proportion as they seemed to be, they had begot him.

Eventually he went out. The incessant rocking of the caravan, its hollow booming in the wind, had begun to infuriate him. He hurried along the road between the pines; wind sifted through needles. On the main road buses ran to Liverpool. But he'd already been there several times. He caught a bus to the opposite terminus.

The bus was almost empty. A few passengers rattled in their lighted pod over the bumpy country roads. Darkness streamed by, sometimes becoming dim hedges. The scoop of the headlamps set light to moths, and once to a squirrel. Ahead the sky glowed, as if with a localised dawn. Lights began to emerge from behind silhouetted houses; streets opened, brightening.

The bus halted in a square, beside a village cross. The passengers hurried away, snuggling into their collars. Almost at once the street was deserted, the bus extinguished. Folded awnings clattered, tugged by the wind. Perhaps after all he should have gone into the city. He was stranded here for – he read the timetable: God, two hours until the last bus.

He wandered among the grey stone houses. Streetlamps glared silver; the light coated shop windows, behind whose flowering of frost he could see faint ghosts of merchandise. Curtains shone warmly, chimneys smoked. His heels clanked mechanically on the cobbles. Streets, streets, empty streets. Then the streets became crowded, with gleaming parked cars. Ahead, on the wall of a building, was a plaque of coloured light. FOUR IN THE MORNING. A club.

He hesitated, then he descended the steps. Maybe he wouldn't fit in with the brand-new sports car set, but anything was better than wandering the icy streets. At the bottom of the stone flight, a desk stood beside a door to coloured dimness. A broken-nosed man wearing evening dress sat behind the desk. "Are you a member, sir?" he said in an accent that was almost as convincing as his suit.

Inside was worse than Michael had feared. On a dance floor couples turned lethargically, glittering and changing colour like toy dancers. Clumps of people stood shouting at each other in county accents, swaying and laughing; some stared at him as they laughed. He heard their talk:

motorboats, bloody bolshies, someone's third abortion. He didn't mind meeting new people – he'd had to learn not to mind – but he could tell these people preferred, now they'd stared, to ignore him.

His three pounds' membership fee included a free drink. I should think so too, he thought. He ordered a beer, to the barman's faint contempt. As he carried the tankard to one of the low bare tables he was conscious of his boots, tramping the floorboards. There was nothing wrong with them, he'd wiped them. He sipped, making the drink last, and gazed into the beer's dim glow.

When someone else sat at the table he didn't look at her. He had to glance up at last, because she was staring. What was the matter with her, was he on show? Often in groups he felt alien, but he'd never felt more of a freak than here. His large-boned arms huddled protectively around him, his gawky legs drew up.

But she was smiling. Her stare was wide-eyed, innocent, if somehow odd. "I haven't seen you before," she said. "What's your name?"

"Michael." It sounded like phlegm; he cleared his throat. "Michael. What's yours?"

"June." She made a face as though it tasted like medicine.

"Nothing wrong with that." Her hint of dissatisfaction with herself had emboldened him.

"You haven't moved here, have you? Are you visiting?"

There was something strange about her: about her eyes, about the way she seemed to search for questions. "My parents have a caravan," he said. "We're in the Pine Dunes Caravanserai. We docked just last week."

"Yeah." She drew the word out like a sigh. "Like a ship. That must be fantastic. I wish I had that. Just to be able to see new things all the time, new places. The only way you can see new things here is taking acid. I'm tripping now."

His eyebrows lifted slightly; his faint smile shrugged.

"That's what I mean," she said, smiling. "These people here would be really shocked. They're so provincial. You aren't."

In fact he hadn't been sure how to react. The pupils of her eyes were expanding and contracting rapidly, independently of each other. But her small face was attractive, her small body had large firm breasts.

"I saw the moon dancing before," she said. "I'm beginning to come down now. I thought I'd like to look at people. You wouldn't know I was tripping, would you? I can control it when I want to."

She wasn't really talking to him, he thought; she just wanted an audience to trip to. He'd heard things about LSD. "Aren't you afraid of starting to trip when you don't mean to?"

"Flashbacks, you mean. I never have them. I shouldn't like that." She gazed at his scepticism. "There's no need to be afraid of drugs," she said. "All sorts of people used to trip. Witches used to. Look, it tells you about it in here."

She fumbled a book out of her handbag; she seemed to have difficulty in wielding her fingers. *Witchcraft in England*. "You can have that," she said. "Have you got a job?"

It took him a moment to realise that she'd changed the subject. "No," he said. "I haven't left school long. I had to have extra school because of all the moving. I'm twenty. I expect I'll get a job soon. I think we're staying here."

"That could be a good job," she said, pointing at a notice behind the bar: TRAINEE BARMAN REQUIRED. "I think they want to get rid of that guy there. People don't like him. I know a lot of people would come here if they got someone friendly like you."

Was it just her trip talking? Two girls said goodbye to a group, and came over. "We're going now, June. See you shortly."

"Right. Hey, this is Michael."

"Nice to meet you, Michael."

"Hope we'll see you again."

Perhaps they might. These people didn't seem so bad after all. He drank his beer and bought another, wincing at the price and gazing at the job notice. June refused a drink: "It's a downer." They talked about his travels, her dissatisfactions and her lack of cash to pay for moving. When he had to leave she said "I'm glad I met you. I like you." And she called after him "If you got that job I'd come here."

II

Darkness blinded him. It was heavy on him, and moved. It was more than darkness: it was flesh. Beneath him and around him and above him, somnolent bodies crawled blindly. They were huge; so was he. As they shifted incessantly he heard sounds of mud or flesh.

He was shifting too. It was more than restlessness. His whole body felt unstable; he couldn't make out his own form – whenever he seemed to perceive it, it changed. And his mind; it felt too full, of alien chunks that ground harshly together. Memories or fantasies floated vaguely through him. Stone circles. Honeycombed mountains; glimmering faces like a cluster of bubbles in a cave mouth. Enormous dreaming eyes beneath stone and sea. A labyrinth of thorns. His own face. But why was his own face only a memory?

He woke. Dawn suffocated him like grey gas; he lay panting. It was all right. It hadn't been his own face that he'd seemed to remember in the dream. His body hadn't grown huge. His large bones were still lanky. But there was a huge figure, nonetheless. It loomed above him at the window, its spread of face staring down at him.

He woke, and had to grab the dark before he could find the light switch. He twisted himself to sit on the edge of the settee, legs tangled in the blankets, so as not to fall asleep again. Around him the caravan was flat and bright, and empty. Beyond the ajar door of his parents' room he could see that their bed was smooth and deserted.

He was sure he'd had that dream before – the figure at the window. Somehow he associated it with a windmill, a childhood memory he couldn't locate. Had he been staying with his grandparents? The dream was fading in the light. He glanced at his clock: two in the morning. He didn't want to sleep again until the dream had gone.

He stood outside the caravan. A wind was rising; a loud whisper passed through the forest, unlit caravans rocked and creaked a little at their moorings; behind everything, vast and constant, the sea rushed vaguely. Scraps of cloud slid over the filling moon; light caught at them, but they slipped away. His parents hadn't taken the car. Where had they gone? Irrationally, he felt he knew, if only he could remember. Why did they go out at night so much?

A sound interrupted his musing. The wind carried it to him only to snatch it away. It seemed distant, and therefore must be loud. Did it contain words? Was someone being violently ill, and trying to shout? The moon's light flapped between a procession of dark clouds. A drunk, no doubt, shouting incoherently. Michael gazed at the edge of the forest and wondered about his parents. Light and wind shifted the foliage. Then he shrugged. He ought to be used to his parents' nocturnal behaviour by now.

He slammed the door. His dream was still clinging to him. There had been something odd about the head at the window, besides its size. Something about it had reminded him unpleasantly of a bubble. Hadn't that happened the first time he'd had the dream? But he was grinning at himself: never mind dreams, or his parents. Think of June.

She had been in the club almost every evening since he'd taken the job, a month ago. He had dithered for a week, then he'd returned and asked about the notice. Frowning, the barman had called the manager – to throw Michael out? But June had told them her parents knew Michael well. "All right. We'll give you six weeks and see how you do." The barman had trained him, always faintly snooty and quick to criticise. But the customers had begun to prefer Michael to serve them. They accepted him, and he found he could be friendly. He'd never felt less like an outsider.

So long as the manager didn't question June's parents. June had invited Michael to the cottage a couple of times. Her parents had been polite, cold, fascinated, contemptuous. He'd tried to fit his lanky legs beneath his chair, so that the flares of his trousers would cover up his boots – and all the while he'd felt superior to these people in some way, if only he could think of it. "They aren't my kind of people either," June had told him, walking to the club. "When can we go to your caravan?"

He didn't know. He hadn't yet told his parents about her; the reaction to the news of his job hadn't been what he'd hoped. His mother had gazed at him sadly, and he'd felt she was holding more of her feelings hidden, as they all had to in the cramped caravan. "Why don't you go to the city? They'll have better jobs there."

"But I feel at home here."

"That's right," his father had said. "That's right." He'd stared at Michael strangely, with a kind of uneasy joy. Michael had felt oppressed, engulfed by the stare. Of course there was nothing wrong, his father had become uneasy on hearing of his son's first job, his first step in the world, that was all.

"Can I borrow the car to get to the club?"

His father had become dogmatic at once; his shell had snapped tight. "Not yet. You'll get the key soon enough."

It hadn't seemed worth arguing. Though his parents rarely used the car at night, Michael was never given the key. Where did they go at night? "When you're older" had never seemed much of an explanation. But surely their nocturnal excursions were more frequent now they'd docked at Pine Dunes? And why was his mother so anxious to persuade him to leave?

It didn't matter. Sometimes he was glad that they went out; it gave him a chance to be alone, the caravan seemed less cramped, he could breathe freely. He could relax, safe from the threat of his father's overwhelming presence. And if they hadn't gone out that night he would never have met June.

Because of the wanderings of the caravan he had never had time for close friendships. He had felt more attached to this latest berth than to any person – until he'd met June. She was the first girl to arouse him. Her small slim body, her bright quick eyes, her handfuls of breast – he felt his body stirring as he thought of her.

For years he'd feared he was impotent. Once, in a village school, a boy had shown him an erotic novel. He'd read about the gasps of pleasure, the creaking of the bed. Gradually he'd realised why that troubled him. The walls of the caravan were thin; he could always hear his father snoring or wheezing, like a huge fish stranded on the shore of a dream. But he had never heard his parents copulating.

Their sexual impulse must have faded quickly, soon after he was born – as soon, he thought, as it had served its purpose. Would his own be as feeble? Would it work at all? Yes, he'd gasped over June, the first night her parents were out. "I think it'd be good to make love on acid," she'd said as they lay embraced. "That way you really become one, united together." But he thought he would be terrified to take LSD, even though what she'd said appealed deeply to him.

He wished she were here now. The caravan rocked; his parents' door swung creaking, imitated by the bathroom door, which often sprang open. He slammed them irritably. The dream of the bubbling head at the window – if that had been what was wrong with it – was drifting away. Soon he'd sleep. He picked up *Witchcraft in England*. It looked dull enough to help him sleep. And it was June's.

Naked witches danced about on the cover, and on many of the pages. They danced obscenely. They danced lewdly. They chanted obscenely. And so on. They used poisonous drugs, such as belladonna. No doubt that had interested June. He leafed idly onwards; his gaze flickered impatiently.

Suddenly he halted, at a name: Severnford. Now that was interesting. We can imagine, the book insisted, the witches rowing out to the island in the middle of the dark river, and committing unspeakable acts before the pallid stone in the moonlight; but Michael couldn't imagine anything of the kind, nor did he intend to try. Witches are still reputed to visit the island, the book told him before he interrupted it and riffled on. But a few pages later his gaze was caught again.

He stared at this new name. Then reluctantly he turned to the index. At once words stood out from the columns, eager to be seen. They slipped into his mind as if their slots had been ready for years. Exham. Whitminster. The Old Horns. Holihaven. Dilham. Severnford. His father had halted the caravan at all of them, and his parents had gone out at night.

He was still staring numbly at the list when the door snapped open. His father glanced sharply at him, then went into the bedroom. "Come on," he told Michael's mother, and sat heavily on the bed, which squealed. To Michael's bewildered mind his father's body seemed to spread as he sat down, like a dropped jelly. His mother sat obediently;

her gaze dodged timidly, she looked pale and shrunken – by fear, Michael knew at once. "Go to bed," his father told him, raising one foot effortlessly to kick the door shut. Almost until dawn Michael lay in the creaking unstable dark, thinking.

III

"You must have seen all sorts of places," June said.

"We've seen a few," said Michael's mother. Her eyes moved uneasily. She seemed nervously resentful, perhaps at being reminded of something she wanted desperately to forget. At last, as if she'd struggled and found courage, she managed to say "We may see a few more."

"Oh no we won't," her husband said. He sat slumped on the settee, as though his body were a burden he'd had to drop there. Now that there were four people in the caravan he seemed to take up even more room; his presence overwhelmed all the spaces between them.

Michael refused to be overwhelmed. He stared at his father. "What made you choose the places we've lived?" he demanded.

"I had my reasons."

"What reasons?"

"I'll tell you sometime. Not now, son. You don't want us arguing in front of your girlfriend, do you?"

Into the embarrassed silence June said "I really envy

you, being able to go everywhere."

"You'd like to, would you?" Michael's mother said.

"Oh yes. I'd love to see the world."

His mother turned from the stove. "You ought to. You're the right age for it. It wouldn't do Michael any harm, either."

For a moment her eyes were less dull. Michael was glad: he'd thought she would approve of June's wanderlust – that was one reason why he'd given in to June's pleas to meet his parents. Then his father was speaking, and his mother dulled again.

"Best to stay where you're born," his father told June. "You won't find a better place than here. I know what I'm talking about."

"You should try living where I do. It'd kill your head in no time."

"Mike feels at home here. That's right, isn't it, son? You tell her."

"I like it here," Michael said. Words blocked his throat. "I mean, I met you," he hawked at June.

His mother chopped vegetables: *chop, chop, chop* – the sound was harsh, trapped within the metal walls. "Can I do anything?" June said.

"No thank you. It's all right," she said indifferently. She hadn't accepted June yet, after all.

"If you're so keen on seeing the world," his father demanded, "what's stopping you?"

"I can't afford it, not yet. I work in a boutique, I'm saving the money I'd have spent on clothes. And then I can't drive. I'd need to go with someone who can."

"Good luck to you. But I don't see Mikey going with you."

Well, ask me! Michael shouted at her, gagged (by his unsureness: she mightn't have had him in mind at all). But she only said "When I travel I'm going to have things from everywhere."

"I've got some," he said. "I've kept some things." He carried the cardboard box to her, and displayed his souvenirs. "You can have them if you like," he said impulsively; if she accepted he would be more sure of her. "The torch only needs batteries."

But she pushed the plastic faces aside, and picked up the ring. "I like that," she said, turning it so that its colours spilled slowly over one another, merging and separating. She whispered "It's like tripping."

"There you are. I'm giving it to you."

His father stared at the ring, then a smile spread his mouth. "Yes, you give her that. It's as good as an engagement, that ring."

Michael slid the ring onto her finger before she could change her mind; she had begun to look embarrassed. "It's lovely," she said. "Have we time for Mike to take me for a walk before dinner?"

"You can stay out for an hour if you like," his mother

said, then anxiously: "Go down to the beach. You might get lost in the woods, in the fog."

The fog was ambiguous: perhaps thinning, perhaps gathering again. Inside a caravan a radio sang Christmas carols. A sharp-edged bronze sun hung close to the sea. Sea and fog had merged, and might be advancing over the beach. June took Michael's hand as they climbed the slithering dunes. "I just wanted to come out to talk," she explained.

So had he. He wanted to tell her what he'd discovered. That was his main reason for inviting her: he needed her support in confronting his parents, he would be too disturbed to confront them alone – he'd needed it earlier when he'd tried to interrogate his father. But what could he tell her? I've found out my parents are witches? You know that book you lent me—

"No, I didn't really want to talk," she said. "There were just too many bad vibes in there. I'll be all right, we'll go back soon. But they're strange, your parents, aren't they? I didn't realise your father was so heavy."

"He used to be like me. He's been getting fatter for the last few months." After a pause he voiced his worst secret fear: "I hope I never get like him."

"You'll have to get lots of exercise. Let's walk as far as the point."

Ahead along the beach, the grey that lay stretched on the sea was land, not fog. They trudged toward it. Sand splashed from his boots; June slid, and gripped his hand.

He strained to tell her what he'd found out, but each phrase he prepared sounded more absurd: his voice echoed hollowly, closed into his mind. He'd tell her – but not today. He relaxed, and felt enormously relieved; he enjoyed her hand small in his. "I like fog," she said. "There are always surprises in it."

The bronze sun paced them, sinking. The sea shifted restlessly, muffled. To their left, above the dunes, trees were a flat mass of prickly fog. They were nearly at the point now. It pulled free of the grey, darkening and sharpening. It looked safe enough for them to climb the path.

But when they reached the top it seemed hardly worth the effort. A drab patch of beach and dunes, an indistinct fragment of sea scattered with glitterings of dull brass, surrounded them in a soft unstable frame of fog. Otherwise the view was featureless, except for a tree growing beside the far dunes. Was it a tree? Its branches seemed too straight, its trunk too thick. Suddenly troubled, Michael picked his way over the point as far as he dared. The fog withdrew a little. It wasn't a tree. It was a windmill.

A windmill by the sea! "My grandparents lived here," he blurted.

"Oh, did they?"

"You don't understand. They lived near that windmill. It's the same one, I know it is."

He still wasn't sure whether she felt his confusion. Memories rushed him, as if all at once afloat: he'd been lying on the settee in his grandparents' decrepit caravan, the huge head had loomed at the window, vague with dawn. It must have been a dream then too.

He followed June down the path. Chill fog trailed them, lapping the point. His thoughts drifted, swirling. What did his discovery mean? He couldn't remember his grandparents at all, not even what they'd looked like. They had been his father's parents – why had the man never mentioned them? Why hadn't he remarked that they'd lived here? The sun slid along the rim of the sea, swollen as though with glowing blood. Had his grandparents also been witches?

"Did Mike's grandparents live here, then?" June said.

His mother stared at her. The spoon and saucepan she was holding chattered like nervous teeth. He was sure she was going to scream and throw everything away – the utensils, her self-control, the mask behind which she'd hidden to protect him: for how long? For the whole of his childhood? But she stammered "How did you know that?"

"Mike told me. The windmill just reminded him."

"Is dinner ready?" Michael interrupted. He wanted to think everything out before questioning his father. But June was opening her mouth to continue. The caravan was crowded, suffocating. Shut up! he screamed at her. Get out! "Were they born here, then?" June said.

"No, I don't think so." His mother had turned away and was washing vegetables. June went to hold the dishes. "So why did they come here?" she said.

His mother frowned, turning her back; within her frown she was searching. "To retire," she said abruptly.

His father nodded and smiled to himself, squeezing forward his ruff of chins. "You could retire from the human race here," June said sourly, and he wheezed like a punctured balloon.

As the four ate dinner, their constraint grew. Michael and June made most of the conversation; his parents replied shortly when at all, and watched. His mother observed June uneasily; he read dislike in her eyes, or pity. He felt irritably resentful, her uneasiness made his skin nervous. Night edged closer to the windows, blank-faced.

His father leaned back as if his weight had toppled the chair, which creaked loudly. He patted his quaking stomach. "Just storing it up for the winter," he said, winking at June.

His arms flopped around her shoulders and Michael's. "You two go well together. Don't they, eh?"

But his wife said only "I'm going to bed now. I'm very tired. Perhaps we'll see you again," which sounded like dutiful politeness.

"I hope so," June said.

"I know we will," Michael's father said expansively.

Michael walked June to the bus-stop. "I'll see you at the club," she said through a kiss. Smouldering cones of yellow light led the bus away, and were engulfed. As he walked back, twisted shapes of fog bulked between the trees. Nearby in the dark, something shifted moistly.

He halted. What had it been? Blurred trees creaked with a deadened sound, thin trails of fog reached out for him from branches. He'd heard a shifting, deep in the dark. A vague memory plucked at him. He shivered as if to shake it free, into the chill clinging night. A restless moist shifting. He felt as though the depths of the forest were reaching for his mind with ambiguous tatters of grey. He strode rapidly towards the invisible light. Again he heard the slow moist shifting. Only the sea, he told himself. Only the sea.

IV

As he emerged into the open, the clouds parted and the moon rolled free. The enormous shape in the open space glistened with moonlight. The unstable head turned its crawling face towards him.

The dream trailed him to Liverpool, to the central library, although the space and the head had faded before he could make them out – if indeed he had wanted to. A rush of rain, and the bright lights of the library, washed the dream away. He hurried up the wide green stairs to the Religion and Philosophy section.

He pulled books from the shelves. *Lancashire Witches*. *North-West Hauntings*. *Ghostly Lancashire*. The banality of their covers was reassuring; it seemed absurd that his parents could be mixed up in such things. Yet he couldn't quite laugh. Even if they were, what could he do? He slammed the books angrily on a table, startling echoes.

As he read he began to feel safer. Pine Dunes wasn't indexed in North-West Hauntings. His attention strayed fascinated into irrelevances. The hanged man's ghost in Everton Library. The poltergeist of the Palace Hotel, Birkdale. Jokey ghost stories in Lancashire dialect, ee lad. Rain and wind shook the windows, fluorescent light lay flat on the tables. Beyond a glass partition people sat studying, library staff clattered up and down open staircases, carrying scraps of paper. Reassured, he turned to *Lancashire Witches*. Pine Dunes. It was there, on three pages.

When he made himself search the pages they didn't say much. Over the centuries, witches had been rumoured to gather in the Pine Dunes forest. Was that surprising? Wouldn't they naturally have done so, for concealment? Besides, these were only rumours; few people would have bothered struggling through the undergrowth. He opened *Ghostly Lancashire*, expecting irrelevances. But the index showed that Pine Dunes covered several pages.

The author had interviewed a group the other books ignored: the travellers. Their stories were unreliable, he warned, but fascinating. Few travellers would walk the Pine Dunes road after dark; they kept their children out of the woods even by day. A superstitious people, the author pointed out. The book had been written thirty years ago, Michael reminded himself. And the travellers gave no reason for their nervousness except vague tales of something unpleasantly large glimpsed moving beyond the most distant trees. Surely distance must have formed the trees into a solid wall; how could anyone have seen beyond?

One traveller, senile and often incoherent, told a story. A long time ago he, or someone else – the author couldn't tell – had wandered back to the travellers' camp, very drunk. The author didn't believe the story, but included it because it was vivid and unusual. Straying from the road, the man had become lost in the forest. Blinded by angry panic, he'd fought his way towards an open space. But it wasn't the camp, as he'd thought. He had lost his footing on the slippery earth and had gone skidding into a pit.

Had it been a pit, or the mouth of a tunnel? As he'd scrabbled, bruised but otherwise unhurt, for a foothold on the mud at the bottom, he'd seen an opening that led deeper into darkness. The darkness had begun moving slowly and enormously towards him, with a sound like that of a huge shifting beneath mud – darkness which had parted loudly, resolving itself into several sluggish forms that glistened dimly as they advanced to surround him. Terror had hurled him in a leap halfway up the pit; his hands had clamped on rock, and he'd wrenched himself up the rest of the way. He'd run blindly. In the morning he'd found himself full of thorns on a sprung bed of undergrowth.

So what did all that prove? Michael argued with himself on the bus to Pine Dunes. The man had been drunk. All right, so there were other tales about Pine Dunes, but nothing very evil. Why shouldn't his parents go out at night? Maybe they were ghost-hunters, witch-hunters. Maybe they were going to write a book about their observations. How else could such books be written? His mind was becoming desperate as he kept remembering his mother's masked fear.

His parents were asleep. His father lay beached on the bed, snoring flabbily; beyond his stomach his wife could hardly be seen. Michael was glad, for he hadn't known what to say to them. He wheeled out the bicycle he'd bought from his first month's wages.

He cycled to the Four in the Morning. His knees protruded on either side of him, jerking up and down. Hedges sailed by slowly; their colours faded and dimmed into twilight. The whirr of his dynamo caught among the leaves. He struggled uphill, standing on the pedals. Dim countryside opened below him, the sea glinted dully. As he poised on the edge of the downhill rush he knew how he could unburden himself, or begin to. Tonight he would tell June everything.

But she didn't come to the club. People crowded in; the lights painted them carelessly monochrome. Discotheque records snarled and thumped, swirls of tobacco-smoke glared red, pink, purple. Michael hurried about, serving. Dim wet discoloured faces jostled to reach him, shouting "Mike! Mike!" Faces rose obsessively to the surface of the jostling: June's, who wasn't there; his mother's, her eyes trying to dodge fear. He was suffocating. His frustration gathered within him; he felt swollen, encumbered. He stared at luridly pink smoke while voices called. "I've got to go home," he told the barman.

"Had enough, have you?"

"My parents aren't well. I'm worried."

"Strange you didn't say so when you came in. Well, I've managed by myself before." He turned away, dismissing Michael. "You'll have to make do with me tonight," he told the shouting.

The last of the lit streets faded behind Michael. The moon was full, but blurred by unkempt fields of cloud; it showed him only a faint windy swaying that surrounded him for miles. When he confronted his father, what would his mother do? Would she break down? If she admitted to witchcraft and said it was time Michael knew, the scene would be easier – if she did. The moon struggled among plump clouds, and was engulfed.

He cycled fast up the Pine Dunes road. Get there, don't delay to reconsider. Gravel ground together squeaking beneath his wheels; his yellow light wobbled, plucking at trees. The depths of the forest creaked; distant tree trunks were pushed apart to let a huge unstable face peer through. He was overtired – of course there was nothing among the far trees but dark. He sped into the Caravanserai; random patches of unlit caravans bobbed up and faded by. His caravan was unlit too.

Perhaps his parents weren't there. He realised furiously that he felt relieved. They were in there all right, they'd be asleep. He would wake his father, the man might betray himself while still half-asleep. He'd dazzle his father awake, like an interrogator. But his parents' bed was empty.

He punched the wall, which rang flatly. His father had outwitted him again. He stared around the room, enraged. His father's huge suits dangled emptily, like sloughed skin; his mother's clothes hid in drawers. His father's metal box of books sat on top of the wardrobe. Michael glanced resentfully at it, then stared. It was unlocked.

He lifted it down and made to sit on his parents' bed. That made him feel uneasy; he carried the box into the main room. Let his father come in and find him reading. Michael hoped he would. He tugged at the lid, which resisted then sprang open with a loud clang.

He remembered that sound. He'd heard it when he was quite young, and his mother's voice, pleading: "Let him at least have a normal childhood." After a moment he'd heard the box closed again. "All right. He'll find out when it's time," he'd heard his father say.

The box contained no printed books, but several notebooks. They had been written in by numerous people; the inks in the oldest notebook, whose spine had given way, were brown as old bloodstains. Some of the writing in the latest book was his mother's. Odd pages showed rough maps: The Old Horns, Exham, Whitminster, though none of Pine Dunes. These he recognised; but he couldn't understand a word of the text.

Most of it was in English, but might as well not have been. It consisted largely of quotations copied from books; sometimes the source was indicated – Necro, Revelations Glaaki, Garimiaz, Vermis, Theobald, whatever they were. The whole thing reminded him of pamphlets issued by cranky cults – like the people who gave all their worldly goods to a man in America, or the others who'd once lured Michael into a seedy hotel for a personality profile, which they'd lied would be fun. He read, baffled.

After a while he gave up. Even the entries his mother had written made no sense. Some of the words he couldn't even pronounce. Kuthullhoo? Kuthoolhew? And what was supposed to be so Great about it, whatever it was?

He shrugged, sniggering a little. He didn't feel so worried now. If this was all his parents were involved in, it seemed silly but harmless. The fact that they'd concealed it from him so successfully for so long seemed to prove as much. They were so convincingly normal, it couldn't be anything very bad. After all, many businessmen belonged to secret societies with jargon nobody else could understand. Maybe his father had been initiated into this society as part of one of the jobs he'd taken in his wanderings!

One thing still troubled Michael: his mother's fear. He couldn't see what there was to fear in the blurred language of the notebooks. He made a last effort, and let the books fall open where they would – at the pages that had been read most frequently.

What a waste of time! He strained his mind, but the pages became more bewildering still; he began to laugh. What on earth was "the millennial gestation"? Something to do with "the fosterling of the Great Old Ones"? "The hereditary rebirth"? "Each of Its rebirths comes closer to incarnation"? "When the mind opens to all the dimensions will come the incarnation. Upon the incarnation all minds will become one." Ah, that explains it! Michael sniggered wildly. But there was more: "the ingestion," "the mating beyond marriage," "the melting and merging" —

He threw the book angrily into the box. The skin of his eyes crawled hotly; he could hardly keep them open, yet he was wasting his time reading this. The caravan rocked as something huge tugged at it: the wind. The oldest, spineless, notebook began to disintegrate. As he knocked it square, an envelope slipped out.

It was addressed in his father's large handwriting; the last word had had to be cramped. TO MICHAEL: NOT TO BE OPENED UNTIL AFTER I AM GONE. He turned it over and began to tear, but his hand faltered. He'd been unreasonable enough to his father for one day. After a moment he put the envelope unopened in his pocket, feeling sly and ashamed. He replaced the box, then he prepared to sleep. In the dark he tried to arrange his limbs on the sagging settee. Rocking, the caravan sounded like a rusty cradle.

He slept. He wasn't sure whether he was asleep when he heard his mother's low voice. He must be awake, for he could feel her breath on his face. "Don't stay here." Her voice trembled. "Your girlfriend's got the right idea. Go away with her if that's what you want. Just get away from here."

His father's voice reached for her out of the dark. "That's enough. He's asleep. You come to bed."

Silence and darkness settled down for the night. But in the night, or in Michael's dream, there were noises: the stealthy departure of a car from the park; heavy footsteps trying not to disturb the caravan; the gingerly closing of his parents' door. Sleep seemed more important.

His father's voice woke him, shouting into the bedroom. "Wake up. The car's gone. It's been stolen."

Daylight blazed through Michael's eyelids. He was sure at once what had happened. His father had hidden the car, so that nobody could get away. Michael lay paralysed, waiting for his mother's cry of panic. Her silence held time immobile. He squeezed his eyelids tighter, filling his eyes with red.

"Oh," his mother said at last, dully. "Oh dear."

There was more in her voice than resignation: she sounded lethargic, indifferent. Suddenly Michael remembered what he'd read in June's book. Witches used drugs. His eyes sprang wide. He was sure that his father was drugging his mother.

V

It didn't take the police long to find the car, abandoned and burnt out, near the windmill. "Kids, probably," one of the policemen said. "We may be in touch with you again." Michael's father shook his head sadly, and they left.

"I must have dropped the car keys while we were out." Michael thought his father hardly bothered to sound convincing. Why couldn't he tell the man so, confront him? Because he wasn't sure; he might have dreamed the sounds last night— He raged at his own cowardice, staring at his mother. If only he could be certain of her support! She wandered desultorily, determinedly cleaning the caravan, as though she were ill but expecting company.

When his gagged rage found words at last it weakened immediately. "Are you all right?" he demanded of her, but then could only stammer "Do you think you'd better see a doctor?"

Neither of his parents responded. His unsureness grew, and fed his frustration. He felt lethargic, unable to act, engulfed by his father's presence. Surely June would be at the club tonight. He had to talk to someone, to hear another interpretation; perhaps she would prove that he'd imagined everything.

He washed and shaved. He was glad to retreat, even into the cramped bathroom; he and his parents had been edging uneasily around one another all day – the caravan made him think unpleasantly of a tin can full of squirming. As he shaved, the bathroom door sprang open, as it often did. His father appeared behind him in the mirror, staring at him.

Steam coated the mirror again. Beneath the steam, his father's face seemed to writhe like a plastic mask on fire. Michael reached to clear the mirror, but already his father and the man's emotions were upon him. Before Michael could turn his father was hugging him violently, his flesh quivering as though it would burst. Michael held himself stiff, refusing to be engulfed. What are you doing? Get away! In a moment his father turned clumsily and plodded out. The caravan rumbled, shaking.

Michael sighed loudly. God, he was glad that was over. He finished shaving and hurried out. Neither of his parents looked at him; his father pretended to read a book, and whistled tunelessly; his mother turned vaguely as he passed. He cycled to the club.

"Parents all right?" the barman said indifferently.

"I'm not sure."

"Good of you to come." Perhaps that was sarcasm. "There's some things for you to wash."

Michael could still feel his father's clinging embrace; he kept trying to wriggle it away. He welcomed the press of bodies at the bar, shouting "Mike!" – even though June wasn't among them. He welcomed the companionship of ordinary people. He strode expertly about, serving, as the crowd grew, as smoke gathered. He could still feel swollen flesh pressed hotly against his back. He won't do that to me again, he thought furiously. He'll never— A tankard dropped from his hand, beneath a beer-tap. "Oh my God," he said.

"What's up with you now?" the barman demanded.

When his father had embraced him, Michael had thought of nothing but escape. Now at last he realised how final his father's gesture had been. "My parents," he said. "They're, they're worse."

"Just sent you a message, did they? Off home again now, I suppose? You'd better see the manager, or I will— Will you watch that bloody beer you're spilling!"

Michael slammed shut the tap and struggled through the crowd. People grimaced sympathetically at him, or stared. It didn't matter, his job didn't matter. He must hurry back to head off whatever was going to happen. Someone bumped into him in the doorway, and hindered him when he tried to push them aside. "What's the matter with you?" he shouted. "Get out of the way!" It was June.

"I'm really sorry I didn't come last night," she said. "My parents dragged me out to dinner."

"All right. Okay. Don't worry."

"You're angry. I really am sorry, I wanted to see you— You're not going, are you?"

"Yes, I've got to. Look, my parents aren't well."

"I'll come back with you. We can talk on the way. I'll

help you look after them." She caught at his shoulder as he tried to run upstairs. "Please, Mike. I'll feel bad if you just leave me. We can catch the last bus in five minutes if we run. It'll be quicker than your bike."

God! She was worse than his father! "Listen," he snarled, having clambered to street level. "It isn't ill, they aren't ill," he said, letting words tumble wildly as he tried to flee. "I've found out what they do at night. They're witches."

"Oh no!" She sounded shocked but delighted.

"My mother's terrified. My father's been drugging her." Now that he was able to say so, his urgency diminished a little; he wanted to release all he knew. "Something's going to happen tonight," he said.

"Are you going to try and stop it? Let me come too. I know about it. I showed you my book." When he looked doubtful she said "They'll have to stop when they see me."

Perhaps she could look after his mother while he confronted his father. They ran to the bus, which sat unlit in the square for minutes, then dawdled along the country roads, hoping for passengers who never appeared. Michael's frustration coiled tighter again. He explained to June what he'd discovered: "Yeah," she kept saying, excited and fascinated. Once she began giggling uncontrollably. "Wouldn't it be weird if we saw your father dancing naked?" He stared at her until she said "Sorry." Her pupils were expanding and contracting slightly, randomly.

As they ran along the Pine Dunes road the trees leaned

closer, creaking and nodding. Suppose his parents hadn't left the caravan yet? What could he say? He'd be tongue-tied again by his unsureness, and June would probably make things worse. He gasped with relief when he saw that the windows were dark, but went inside to make sure. "I know where they've gone," he told June.

Moonlight and unbroken cloud spread the sky with dim milk; dark smoky breaths drifted across the glow. He heard the incessant restlessness of the sea. Bare black silhouettes crowded beside the road, thinly intricate against the sky. He hurried June towards the path.

Why should his parents have gone that way? Something told him they had – perhaps the maze he remembered, the tunnel of undergrowth: that was a secret place. The path wound deeper into the woods, glinting faintly; trees rapidly shuttered the glow of the moon. "Isn't this fantastic," June said, hurrying behind him.

The pines gave out, but other trees meshed thickly overhead. The glimpses of flat whitish sky, smouldering with darker cloud, dwindled. In the forest everything was black or blanched, and looked chill, although the night was unseasonably mild.

Webs of shadow lay on the path, tangling Michael's feet; tough grass seized him. Bushes massed around him, towering, choking the gaps between trees. The glimpses of sky were fewer and smaller. "What's that?" June said uneasily.

For a moment he thought it was the sound of someone's foot, unplugging itself from the soft ground: it sounded like a loud slow gulp of mud. But no, it wasn't that. Someone coughing? It didn't sound much like a human cough. Moreover, it sounded as though it were straining to produce a sound, a single sound; and he felt inexplicably that he ought to know what that was.

The bushes stirred, rattling. The muddy sound faded, somewhere ahead. There was no point in telling June his vague thoughts. "It'll be an animal," he said. "Probably something's caught it."

Soon they reached the tunnel. He knelt at once and began to crawl. Twigs scraped beside his ears, a clawed dry chorus. He found the experience less disturbing now, less oppressive; the tunnel seemed wider, as though someone stout had recently pushed his way through. Behind him June was breathing heavily, and her voice fluttered in the dark. "There's something following us outside the tunnel," she said tightly, nervously.

He crawled quickly to the end and stood up. "There's nothing here now. It must have been an animal."

He felt odd: calm, safe, yet slyly and elusively excited. His eyes had grown equal to the dark. The trees were stouter, and even closer; they squeezed out masses of shrub between them. Overhead, a few pale scraps of sky were caught in branches. The ground squelched underfoot, and he heard another sound ahead: similar, but not the same.

June emerged panting. "I thought I'd finished tripping. Where are we going?" she said unevenly. "I can't see."

"This way." He headed at once for a low opening in the tangled growth. As he'd somehow expected, the passage twisted several times, closing almost impenetrably, then widened. Perhaps he'd noticed that someone before him had thrust the bushes apart.

"Don't go so fast," June said in the dark, almost weeping. "Wait for me."

Her slowness annoyed him. His indefinable excitement seemed to affect his skin, which crawled with nervousness like interference on the surface of a bubble. Yet he felt strangely powerful, ready for anything. Wait until he saw his father! He stood impatiently, stamping the mushy ground, while June caught up with him. She gripped his arm. "There it is again," she gasped.

"What?" The sound? It was only his feet, squelching. But there was another sound, ahead in the tangled creaking dark. It was the gurgling of mud, perhaps of a muddy stream gargling ceaselessly into the earth. No: it was growing louder, more violent, as though the mud were straining to spew out an obstruction. The sound was repeated, again and again, becoming gradually clearer: a single syllable. All at once he knew what it was. Somewhere ahead in the close dark maze, a thick muddy voice was struggling to shout his name.

June had recognised the sound too, and was tugging at

his arm. "Let's go back," she pleaded. "I don't like it. Please."

"God," he scoffed. "I thought you were going to help me." The muddy sounds blurred into a mumble, and were gone. Twigs shook in the oppressive dark, squeaking hollowly together. Suddenly, ahead of him, he heard his father's voice; then, after a long silence, his mother's. Both were oddly strained and muffled. As though this were a game of hide and seek, each had called his name.

"There," he said to June. "I haven't got time to take you back now." His excitement was mounting, his nervous skin felt light as a dream. "Don't you want to look after my mother?" he blurted.

He shouldered onwards. After a while he heard June following him timidly. A wind blundered through the forest, dragging at the bushes. Thorns struggled overhead, clawing at the air; the ground gulped his feet, sounding to his strained ears almost like words. Twice the walls of the passage tried to close, but someone had broken them apart. Ahead the passage broadened. He was approaching an open space.

He began to run. Bushes applauded like joyful bones. The thick smoky sky rushed on, fighting the moonlight. The vociferous ground was slippery; he stumbled as he ran, and almost tripped over a dark huddle. It was his parents' clothes. Some of them, as he glanced back impatiently, looked torn. He heard June fall slithering against bushes. "Don't!" she cried. But he had reached the space.

It was enclosed by trees. Ivy thickened the trunks, and had climbed to mat the tangle overhead; bushes crowded the cramped gaps between the trees. In the interstices of the tangle, dark sky smouldered.

Slowly his eyes found the meagre light; outlines gathered in the clearing, dimmer than mist. Bared wooden limbs groped into the space, creaking. The dimness sketched them. He could see now that the clearing was about thirty feet wide, and roughly circular. Dimness crawled on it, as though it were an infested pond. At the far side, a dark bulk stood between him and the trees.

He squinted painfully, but its shape persisted in eluding him. Was it very large, or was the dark lying? Across the clearing mud coughed and gurgled thickly, or something did. Dimness massed on the glistening shape. Suddenly he saw that the shape was moving lethargically, and alive.

June had hung back; now she ran forwards, only to slip at the edge of the clearing. She clutched his arm to steady herself, then she gazed beyond him, trembling. "What is it?" she cried.

"Shut up," he said savagely.

Apart from her interruption, he felt more calm than he had ever felt before. He knew he was gazing at the source of his dreams. The dreams returned peacefully to his mind and waited to be understood. For a moment he wondered whether this was like June's LSD. Something had been added to his mind, which seemed to be expanding awesomely. Memories floated free, as though they had been coded deep in him: wombs of stone and submarine depths; hovering in a medium that wasn't space, somehow linked to a stone circle on a hill; being drawn closer to the circle, towards terrified faces that stared up through the night; a pregnant woman held writhing at the centre of the circle, screaming as he hovered closer and reached for her. He felt primed with centuries of memories. Inherited memories, or shared; but whose?

He waited. All was about to be clarified. The huge bulk shifted, glistening. Its voice, uncontrollably loud and uneven, struggled muddily to speak. The trees creaked ponderously, the squashed bushes writhed, the sky fled incessantly. Suddenly, touched by an instinct he couldn't define, Michael realised how he and June must look from the far side of the clearing. He took her arm, though she struggled briefly, and they stood waiting: bride and bridegroom of the dark.

After a long muddy convulsion in the dimness, words coughed free. The voice seemed unable to speak more than a phrase at a time; then it would blur, gurgling. Sometimes his father's voice, and occasionally his mother's – high-pitched, trembling – seemed to help. Yet the effect was disturbing, for it sounded as though the muddy voice were attempting muffled imitations of his parents. He held himself calm, trusting that this too would be clarified in due course.

The Great Old Ones still lived, the halting voice gurgled loudly. Their dreams could reach out. When the human race was young and strayed near the Old Ones the dreams could reach into the womb and make the unborn in their image. Something like his mother's voice spoke the last words, wavering fearfully. June struggled, but he gripped her arm.

Though the words were veiled and allusive, he understood instinctively what was being said. His new memories were ready to explain. When he read the notebooks again he would understand consciously. He listened and gazed, fascinated. He was in awe of the size of the speaking bulk. And what was strange about the head? Something moved there, rapid as the whirl of colours on a bubble. In the dark the face seemed to strain epileptically, perhaps to form words.

The Old Ones could wait, the voice or voices told him. The stars would come right. The people the Old Ones touched before birth did not take on their image all at once but gradually, down the centuries. Instead of dying, they took on the form that the Old Ones had placed in the womb of an ancestor. Each generation came closer to the perfect image.

The bulk glistened as though flayed; in the dimness it looked pale pink, and oddly unstable. Michael stared uneasily at the head. Swift clouds dragged darknesses over the clearing and snatched them away. The face looked so huge, and seemed to spread. Wasn't it like his father's face? But the eyes were swimming apart, the features slid uncontrollably across the head. All this was nothing but the antics of shadows. A tear in the clouds crept toward the dimmed moon. June was trying to pull away. "Keep still," he snarled, tightening his grip.

They would serve the Old Ones, the voice shouted thickly, faltering. That was why they had been made: to be ready when the time came. They shared the memories of the Old Ones and at the change their bodies were transformed into the stuff of the Old Ones. They mated with ordinary people in the human way, and later in the way the Old Ones had decreed. That way was

June screamed. The tear in the clouds had unveiled the moon. Her cry seemed harsh enough to tear her throat. He turned furiously to silence her; but she dragged herself free, eyes gaping, and fled down the path. The shadow of a cloud rushed towards the clearing. About to pursue June, he turned to see what the moon had revealed.

The shadow reached the clearing as he turned. For a moment he saw the huge head, a swollen bulb which, though blanched by moonlight, reminded him of a mass dug from within a body. The glistening lumpy forehead was almost bare, except for a few strands that groped restlessly over it – strands of hair, surely, though they looked like strings of livid flesh.

On the head, seeming even smaller amid the width of

flesh, he saw his mother's face. It was appallingly dwarfed, and terrified. The strands flickered over it, faster, faster. Her mouth strained wordlessly, gurgling.

Before he could see the rest of the figure, a vague gigantic squatting sack, the shadow flooded the clearing. As it did so, he thought he saw his mother's face sucked into the head, as though by a whirlpool of flesh. Did her features float up again, newly arranged? Were there other, plumper, features jostling among them? He could be sure of nothing in the dark.

June cried out. She'd stumbled; he heard her fall, and the thud of her head against something: then silence. The figure was lumbering towards him, its bulk quaking. For a moment he was sure that it intended to embrace him. But it had reached a pit, almost concealed by undergrowth. It slid into the earth, like slow jelly. The undergrowth sprang back rustling.

He stood gazing at June, who was still unconscious. He knew what he would tell her: she had had a bad LSD experience, that had been what she'd seen. LSD reminded him of something. Slowly he began to smile.

He went to the pit and peered down. Faint sluggish muddy sounds retreated deep into the earth. He knew he wouldn't see his parents for a long time. He touched his pocket, where the envelope waited. That would contain his father's explanation of their disappearance, which he could show to people, to June.

Moonlight and shadows raced nervously over the pit. As he stared at the dark mouth he felt full of awe, yet calm. Now he must wait until it was time to come back here, to go into the earth and join the others. He remembered that now; he had always known, deep in himself, that this was home. One day he and June would return. He gazed at her unconscious body, smiling. Perhaps she had been right; they might take LSD together, when it was time. It might help them to become one.

IN SILENCE, IN DYING, IN DARK

CALEB WEINHARDT

I wear my best suit to be buried in. I go the whole day in it, but no one has a kind word to say. Not even Netta. She doesn't notice the silver cufflinks she gave me; just looks on past.

This has become comfortable, common. It's a burden lifted—much lighter than stifling skirts and strangling corsets that could not contain all of me. I was always spilling out; everyone else could see that and looked disdainfully at my excess. An obvious miscommunication between myself and God.

But in my best suit, I am invisible.

On my funeral day, I watch Netta dress in black. A veil hides her face away. It belonged to her mother, and shows its age in holes and tears. She walks with slow, deliberate paces, not lifting her head to the ferryman or the few guests who come to console her. I would offer her my hand if I could.

But when they go to lower me into the ground, there is a hitch. A message passed from a sweating priest, a glance at Netta that changes everything.

Did she know? She must have known.

The service is halted. My employer from the print shop has come too, fuming from the ears. He hands Netta a letter written in my hand, confirming the accusations.

She feigns shock. Disbelief. It's what I would tell her to do. It will only buy her time, some small change she might use to flee the city. But I am here, tethered to the body that has not yet fallen into the ground.

Dirt is wiped away. A casket carried back on wearier shoulders.

༺༻

I worked at the printers for nine years. What good it does me now. I was young and fresh-faced, Netta always scrubbing ink stains from my shirts. There was a thrill to it then, for folks to look at me without a second glance. To nod, to say *yes*, to stamp my papers. My employer, Graham, was grim and gray-faced, with a mustache that twitched as he examined my work. This was how he communicated his approval or disapproval, without looking me in the eye. I came to learn that this was the way things were done between men.

There was something said in the absence. There was a

trust he need not look deeper.

But also something missed. Because the papers that run after my death claim I had a woman's eyes, and that everyone knew this. I watch Graham print those words, the ink seeping into his skin. If only, he wishes, he had looked closer.

I started there after I'd met Netta. We came to Boston together, hoping to disappear for a while. And she was right—no one looked at us strangely as husband and wife. It was easier to find work, and soon we had our own apartment with creaky floors and dusty furniture that started to take on the salt of our sweat.

⁂

I am in the coach with Netta when she rides back to the coroner, her hands tucked inside each other. She looks pale and ghostly, watching rain tap against the window. Away from the small plot at the cemetery she spent all our savings on.

I reach across and touch her hands, try to pull them apart. When they fall open, she looks up at me, bewildered.

She does not see that I am here with her.

⁂

She doesn't know the lengths I went to. Late nights in the shop when everyone else had already gone home to their wives, printing page after page so they would all be there for Graham in the morning, so he would nod without looking me in the eye and leave me a tip. And then I would crawl into bed alongside Netta when the sun was nearly up.

I never told her about the letters. They came at regular intervals, every few months, then closer together. I anticipated their arrival and hid them. *It's time to send more money,* they said. Signed, *X*.

You know who. For a secret safely kept.

It was something I had to do, for Netta and for the life we had built together.

Once, I came close to confessing, ready to spill all onto the page and rid us both of the blade that swung nearer and nearer. Someone from my old life with a grudge—why should they hold so much power? It would be so easy to work it into the back pages of the newspaper, where no one would notice until it was too late.

But then I saw Netta fussing with her hair before church, how all she knew was that the strife was long behind us, and I could not take that away from her.

The page I wrote left my mind. It sat buried with my other work, pushing its way to the surface like a splinter.

Each time the letters came, the sum grew larger. I tried my best to keep this from her, but she must have noticed the money slowly leaving our accounts. Perhaps she suspected gambling or another woman. These were preferable answers. The silence between us widened.

The lights are off when she arrives, and I follow behind. Even the dead must sleep sometimes. But the coroner switches them back on for her, bright and blistering. There is Graham with him, and the magistrate, and the priest, and the barrister. They wear a gallery of expressions when Netta comes in, from disgust to amusement to *look what we're going to show you*.

Netta, already thinking of her defense, shows nothing discernible. She hardly speaks. She follows them down the long hall.

※

My fear of the letters was misplaced, when something much more pressing lay at my doorstep. I should have feared the young pageboy that came in the mornings to collect his papers. I should have noticed his sunken eyes, the way he turned away to hack into his sleeve. But I was printing pages and paying off debt, and didn't notice until the first spatter of blood.

I kept this from Netta too. Didn't want to worry her. I stayed working as long as I could, my skin turning pale from the dim light, washed in blue. My eyesight was poor from squinting and darkness. The cough came and got stronger, and soon I couldn't catch my breath.

She was angry, yes. She shouted and threw things. *We could have gotten help*, she said. *You should have told me.* She tried to convince me to see a doctor, but I, thinking of how they would use their tools to look inside me, refused. There were secrets I had worked so hard to keep, and I would not let illness undo them. She said that didn't matter now.

But I was quiet in my stubbornness. The illness persisted, and so did Netta's fury.

◈

I would prefer her rage now over her quiet. I want it to rip from her throat for me, to deafen the room. I want her to make them cower and tremble in the face of it.

But I can't make a sound, and neither can Netta. The two of us must stand and watch as they disrobe my body.

It is not kind. It is not ceremonial. Netta does not want to, but they make her look. I have no choice. I feel every inch of it.

I no longer wear my nice black suit. I am no longer invisible. Skin falls over bones in peaks and valleys. Eyelids shut. And once they are complete with the surface, having investigated every part of it, they peel that away too to see what lies underneath.

As they cut and carve, I see a creature emerge that no longer looks like me. This thing is fleshy with categorizable organs and a message to be decoded.

Do you see now? They ask Netta. Half-toothy smiles—they are so proud of their amateur detective work, their butchery.

Netta nods with dull eyes. She turns back through the

door to the office where she must sign some papers, and brushes right past me. I can see the change in her, the hairs that rise on her skin, but she only pauses shortly before she goes.

⁂

Netta does not see my body again, once in the hands of the state. That is how she will remember me—splayed out and gutted for inquisitors, thoroughly defined and documented. That is how she will be known—the widow who is not a widow, the woman who was deceived and yet also complicit.

But in time, she moves on. She marries. She leaves the city.

And I stay. I wander as far as the cemetery and the print shop and the outskirts of town, but can go no further. I linger until the places become unfamiliar and new.

My body does not lie in a grave with my name, but an unmarked hole in the dirt. It welcomes me hungrily into its darkness—the hole was alone, too, before I came. And now we rot together. Roots embrace me.

It happens day by day, not all at once. A gradual loss of feeling, a transparency in my fingertips. A thinning. I lose my hair and my tongue. Earth fills my mouth until only teeth are left. And sometime, after many years and many lifetimes, I return to nothing.

ONE OF THOSE GIRLS

PREMEE MOHAMED

At first, Benny debated wrapping the suicide note around the plastic stick, or taping them together (because what if, in the chaos of discovering her body, the proof was lost?). But an envelope would be best, she decided. It would look neat, professional. It would show that she had *thought this through*, the final, rational act of eighteen years spent thinking things through.

Except this one thing, of course. She tilted the stick to better catch the hazy afternoon light: still two blue lines. Would the chemicals fade and make her seem a liar afterwards? Everything faded—ink, book covers, fabric dye, wallpaper. Well, she would just have to do it soon, then.

She closed her eyes, feeling the weak sun on her face. Her first year of university, the semester not even half over, and instead of reviewing her calculus notes she was deciding whether to kill herself now, or be caught trying to get an abortion and die that way. That was a kind of calculus too, she supposed.

"Beni*aaaaa*? Are you coming to eat?"

Benny shoved the plastic stick under the untidiest heap of papers on her desk and ran to open the door. "Yes, Ma."

Her mother was short, powerfully built, and even in the soft swags of her housecoat she gave the impression of something adamantine. A few bright flecks—turmeric or curry powder—gleamed golden on the edge of her eyeglasses. She peered over Benny's shoulder, narrowing her eyes, and for a split second Benny's fear felt more vast than the sight of the second blue line appearing in the stick, like a sea monster slowly but inexorably surfacing to savage and eat her: *Oh no, I left the box on the desk, Jesus God, or the instructions sheet—*

"Clean your room," her mother said after a moment that felt like an eternity. "How can you study like that?"

"Sorry. Right after dinner."

As she ate, she drafted the interrupted suicide note in her head. Her heart was still pounding from the near-miss. Hers wasn't like the families on TV, who would have been all "These things happen" and "Let's talk about supporting you and the baby." She'd heard enough stories to know exactly what would happen instead. In a family where even minor mistakes resulted in draconian punishments (so you never dared make the same one twice), this—the biggest mistake imaginable—would incur whatever went beyond draconian. No, her way would be easier. Neater. It might even be expected from little Benny, the most risk-averse, anxious-to-please, goody-two-shoes.

Dear all, she wrote on the imagined sheet of paper, *please accept the enclosed item as confirmation of my resignation...*

Above the sink, the white lace curtain briefly billowed out, the play of shadows forming the shape of a woman: pregnant, not billowed but *bellied*, swaybacked, faceless except for the shattered *O* of a shrieking mouth.

Benny flinched, dropping her fork. Her mother said, "What happened?"

"Nothing. Sorry. Bit my tongue."

The shape was gone. A week ago, Benny would have screamed; now, although startled, she had developed the resignation of familiarity. She ducked her head, telling herself she hadn't seen it, it was nothing, *Psychosomatic, that's the word—seeing things from stress.*

⁂

It was an hour and a half to campus; her friends often asked why she didn't just move into residence (white friends, anyway—anyone Asian or West Indian already knew). Benny had scholarship money, she qualified for a spot, surely—"I don't mind," she repeated. "I study on the bus, it's fine. I like the quiet time." It was weak, but it sounded better than saying *I'm not allowed to move out.* They didn't get it; they thought legal adulthood severed the bond like a guillotine blade. There probably were families like that, she reflected. Not hers. The fight over her moving out was one of the things she wanted to push as far down into the incinerator of her memory as possible. She shouldn't even have asked; they still brought it up. *How could you? How could you say such a thing to your family?*

She sat at the back of the bus today, watching people get on and off with a kind of fretful wariness. Students, office workers, a dozen old mainland Chinese ladies hopping on for their weekly girls' breakfast, a bunch of young Black kids in private-school uniforms (grey blazer, red tie), then some elderly Indian women in full saris and jewellery (at this hour of the morning!) headed to the fancy shops...

Benny was studying not faces but the gaps between them, where the pregnant woman in white often appeared, silently screaming. The woman seemed to live within that interstitial plane, an optical illusion formed by negative space. Benny had been frightened the first time, sure that she'd seen a ghost, or worse—a demon, a vampire, something else she didn't believe in—and had simply gotten off the bus in a blind panic and vomited, she believed from the shock, into a trashcan on Sheppard Ave.

Of course it hadn't been shock.

Benny had no idea how her brain had come up with

this, or whether the apparition was *real* in some way (no one else seemed to see it) and not other ways. She did not even know whether this was some kind of known quantity, something from a pantheon of minor scaries... her parents always refused to tell her anything about Guyana, any legends, myths. They occasionally leaked a few superstitions, like an aunt telling a pregnant cousin that she mustn't go anywhere alone, but always with another woman (and, if possible, carrying a stick). But that was a vault that was closed to her, filled with knowledge that had no impact on their lives here in Canada.

Anyway, it was nothing, nothing. *Not real. Things that aren't real can't hurt you.*

Benny got off at her stop and stepped out of the swirl of students, watching as the streams divided, poured into doorways, leaving a few stragglers running to get to their classes. No woman in white.

"Hey."

Benny turned: a blaze of red hair and red jacket, her friend Melissa, her oldest friend and the only one her parents grudgingly tolerated when she called the house. "Hey," she said. "Thanks for coming. I mean, thanks for setting this up, for... for everything..."

"Ben, it's OK," Melissa said. She punched Benny lightly on the arm. "I'm just glad I could, like, throw myself on the grenade for you. I can't *believe* you thought it'd be easier to off yourself than to just find an appointment."

"It's not that I thought it'd be *easier*, it's just..." Benny trailed off, tears stinging her eyes. Melissa didn't understand, she'd never understand, just as she wouldn't understand the reality or unreality of the woman in white. "It's not about easy or hard, it's like... I'm not the *kind* of person who does this, I'm not someone who *can* do this. We've known each other since we were like, what, ten years old? It's..."

Melissa nodded uncertainly. Benny gave up. It was about her parents, about how the verb *parenting* was only ever a synonym for fear and control, about a regimented world in which things like this never had to be discussed because they hadn't raised a daughter who would need it. She had been hammered too flat for too long to be otherwise now; they had crafted her into an instrument that could only be employed by their hands, of no use to others. That was why she needed Melissa for this.

"Everything's fucked up," Benny finally finished.

"Hell yeah. But I'm not gonna leave you. You're turning green, are you gonna throw up?"

"Don't think so."

"Well, I got mints in my bag if you feel sick. Plus, I asked Wing to take notes for us in linear algebra. But we'd better get going. They're pretty strict about the appointment times."

Benny had expected picketers, as they occasionally saw on campus—strident, shiny-faced religious types holding signs with graphic pictures of dismembered fetuses—but the building hadn't attracted more than its regular share of foot traffic. It lurked quietly at the back of a parking lot that it shared with a half-dozen other stores listed on the CUSTOMER PARKING ONLY sign. "Oh my *God*," Benny laughed, pointing.

"What?" said Melissa.

"Nancy's Baby Boutique. Two doors down from an abortion clinic."

"In*cred*ible. What else is here? Oh, there's a plumbing place, boring... there's a..."

"Benita?"

Benny froze at the voice; for a split second she thought her bladder might let go, dimly thinking *Oh, I thought that didn't happen till you were further along, guess I'm just a gifted kid in everything*. She turned, already picking through excuses in her head, you couldn't really lie to old women, they knew too much, but what she might have was a *tiny* bit of plausibility, because they were still in the parking lot.

"Hi, Aunty."

Her aunt smiled, a brittle, suspicious expression that didn't reach her eyes. "You don't have class?" she said. "Your mama said you left at six like usual for your early class."

Benny almost rolled her eyes. This was the problem with her apartment: not just that three other units in the building were occupied by aunts, uncles, and cousins, but that they were incurable goddamned busybodies who did nothing but watch the front walk and gossip all day. "Class was cancelled," she said.

"For the whole day?"

"No, just that one."

"So what are you doing out here? You're pretty far from school, nuh?"

None of your goddamned business! "We're, uh," Benny said. *Think! It's going to get back to Mom and Dad anyway. Make it sound legit but something they can't check.* "We're doing a project for our engineering class," she said, gesturing at the plumbing store. "We're building, uh..."

"A water treatment system," Melissa said brightly. "This was the only place we could get everything."

"Well! You go on in and shop, I just need to stop in at Spice Village here to get some saltfish and dry goods, and then I'll give you a ride back so you don't have to take the nasty bus—how's that?"

"No, no," Benny said, resisting a powerful urge to look at her watch. Were they already late? How long would the clinic wait for a patient? They had only gotten this slot because of a cancellation—it would be weeks till the next one. Surely... "No, Aunty. We don't want to hold you up."

"It's no trouble! This isn't a safe neighbourhood for girls to walk alone!"

Melissa glanced at her watch then, and Benny did not

even need to see her friend's restrained wince to know that they were too late. She stood very still for a moment, feeling the swell of rage and despair and injustice and futility, then pushing it back down. "Thanks!" she forced herself to say. "We'll just be a few minutes."

"Take yuh time, girls," her aunt said airily, shepherding them toward the plumbing store, where the cashier gave them a startled look through the plate-glass window.

Next to her in the back seat of her aunt's SUV, Melissa scribbled quickly on the back of the receipt, *It's OK. Call 4 another appt SOON.*

Benny nodded, still rattled by how close she had come to freedom, as if a door had been slammed in her face. She wrote, *Do u think I should tell him?*

Melissa thought for a second, then wrote back, *Why?*

―※―

It was a good question; Benny did not have an answer. In this at least she was on the same page as her family, who had drilled into her from an early age that the only thing worse than creating dirty laundry was airing it out. And she understood that to an extent. They had come from lives of poverty and desperation, accepting this cold wild land only inasmuch as it might raise them at least a little from the mire of their history.

And their kids must be better still—sheltered and educated, snipped and bent into two perfect creatures: a white one assimilated into this new society, and a brown one retaining all the qualities of home. The only unbreakable rule was to keep up the façade. If white people saw immigrants acting like... like *sluts* or *savages* or *thieves* or *animals*, that would be the only thing they would remember forever, and everyone would suffer.

Keep it in the family. Hush it up. And for God's sake, be classy about it.

And yet: she had not gotten knocked up on her goddamn *own*. She had lost her virginity (willingly, awkwardly) to someone who had condoms and, as far as she could tell in the shameful darkness, used them correctly.

So even if this wasn't entirely his fault, it was not entirely hers either. She had grown up taking the blame for everything, but for this it was *scientifically impossible* to shoulder the full burden.

She paused in front of his office door, only half-seeing the name placard (*Dr. R. MacClain – Assistant Prof – Physics Dept*), her hand held up as if to knock. Now she did feel sick, a creeping liquid heat moving up her throat. She went to the fountain, drank deeply of the mineral-tasting water, put two of Melissa's Altoids in her mouth, returned.

As she lifted her hand again, the door swung open and he stared down at her: a tall, pale man in a crisp blue shirt, his blond hair slipping over his collar as he reared his head back in surprise. With a little start she realized it had been almost three weeks since she'd seen him, since she'd run her hands through his silky hair, liking the texture, not telling him, waiting for him to invite her to speak.

"Robert, we really need to talk. It's been almost a month," she said quickly, reciting her memorized speech before she could chicken out. "I have to—"

"Ah, Benita!" he said loudly. "I'm sorry I can't help with your assignment, we were just headed out." He opened the door fully to let someone pass out of the office, a pretty, heavyset woman in an unbuttoned black coat, her hand smoothing the brightly patterned dress draping the prominently curved abdomen. "My wife, Alison. Alison, this is Benny—" He hesitated for a fraction of a second, just long enough for Benny to realize, with ugly clarity, *He doesn't remember my last name.*

"One of my physics 238 students," he concluded. "I've told all my kids they can come see me outside of office hours, but tonight just doesn't work; I stopped in to drop off some books, and then we're headed over to the theatre for a charity show. The med students, you know."

"Oh," Benny heard her mouth say. "Uh, I've heard a lot about that show. It's OK, Dr. M, it was last week's assignment I wanted to ask about. It's not a rush or anything."

"Well, all right." His eyes twinkled benevolently as he ushered both women along the hallway. Benny could not stop staring at his pregnant wife, her plain gold band; Robert did not wear his ring. She supposed Alison didn't mind. Her grey eyes were lively and intelligent, and rested on Benny now with a certain sympathy or nostalgia or something equally innocent, so that Benny abruptly perceived herself as seen from the outside: a dark-skinned brown girl with coarse black hair in an unraveling braid, smeared glasses, a backpack half as big as she was. *Poor young thing, I remember my undergraduate days*—something like that.

Benny's ears were ringing as if she had hit her head. She fled, muttering something about variables, looking at her feet. Pacing her, just visible, was the woman in white, her pale legs hovering above the ground, and was that a black coat wrapped around her white dress, like a bad joke?

"Stop it," Benny whispered. "*I* didn't know he was fucking *married*. Don't you think I have enough problems? Leave me *alone*."

※

She thought about calling Melissa and saying *I'm losing my mind*; she thought about calling campus mental-health services; she could not imagine the conversation that would follow. What *would* someone do with a pregnant girl who was going insane? It would have been so easy, so rational, to tell herself that it wasn't the pregnancy itself that was doing it but her fixation on it, the way it scraped at her every waking thought, ripping off the previous day's scabs; under these conditions, of *course* she was seeing a ghostly pregnant woman. The ghost was a symbol, or a metonymy, or whatever the term was, she couldn't remember.

Yet she couldn't tell herself that, because the dreams had started before she knew she was pregnant—before she *could* have known, if her math was right.

She thought about sending a letter to the school newspaper naming names, and then killing herself.

She thought about next year, which was not the first of the new millennium (that would be the year after), and the new year's parties she would not attend or even be invited to.

She thought about the family wedding where her cousin had dumped a crying baby on her, "I'll be back in a second," and gone off to dance, and Benny had wandered around trying to shush the sodden lump, or hand it off to someone, and how the rest of her family had laughed at her distress and told her to get used to it. *Get used to it, that'll be life after you get married, and you know we're only sending you to school to find a husband...*

She thought about starving herself; maybe that would kill the unwanted thing and spare her.

She thought about running away, then shuddered at what would happen after the uproar and the return home, when all the TV cameras had left.

She thought about confessing and just letting them kill her.

She thought about screaming back at the woman in white, but not silently.

The theatre was stuffy, as if at some point a sound producer had complained about the loudness of the ventilation and building services had shut it down instead of fixing it. Benny felt light-headed from the heat and, she suspected, the carbon dioxide levels, but pleasantly so; she had never gotten drunk (*no harm in doing it now, I suppose*) but this was how she imagined it: sweaty, dizzy, free from worry and shame. Newly released from prison, or about to be.

She and Melissa had holed up in a friend's dorm room and called clinics and hospitals all day, threading the needle between "Well it's not technically an emergency" and "It's not optional, though." At last, they snagged another appointment—six weeks from now, so she might be starting to show, but that was a problem for the future. Tonight they could celebrate, within the limits of getting Benny home by 10 p.m. And Melissa had promised this play was her kind of thing: uncomplicated, funny, dark.

"And nothing about babies, right?" Benny whispered as the curtain inched upwards.

Melissa chuckled. "I swear," she whispered back. "No babies, no kids, no pregnant bellies, no sex, just four friends going on a road trip and coming back with three."

"Oh, *murder*. Murder's fine."

The director came on-stage and delivered a shaky speech about the play; Benny thought it was clear that he wanted to be backstage. The four friends, graceful boys in upper-class stiff, formal 1950s outfits, walked on and arranged themselves on the couches in postures of relaxation.

And from behind them, unbidden, her hands out as if navigating a private darkness, despite the bright lights of the stage, came the woman in white: clearer than Benny had ever seen her, the black hair writhing over her shoulders, the translucent dress showing the full curve of the heavy belly, dark smudge of her pubis half-hidden by the overhang, her white limbs not the colour of skin but of bone. The faceless face turning to the audience, seeking, sightless and soundless over the void of her open mouth.

Benny choked on a scream, and thought abandoned her. All she could think of was getting out, out, *away, now*. Breathlessly she eeled past the three people at the end of the row, stumbling on the stairs, taking them three at a time to the closest exit door. Three panicked shoves and it finally spat her into the empty lobby.

She was shaking, sweat trickling down her face, stomach churning. Staring at the carpet helped—a busy pattern of yellow and red on a dark blue ground. Air, she needed air. Low oxygen in there. Scientific. Melissa would come looking for her but that was all right, she'd be back by then. Quick walk.

Outside was better, the fresh air settling her stomach; she looked up instinctively at the night sky, but there were too many lights to see stars. One lap around the building would take five or ten minutes, and then she'd go back in. It was fine. Fine.

She was almost around the third corner when she spotted the man on the sidewalk, moving perpendicular to her, heading for the street. She didn't even recognize him with her eyes, it felt more like her whole body knew, striking her with a familiarity that she did not, even now, mistake for love, for the tenderness one feels for the beloved unaware they are being watched.

He hadn't seen her; for a second she considered letting him go on. But they were alone, and he still didn't know, and the confusing blend of betrayal and jealousy and relief and anger she'd felt when she saw his wife last week returned to her like a shock of cold water.

The problem was solved but he was *not* going to escape unmarked if she wasn't.

"Rob."

He turned, and even in the sickly yellow lights she saw on his face the desire to run—he mastered it, and even managed a smile. "Benny. Hi."

Benny. Hi. The best he could do for someone he had slept with, on and off, for five weeks. *OK.* "Here for the show?" she said.

"Uh, no. Just headed back to my office to... where's your coat? You must be freezing."

"I have to tell you something," she said.

"... Well, let's go inside, and—"

"It'll only take a second," Benny said. And he clearly guessed, because he stayed, gnawing on his lower lip, something in his eyes not like fear but distaste: Was this blackmail, would she go to the Dean, what proof did she have, would it be her word against his, it was just a little fling—"I'm pregnant," she said.

For a horrible moment his mouth contorted around a reflexive *Congratulations!* before he visibly got ahold of himself and said, "Are you suggesting that your condition is somehow related to me?"

Benny blinked incredulously. Was *he* suggesting that she was the Virgin Mary? Or—no, of course not. She narrowed her eyes, feeling the white heat of anger overtake her anxiety. *Don't talk back*, she heard her parents scream at her, same tone, same cadence, year after year. *Shut up and listen. Shut up and listen.*

Not this time.

"It sounds like *you're* suggesting that I've slept with enough guys to not know who the father is," she said, her voice shaking. "But you're the reason for the condition, in case I'm not making myself clear. I thought..."

Her eyes grew hot as she groped for a way to finish the sentence. She hadn't thought they'd end up together; she was young and she was sheltered but no one was *that* naïve. But she hadn't thought this would happen, and she hadn't thought he'd disappear if something like this happened. He hadn't wanted this; neither had she. Surely that put them on the same side. Yet he was acting like a boy her age, frantically trying to shift the blame, calculating a way to salvage at least *his* future, and who cared whether hers or the baby's were over.

"I think you'd have a difficult time proving that," he said.

"I think paternity testing is pretty good these days," she said. *And anyway, in a few weeks it won't matter. I just thought you should know...* no, she refused to let him off scot-free, she would not take the entire fall on her own. She squared her shoulders, or tried to. The wind was biting through her thin sweater, and she wanted to wrap her arms around herself. "I'm getting an abortion," she said. "And you're paying for it."

He laughed, a small, condescending sound, as if he had finally found his footing on the unstable ground of the conversation, and had spotted a chance to knock her off-balance.

"Well, let's look at this scientifically," he said. She took a step back, instinctively, from the tone. "You're not negotiating very well, Benita. If I refuse to pay up—which I do—you're going to get the abortion anyway, aren't you? So you won't *have* any evidence for a paternity test. Your other option is to cancel the appointment if I don't give you the money, and, perhaps, attempt to go public—and get a *court-mandated* paternity test once it's born. But you don't want that, do you? You want to keep it quiet. You want to make it go away as much as I do. So why are you even telling me?"

"Because it's half your fucking child," she said flatly. "And it's half your fucking fault. And you want to pretend this was nothing, this meant nothing, I meant nothing. How many undergraduates have you fucked, Rob? How many girls did you offer extra help, and then start calling yourself their *best friend*, and then putting your hand on their leg? You were too good at it for me to have been the first. Were they all even legal?"

The slap startled her, partly because she hadn't expected it and partly because it was so weak, compared to her father's, that she instantly thought of the stage fights the actors might be having right now. She laughed before she could stop herself, and didn't see his hand rise again.

The second slap was less of a surprise (*Who stops at one?* she thought dazedly) and much harder, right from his shoulder. She stumbled out of range, shocked when he followed, shoving her into the darkness of the loading dock behind the theatre. His face was a mask of animal rage as he grappled with her, first snatching at her sweater and then her throat, his cold fingers unyielding as metal.

This wasn't really happening, it couldn't be. He was a professor, a math nerd, in a second he would remember what he was and who he was and he'd let go—

"You little *bitch*," he whispered, dropping his messenger bag on the concrete dock to free both hands. "If you think you can talk to *me* like that—"

Benny clawed at his hands, her kicking weakening

by the second. She only distantly felt his grip tighten, overwhelmed by dizziness and cold, the faraway lights of the parking lot dimming from yellow to grey. Her mouth opened in an airless scream.

And behind him, the woman in white appeared.

Real? Not-real? He surely felt her hand on his shoulder—felt it, she could see it in his face—and as he turned, snarling incoherently, Benny could even see what he was thinking: *Oh, it's just another woman, who cares.*

Then he saw her face more clearly, and jerked back, disbelieving at first rather than frightened, loosening his grip on Benny's throat.

The woman in white seized both his wrists and twisted, forward and back, turning her dress into a wild flutter of white; Benny fell awkwardly to the ground. Her vision was still clouded somehow, for she half-saw, half-sensed MacClain and the woman not exchanging blows but wrestling, as if she were trying to take something from him and he, reflexively, not knowing what else to do, was trying to stop her.

There was no blood, no breaking of bone, no tearing of skin. The woman in white swelled—in triumph, Benny thought incoherently—and her thin, blue-white hand shot back to her chest, concealing something, and then she was gone.

MacClain was still alive, sobbing, his silky blond hair askew on the concrete, as Benny scrambled to her feet and ran back to the lobby.

Melissa was already at the far end, a bright spot of red, and she headed for Benny at a run. "Ben! Benny, are you— Jesus!"

The carpet rose to meet her. Cramps, sudden, knifed red-hot through her gut, and for just a second Benny wanted to joke about dinner (cheap pasta at the chain restaurant down the block), maybe to ask Melissa if she'd eaten off her plate, but the pain erased any hint of humour. The blood soaking her corduroy thighs was hot, irregular, coming in pulses. Waves. "What the fuck?" she gasped. "I'm not— I'm not—"

"Don't be stupid," Melissa hissed, as an usher finally clued in and headed toward them. "It's the size of a blueberry at this point, you know that."

"Then what—"

"Call 911!" Melissa shouted over her head, as darkness dragged her down.

"So your parents... freaked out? Didn't freak out? I called a couple times and they said you weren't talking to anyone."

Benny sighed. "They meant *they* didn't want me to talk to anyone. Mom freaked out. Dad... well, the doctor told them it was a 'ruptured cyst' instead of a miscarriage, thank fuck, and when he heard talk of *women parts* he sort of disappeared. But they don't know, so they just freaked out because I was sick."

"Phew."

"Yeah." She pressed her forehead to the window, gazing out at the falling snow. White, untenanted, innocent. "Thanks. For everything."

"That's what friends are for," Melissa said firmly. "Did you ever, uh..."

"Funny story about that," Benny said, lowering her voice as she heard her mother coming down the hallway. "I'll tell you later. It's not really funny. I gotta go. Dinner."

After they ate, she asked her aunt to mail a letter for her; she wasn't supposed to leave the house for a few days.

She had debated writing to Alison; it was not easy to be a pregnant widow, especially with no warning, the heart attack felling MacClain barely a week after the attack at the theatre. Benny had no sympathy for the dead man—no guilt either, only a kind of stunned and horrified relief that now there really was an end. He had not come to justice for attacking her, or anything else, but something else had stepped in to replace justice—had chosen him instead of Alison, him instead of Benny. Benny thought uneasily that it probably didn't always turn out that way.

In the end, all Benny had been able to do was express some vague condolences, and nothing else; she had not even signed her name.

"Got enough postage on it?" her aunt said, taking the envelope delicately and placing it in the side of her purse to stay flat.

"It's local," Benny said. "Thanks, Aunty."

Her mother said, "How yuh feeling, hm? Any more trouble down there?"

Benny shrugged, meeting her mother's gaze steadily, not staring at the floor for once as they spoke. In the hospital, when her mother had come to sign her out, Benny had seen her eyes flick up and over her daughter's shoulder, seeing something there that the staff could not see. One final goodbye, perhaps? Or a final promise?

"I feel OK," she said. "I just need more sleep. But after I get up..."

"Mm?"

"I have some questions for you."

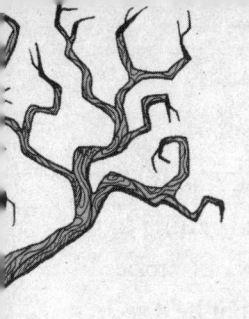

JURACÁN

GABINO IGLESIAS

Manuel looked out the window and wondered if the ropes he'd used to tie his boat down would hold. He knew hurricanes possessed a strength humans couldn't comprehend, and he'd seen winds snap trees in half and tear houses from the ground.

"Your boat will be fine," said Octavio, Manuel's father, from behind him.

"How do you—"

"Your face," said Octavio with a smile that showed his few remaining teeth and multiplied the creases decades under the Caribbean sun had etched into his face. "You get that knot in your forehead every time a hurricane comes. Been doing it since you were a kid."

Manuel had indeed been worried about hurricanes since he was a kid. Some of his fear came from the destruction he knew they brought, but a lot of it had to do with the stories his parents told him. They were also the reason why he was always scared of taking the boat out and getting too close to the reefs bordering San Juan: old spooky stories. He knew ignoring them was the thing to do, but he'd seen enough out in the water and in the woods around his house to know that even the wildest stories had a kernel of truth at their core.

"I think I'm gonna check on the boat real—"

"You'll do no such thing!" Octavio's voice was, for a brief moment, as powerful as it'd ever been. Manuel turned. He saw fear in his father's eyes. That was a rare thing to witness. It sent a shiver down his spine. For the thousandth time, Manuel realized that the toughest part about getting older was watching time pummel his biggest hero into a bent, brittle thing.

"You think that evil spirit you and Mom always talked about is out there?"

Manuel's smile was an attempt to hide his fear and discomfort. His tone was meant to make the whole thing sound ridiculous, nothing more than an old wives' tale from superstitious island people who believed in weird things. Octavio turned his head to the side and nodded. The old man could see right through him. Manuel wanted his father to say something that would make him feel better, but he knew it wouldn't happen and he had no clue how to ask for it.

"It's out there," said Octavio. "It's always out there. I

don't know where it goes when hurricanes stop, but I know it's always... somewhere."

"You really think it took Mom?" The question flew out of his mouth too quickly. The second it passed his lips, Manuel wished he could grab it out of the air and swallow it before it reached his father's ears. He was thirty-three, but talking about his mom always made him feel like he was twelve, scared, and lost.

"There's nothing to think about," said Octavio. "Get away from that window and sit down with me. I have to talk to you."

Manuel turned and went to the kitchen table. A small stack of newspapers sat next to an empty bowl that was supposed to contain fruit but was always empty and the dirty, chipped mug his father used for coffee every morning. They were his things, the little details that made the house his and told Manuel his dad was a presence even when he spent the day watching TV, dozing off, and reminiscing about his years as a fisherman. Manuel pulled out a chair and sat down facing Octavio.

The silence between them was filled by the violent crying of the wind outside and the rattle of their windows as they fought to keep the storm out.

"You've heard the story before, but I want to tell it to you again, this time completely, because I had an awful dream last night and have a bad feeling about this hurricane, son."

Manuel looked at his father. He had nothing to say. He knew the story well and had no desire to hear it again, but the lines on his father's face reminded him of the respect his old man had earned, so he just nodded.

"You already know that your mom and I had been helping a neighbor—Sara was her name—up the mountain whose house was destroyed by Hurricane Georges back in 1998. The rain was coming down hard as we made our way back here with Sara. We were crossing the bridge when... there was a rumbling sound. It was like the earth itself was groaning, cracking open somehow, all that dirt and stone yelling as it tore in half. The sound turned into a roar we could hear even over the wind and the noise the trees were making. Then it dawned on me—it was the river. I'd seen it grow dangerously fast and big before, but never like that. I went to the edge of the bridge and looked down. The water level had gone up and I knew it was a matter of time before the water took the bridge, but we still had time to cross. Well... you know we didn't. The river came down from the mountain, rising like a brown wall of water, mud, trees, and whatever else it had destroyed on its way down. I turned to your mother and..."

Octavio stopped talking. His eyes were shiny with tears, his gaze nailed to the window, where the worsening storm was shaking the trees without mercy. For a few moments, Manuel sat there in silence, respecting his father's moment. Respecting his pain.

"You know this story already," said Octavio all of a sudden, "but this is where the story changes today, son. I've always told you the water came and swallowed the bridge. I've told you that Sara and I made it across, but your mom didn't. That's... not the whole story. I heard a scream as I was looking at the rising river. It made me turn to your mom. I wanted to tell her to hurry up, to grab her hand and run across the bridge together, but when I looked at her, there was something standing next to her, a figure that looked like a big man made of shadow. I saw it for a second before it grabbed your mom like it was hugging her around the waist and jumped with her over the side of the bridge. The neighbor and I panicked. We ran, screaming. We got across just in time. Your mom didn't, but it was because that thing grabbed her. The thing has a name, but I've forgotten it. When you get old, death takes things away from you, and that includes your memories. But I do know what took her. It was the dark demon that travels with every storm. Last night I dreamed that it came back."

The story—boring, painful, tattooed in his heart—was one Manuel knew like the back of his hand, but this time it had changed. He'd grown up missing his mother and thinking the river had taken her. Now his father had told him it'd been... what, a demon? Some storm monster made of shadow? It was nonsense. The old man's mind had to be slipping.

"Dad, that's not—"

"I had a dream, Manuel!" bellowed Octavio. "I saw your mother. She told me the demon was coming back with this storm. She…"

Octavio started crying. He put his head down and covered his face with his hands.

Watching his father cry—a sight he only remembered seeing back when his mother died—broke something deep in Manuel, something without a name he knew no one would be able to fix.

Manuel got up, took a step closer to his dad, and placed his right hand on the old man's trembling left shoulder. The muscles there felt smaller, somewhat shrunken and weak, unlike the ones he remembered.

"Dad, it's OK," said Manuel. "You don't—"

Octavio lifted his bloodshot eyes to his son and grabbed him by the shirt. The move made Manuel want to pull away. A fiery fear made the old man's eyes shimmer. Manuel wondered just how far his father's mind had gone. It had to be the storm, the awful memories brewing inside him for so long, the grief that ate away at him like a cancer and pushed him from the ocean when he could still take the boat out.

"Listen to me, Manuel! Your mother talks to me sometimes, and she's always right. That day I kept you home and your friend Antonio died in the water? Your mother asked me to keep you here. The day I asked you to be careful and that barracuda bit your arm? She told me to ask you to be careful. That time—"

A shriek unlike any Manuel had ever heard interrupted his father. Manuel looked back at the door, the window.

Octavio's gasp and the image of a large dark figure standing outside their window, seemingly impervious to the wind, hit Manuel simultaneously.

Octavio screamed again.

Manuel turned to his father. Octavio's hands flew to his chest.

A sound like a bone breaking beneath thin skin erupted from Octavio's mouth.

Then it all came to Manuel.

His father's story. The dark figure. His mother's death. It was all true.

The thing outside had killed his mother.

Every story about a demon that arrived with the storm was true. He knew it. He had seen things. The danger lurking in the water. The river taking people. His neighbor's baby, who had been born with seven rows of tiny teeth in his mouth and had been buried near the family's chicken coop with his grandmother's rosary stuffed in his mouth as soon as the last hurricane had stopped blowing.

Manuel screamed, almost as loud as the thing outside. He looked at the table for a weapon. The newspapers, empty bowl, and his father's dirty mug looked useless. He turned and ran to the door.

The door didn't want to open, as if someone really strong was holding it from outside. Manuel thought about going to the window and looking out again, but he didn't want to waste time. He kept pulling at the door. Then, it finally blew inward, almost sending Manuel to the floor.

Hurricane Maria entered the house with a howl.

The newspapers on the table erupted into a gray mass that moved around like a flock of startled birds. The chair Manuel had used scraped against the floor. Something fell and broke in the kitchen.

Manuel stepped into the wall of water outside. The wind pushed and pulled at him with a strength he'd never known.

The figure was gone. Manuel screamed again, a sound full of anger, fear, and frustration. He ran back inside.

Closing the door was as hard as getting it open.

With the door finally shut, Manuel turned and looked at his father.

Octavio was slumped on his chair as if someone had dropped him there from a five-story building. His neck sat at a strange angle and his lower legs were obviously broken, the bone pushing against the skin on both legs.

Manuel dropped to his knees. Tears fell from his eyes, their warmth like the caress of a ghost over the cold rain that covered his face.

First his mother, now his father. The loneliness felt like a hole opening up in the center of his heart.

Outside, the wind howled.

THE SAINT IN THE MOUNTAIN

NADIA EL-FASSI

Last night I dreamed about eels, feasting on the milky flesh of some unfortunate, lesser fish. When I woke up my period had come, red smeared on my thighs. It was my second one, and despite the pain, I was no longer afraid of the blood. I cleaned myself and put on a sanitary towel that I had bribed the maids to hide from my mother as they brought in the shopping. I didn't want her to find out I was bleeding. Before I went down to eat, I sprayed a heavy floral perfume across my legs, collarbones, wrists – it was sickly sweet but necessary to mask the blood.

She found me in the kitchen, drizzling honey onto a stack of baghrir.

"Are you sure you need all that honey?" My mother stood at my shoulder, swiped a red-nailed finger across the top pancake and sucked it into her mouth. "Come and eat with me."

I did, squatting down to perch on the low sofa in the morning salon. The maids hadn't opened the shutters yet, but my mother preferred it that way. Even in the dim light, she cut a striking figure in her green gondora, curls piled on top of her head in a way that looked artful and elegant on her, but would have made me look a mess. She was the kind of woman people wanted to compliment, to be seen by. The girls at my madrasah copied her hairstyles and make-up and always asked me what shade of lipstick she wore. They cared more about her than me, and they made sure I knew it.

"You're awake early?" she said.

"I couldn't sleep."

"The heat?"

"Yes."

I didn't like this small talk. She never spoke to me like this without an ulterior motive. I could sense it coming, perhaps one or two sentences away, clawing its greasy way into the space between us.

"You should turn your fan on, so you don't sweat, Mina, it's ruining your skin."

"I'm sorry, Mama."

She clicked her tongue and reached across the table to help herself to my breakfast. As she leaned close, I felt her stiffen.

"You smell different."

Guilt closed my throat. "It's a new perfume."

"No. You're bleeding."

"No, I'm—" She grabbed me by the base of my skull, nails scraping my scalp. I stifled down a pained sound as a cramp bruised my abdomen.

"Don't lie to me, Mina. You got your period. When?"

"Last month."

Her fingers eased a little, but I could already feel a stinging at my hairline where her nails had broken the skin. This close, my mother smelt of brine and cigarette ash and honey.

"Good. It's not too late, then."

"Too late for what?"

"Silly girls ask silly questions," was all she said.

⁂

My mother and father argued in the grand salon after dinner. I had only picked at my part of the tagine plate, nibbling at the beef shin that my father broke up and placed in front of us. When I hadn't finished my food, my mother had eaten it for me. She could eat and eat and never put on weight.

"You're not driving there on your own, Rachid can drive you both," my father said. He had adopted the pleading tone I often heard him use when speaking with my mother, when he knew he was fighting a losing battle.

"No." My mother's voice was raspy, lower than normal. "I am taking her home, and we'll be back next week. Don't push me, Abdel."

It dawned on me that when she said "home", my mother meant to take me to her village. To H_____, where she'd been raised. She barely ever spoke about it, and I had learned not to ask.

Why now was she taking me there?

I peeked around the corner, careful not to lean on the creaking door, and saw my mother standing over my father. It wasn't right... that's the best way I can put it. She was too tall, too straight. I must have leaned on the door anyway, because her eyes flicked to mine, her mouth opened wide in one of her feverish smiles.

⁂

My mother said I could sit in the front seat, now I was nearly a grown-up. My father waved goodbye to us from the doorstep, telling my mother to drive slowly. Her red nails kept clicking on the steering wheel and the car was hot, but when I tried to open my window, she reached her hand back and wound it back up, saying I couldn't open it until we left Salé, so her skin wouldn't take in the fumes.

I thought back on everything I knew about my mother's village. It wasn't much. H_____ was somewhere in the mountains, and once, when I had complained about my walk to school, she told me I should at least be grateful I had a school within walking distance, so it must be a small village too.

I wondered if I still had family there. If my mother

had siblings. I'd heard her on the phone in the kitchen a couple of times, late at night, when she thought no one was listening and the maids had gone to sleep, talking to someone down the line. Her voice would change to a low hiss and I could never make out the words.

I shifted in my seat, earning a glare through the rear-view mirror. The bleeding was worse than yesterday; everything I ate had made me bloat and all my clothes clung to me awkwardly.

After an hour we streamed out of the city and onto the open road. Zeboul shrubs lined the road, the fruits hanging heavy and sweet. The car kicked up dust, but I didn't care, sucking in deep breaths with the window down; the air smelt of asphalt and oranges. She'd finally let me breathe, and like every morsel of affection she gave me, I gobbled it up.

"Are we going to see your family?" I asked. I had picked my questions carefully, as I always did with her.

I fell under her gaze. "In a way."

What way? I almost said, and bit down on my tongue to stop myself.

"There's an important part of our family history up in the mountains, in H_____. It's time for me to finally show it to you."

"Why now, not before?"

"You weren't a woman before, they would have had no need of you."

Who was "they"? Was I only a "woman" now because I had my period? I tried to ask more questions but she didn't like it.

~ ❦ ~

We hadn't passed a car in a while, only the occasional farmer with a mule and wagon. There didn't seem to be any towns this far into the countryside, only small villages cut into the hillside that my mother sped through in seconds. I saw flashes of a few tin roofs, a grocer, a gaggle of hajjis sitting in the shade drinking tea. If there were women and children, they were out of the sun and in the cool, shaded indoors. It was the hottest part of the day. I wished we could stop so I could use the bathroom and wash my face.

The mountains loomed around us, previously indistinguishable from the yellow haze of sky. We cut through them on winding, steep roads. Pink shrubs and heather, olive groves, and further in the distance, the squat white arches of graves poking up from the earth like decaying molars.

My mother didn't even wipe the sweat or dirt from her face, beads of it rolled into her eyes and I watched her blink them away. Her pin curls were coming undone. She drove fast, gripping the steering wheel with a fervour, the map forgotten.

I remained as still as I could so I wouldn't draw her attention even from the corner of her eye. When she was in these moods it was best to make myself as small and still as possible. Not a threat.

I played a game with myself, keeping my burning eyes open as long as I could until my vision swam and blurred like I was underwater, then I'd allow myself to blink. When I grew tired of that, I practised my English in my head. *I go, you go, he goes.*

I fell into my favourite daydream: I would get accepted for a travel-abroad scholarship, just as my cousin Fatiha had done. I would travel to England or America, and I would have oceans and thousands of miles between me and my mother. We would speak on the phone sometimes, because that was safe. She wouldn't be able to reach me in America, and if she came to visit I would have time to prepare. I would go to school, I would have friends that didn't know me only as my mother's daughter, I would shine. Maybe, if someone asked me about my mother I could lie, and tell them that she had died and I would bathe for a moment in their sweet, pitying expression as they imagined me to be a child who had lost a loving mother.

The daydream helped pass the time.

Late afternoon came, the shadows reaching across the side of the car, and we still hadn't eaten.

"Please can we stop? Just for a minute?" I whispered.

Eventually, we saw a man on the side of the road, pulling along a cart piled high with zeboul and oranges and watermelons. Out of the corner of my eye, I saw my mother lick her lips. She wouldn't stop for me, but she would for food.

We pulled over and paid for a watermelon and some zeboul. I ate a few, my mouth filled with honey, almost too sweet, and the soft mounds of the seeds. Like beetle shells. I tried not to bite down, though it went against my instinct.

I watched my mother, in her pretty French-style dress, crouch down on the side of the road and gorge herself on the red flesh of the watermelon until her mouth was stained with it.

"Go buy me another," she told me, and I gave the man five dirhams for another watermelon.

"Where are you both going, then? Don't see many new cars around here," the old man said.

"We're going to H____," I told him. He flinched, as if I'd spat on him.

"Why H____, benti? Don't you know what happens there?" His voice had quietened to a whisper.

"What do you mean?"

"Strange, ancient things live up in these mountains, benti." He said, leaning in. "They say H____ is home to a djinn, an old and powerful one, that takes many shapes. Strange people live there. You should turn around and go home."

"But we're going to visit family? My mother—" A shadow loomed behind me, and my mother snatched the watermelon from my hands.

"What has he been telling you?" she hissed.

The old fruit seller staggered back, made a gesture with his hands. It took me a moment to recognise it, it was something I had seen my maid Maha do on occasion, to ward off evil. My mother grinned, spitting out a watermelon seed at the man's feet.

"Superstitious old bastard," she laughed, and grabbed my wrist, pulling me back to the car. I waited until my heart slowed, unsure why it was even racing in the first place. Djinn were meant to be children's tales; my father used to tell me about them when I couldn't sleep, but his stories only gave me nightmares. They weren't real.

"Mama, the man said— "

"—ignore him. He was talking shit." The words sounded crude in her mouth.

"He said something about a djinn in the mountains."

My mother looked back at me in the rear-view mirror, her expression feverish with anger. Brine scented the air, even though we were miles and miles inland.

"I said ignore him, Mina." She spoke, but her lips barely moved, the sound instead vibrating from within her body. I didn't like the way she said my name. "There is no djinn, there is only the Saint."

We hadn't passed any more villages in over an hour. I rolled my window back up; the mountain air was biting. I really wished we could stop and rest. I wanted to wash; I managed to change my towel earlier but I didn't feel clean. I needed water.

My mother hadn't elaborated on what she meant by the "Saint". Was it just a term of endearment she used for some old grandmother figure? A hajja we had to go and pay our respects to?

It was almost dusk when my mother turned down a side road. I gripped the handle of the side door as the car swerved, tossing dust in our wake. It was barely a road at all, more like a dirt track, only there if you knew where to look. Cacti lined it on either side as it switched back up the hillside. If you were driving past, it would be impossible to tell there was a road here at all.

"We're not far now," my mother said.

"Close to the Saint?"

She nodded and smiled at me with all her teeth. We must have reached the top of the hillside, because evening sunlight blinded me in a sudden rush, and the road flattened. When I could see again, I glanced around.

All the way up here, hidden from view, was a village. No shops, but small houses with thatched roofs, walls made of the same blood orange stone as the ground they stood on. A few donkeys, their ribs on show, were tied to an olive tree. My mother pulled to the side of the road and got out. I reached for my bag.

"Leave it. You won't need it," she said.

I got out of the car and followed her. The air up here was clearer, blowing in from the west. For a moment, I caught a salty, oceanic smell, the same one that had been following me since yesterday, and heard running water, but the mountain around me was shrub dry.

People came out of their houses, keen to see who had driven up here. Strangely, they were all women. Some young, some holding babies against their chests or slung around their backs. You wouldn't know it was the modern world; I couldn't hear the buzz of a single radio, nor were there any cars lining the path.

I didn't like the way they looked at me, those quiet, shiny-eyed women, with the disinterest of a predator that knows its prey will tire eventually. We passed an old woman sitting on her stoop, sifting through lentils for rocks. I recognised the act, because my mother made me do it as punishment when I'd misbehaved. Sometimes, she asked me to eat the little pebbles, and would bend closer to listen to the way they crunched in my mouth, slicing my gums.

My mother grabbed my hand and tugged me further down the main path, the only path. No one spoke to us.

"Can we go? Please," I whispered, pulling at her sleeve.

My mother looked down at my hand on her sleeve as if a small, dirty bug had latched on to her, and shook me off.

"Why would we leave? We've only just got here."

I pulled my hand back, started turning back to the car, but she dug her nails into my wrist, the skin breaking.

I felt in my core then, how wrong this was. I didn't want to meet this Saint, that elicited such fervour from my mother. She was here with me, but I was alone.

There was a white house at the end of the path, behind it only sky. I had a sense of being at the edge of something, a maw that would swallow me up. All around us were more graves, the same shade of bone white.

"Can you feel that, Mina?" my mother said, hushed reverence in her voice.

"Feel what?"

"The Saint, all around us. Be a good girl now and do what I tell you."

I nodded.

"Are you scared?" my mother said, looking down at me. "You don't need to be. I visited the Saint when I was your age too, it's completely natural."

I huffed to myself how all these "completely natural" things felt anything but.

My mother knocked at the door of the white house, and a middle-aged woman opened, a white headscarf wrapped around her hair. Brine and damp hit my nose immediately, coming from inside. Something wet and dark and fishy.

"Khalti." My mother exhaled, and the woman pulled her into a tight hug. After they broke apart, the woman looked at me.

"This is my daughter, Mina."

"Mina," the woman said, tasting my name on her tongue. Like she wasn't accustomed to speaking. She pressed a kiss to each of my cheeks, but her own cheek was clammy and gritted with dried salt.

"Come inside." The woman beckoned us in. I followed my mother, doing as she did and taking my shoes off at the door. The inside of the house was much colder than outside, raising gooseflesh on my skin.

There was very little furniture: a small sink in the corner, and a couple of chairs. My focus was drawn to the centre of the room where a pool was cut into the earth, round as a bulbous eye. I couldn't see how deep it went, nor was I inclined to step closer. There was no lamplight either, the room only lit by the fading sun that came in from one squat window.

"What is this place?" I asked.

My mother turned to me, flashing me a smile, and I caught sight of the other woman. A similar smile tugged at the corners of her mouth.

"Welcome to the door of the Saint," the woman said. "Sit down, over here." She gestured at some woven mats near the pool.

"The door?" I said.

The woman's eyes flicked down to the pool of black water. When she spoke again, it was in a voice of ritual.

"We are but a humble entrance, a place of crossing. You are blessed, Mina, to be in the presence of such a wonder."

"The Saint is here? Are we going to see them?"

"No, Mina," my mother said, reaching out and patting my hand, "you are going to see the Saint. They are waiting for you."

That feverish gleam was back in her eyes, the same expression she had sometimes when I saw her eating, or when she would watch me consume the lentil stones. She knew I couldn't leave; she had me under her thumb.

I told myself that there was nothing to be afraid of, I wanted to believe that she would not do anything to me. There was no way out from here, only the single door behind me and even if I managed to leave, there was only the village at my back, and the silent women.

I wanted to shout at her to save me and take me home and end whatever this was. But more than that, I wanted her to look at me, for once in my life, with something other than loathing. As always, I would do what my mother wanted. Maybe this time it would be different, and I would make her proud.

"Alright. How do I meet the Saint?"

The woman reached for me and pulled me to standing. Without ceremony, she began unbuttoning my dress.

"Stop. What are you doing?"

"Let her, Mina. Or do it yourself." My mother waved a hand.

"Can't I keep my clothes on?"

"No," the woman said, "they would only get wet."

I understood then that they wanted me to get into the pool. The pool that, now I looked again, seemed to writhe in its blackness, too dark to be water, shapes moving just out of sight. I could swim, I wasn't afraid of that. I spent most summers by the sea, staying out in the water as long as I could until my mother dragged me back to sit under the umbrella, scolding me that my skin would become too dark to be pretty. But this was not the clean sea with its brightly darting fish. No water should smell like this or appear so olive black.

The woman tugged my dress down, leaving me shivering with only my sanitary belt wrapped around me. She unclipped my belt, the reddened cotton slipping to the ground. I squeezed my legs together, willing the blood to stay inside me and not drip onto the floor.

"I'll bleed in the water."

"Of course you will, how else will the Saint taste you?" My mother pushed me into the pool. I must have screamed, water filling my mouth, tasting of rotted, over-salted meat.

I kicked and flailed, my hands slipping on the smooth clay of the pool's walls. I treaded water, revolted as I realised I couldn't feel the bottom of the pool beneath my feet. How deep did it go?

My mother and the woman bent over the pool, gazing past me, deeper into the water.

"Let me out!" I screamed, grabbing again at the sides of the pool. I felt a hole, and then another, about the size of my fist. I reached in, hoping I could use them to pull myself out.

But there was something inside the hole. Something moving.

I screamed again, ripping my hand away and splashing back down into the water. I looked about, properly this time, at the walls, noticing they were only smooth at the top, but further down they were pockmarked with more holes. And staring back at me from the holes were dozens of eyes.

One by one, eels slithered out into the pool, the bulky mounds of their mouths nosing at my arms, my legs. Every time they touched me I pulled away, but had to kick my legs back out into the wet, dark mass of fins so I wouldn't drown.

"Please! Get me out!" I begged.

"They have had their fill," I thought I heard the woman say, "now they will take her to the Saint."

The eels wrapped themselves around my torso, their brackish scales sickeningly smooth. Bile rose in my throat.

Tighter, they wove around me, knotting themselves together. I ripped them off, but the eels nipped at my arms and legs until I gave up. There were too many of them, hundreds now, all swarming, twisting about my legs like some disfigured mermaid's tail.

And they pulled. I sank and sucked in a final breath, knowing now that I would not get another.

The dim light of the room didn't carry very far. Soon I found myself immersed in complete darkness, the slick bodies pressing me on all sides. How far would they take me?

The water grew much colder, stabbing my fingers and toes with pins of ice. I was already desperate for breath. The tunnel of darkness was pinpricked with light; a source that was growing larger as I drowned. Only it was all wrong.

The light was a silty green, the water so thick it was almost milky. I watched, helpless, as the eels dragged me down. Long, heaving seconds passed. My breath began to fail, my lungs constricting.

In a strange moment, the eels began to swim faster, and I had the perverse thought that they didn't want me to drown.

The green, source-less light bled into the water all around me, and the water began to feel warmer. I could see now that we were in a kind of underwater cave in the hollow of the mountain. We entered a great, domed room. It was larger than any mosque I'd ever visited, the pale stone walls reminding me of a mausoleum. I had the perverse thought that if I spoke, my voice would echo.

But there was a purpose to the shape of this place, and when I looked up, I understood why. The curved ceiling was covered in a mosaic. Chipped and decaying, it depicted something hideous. Something beautiful. A holy maw. It took every ounce of my strength not to scream.

I still couldn't see the cave bottom, there was too much silt. But in those depths, something stirred.

A large black cloud: I thought at first that it was another tangled mass of eels. But no, it moved in sleek, horrible unison. Eyes appeared all around me, glimmering like pale stars. A congregation of eels, emerging from holes in the walls, stared at me, unmoving as I was pulled down. Their patient watchfulness reminded me of the village women above.

I was certain then, this was a shrine, a tomb of some kind, and it was here I'd meet the Saint. There was no more air in my lungs, softness blurred at the edges of my vision.

The huge cloud moved again, kicking up storms of sediment. It turned, and a dark face rose out of the silt, larger than the body of a whale.

The eels roiled around and through the pump of my slowing heart I heard a vibration, a kind of unholy symphony of calls back and forth. As if the eels that pulled me, and all the others that coated the walls of this tomb, were ululating. Singing.

The face turned to me, its sleek body mostly buried in shadow beneath, crusted with aeons of sediment. Its eyes found mine, and the Saint looked, and it knew me.

I screamed, water flooding my lungs. And in some warped mimicry of my scream, the Saint opened the cavern of its mouth, and out from behind the rows and rows of teeth there swam a tiny silver eel. It reached me in a second, slipping unceremoniously into my mouth, and down my throat. Its fins sliced my tongue, and I couldn't help but taste its skin, acrid slime and salt. I felt the eel settle inside me, and I understood.

She was their queen, their mother. And now she was mine, too. Vast quantities of memories; prayers sent into her depths, thousands of years of being buried in this tomb, the unknowable loss of sunlight, my children growing and dying within me, again and again I felt all their deaths, the taste of their bodies as they returned to me. Sounds that could have been words but that my mind didn't have the facility to comprehend passed through me.

I was no longer just a girl, but a single sliver of a pulsing whole.

And beneath it all, the hunger.

She always fed, but it was never enough. She would never be satiated. She couldn't leave, she was trapped here. That's why she needed me. I would feed her.

The tiny silver eel roiled and wriggled inside me, gnawing at my womb, scraping it all away to bloody pulp. The agony was beyond anything I'd known and I choked on silt.

Finally, gladly, my heart gave out. I don't remember anything after that.

I woke up in the Saint's house, choking on the woven mats. My mother was patting me down with a towel, drying my hair with soft caresses, crooning. The other woman was chafing my legs, and when I looked down I saw they were covered in small bites and bruises. But I was no longer bleeding, the cramps in my belly had gone.

"Well done, habiba. You did so well. I'm so proud of you," my mother said, kissing my cheeks. We both smelled of salt. She had never been this soft with me before. I didn't want her softness now.

They dressed me, and it struck me how little time had passed. It was only just after sunset. I had been gone less than half an hour. I was put into my dress from earlier, the cuffs sticky from the fruits we ate on the road.

I felt it then, a slithering in my belly, my destroyed womb. Hunger. I could have eaten an entire lamb, sucked the marrow from the bone. I wanted sweet and savoury, I wanted to glut myself on it all.

"There, you feel it, don't you?" my mother said, kneeling before me like she was sharing some exciting secret.

I was going to be sick. I fled to the small sink in the corner of the room and retched. Nothing came out, and I spat, watching a trail of silt sink down the plughole. I looked up at myself in the hanging mirror. My eyes were bloodshot, my lips cracked and my hair plastered to my scalp.

It squirmed, slapping inside me, curling and turning. I opened my mouth, wide as I could, and I saw a pair of pale eyes staring back at me from the shallow of my throat.

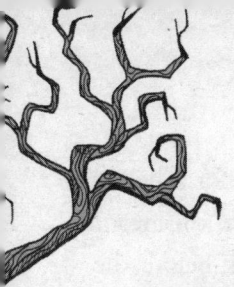

CREPUSCULAR

HAILEY PIPER

The island's sweltering afternoon had its eyes on early evening when Chelsea spotted the thing on the beach below. She could only get a closer look by either hiking back down the slopes to where the boat from Jakarta docked or dropping from the sheer rock cliff at her feet.

"Keep moving, love," Rhianne said, waving a lazy arm ahead. She shrugged against the straps of the four-foot black bundle seated on her back. Sweat dotted her soft brown face, round and exhausted as the moon. "Another hour, then we'll rest."

Chelsea wiped sweat off her reddening brow and hurried to keep up. "But there's a weird thing."

"It's the Pacific," Rhianne said, swatting a quarter-sized fly off her ear. "Everything's either weird or painful."

Black swarms hung in the sticky air, filled with monkeys' hoots, birds' songs, and the roar of insects. The island seemed ready to eat them alive, punishment for Chelsea forgetting its name's spelling and pronunciation. Cha-woo? Cho-wa? She left that knowledge at the dock before the narrow, rocky climb began toward the island's summit.

Chelsea eyed Rhianne's weary shoulders, poking out from her tank top. "I'll carry her this next stretch."

Rhianne shrugged again. "I got her. Hurry along; we'll make the next ridge before Jackie has her next dusk fit."

Chelsea eyed the beach-thing one last time. Shark? Whale? At this distance, the best she could make out was a bluish-green suggestion of appendages groping the white shore the way a shipwrecked sailor might cling to driftwood. The beach-thing seemed dead.

Obtuse rocks jutted from the next slope in untrustworthy perches. The outdoor sauna boiled Chelsea's brain, but the island sported no ski lift to its summit. She and Rhianne could only climb its narrow ascending path between cliffs to the right and a tangled green hell to the left, where they'd been warned by their boatsman that redfurred monkeys ripped skin and gouged eyes.

Chelsea and Rhianne had no business there. Only the island summit could heal little Jackie, carried on Rhianne's back.

They had tried therapy first, back when they thought Jackie suffered a psychological condition, trauma over having left her father in London. The therapist couldn't help, and who could blame him? Neither could psychologists, neurologists, or paranormal experts. A psychic had screamed the family out her business's door when Jackie had read the psychic's memories of locking her own children in a closet for two days.

That was before Jackie's head began its metamorphosis. Before the "fits," as Rhianne called them.

They made the next ridge at her pack's first evening spasm. Jackie was awake too early, the sky still bright and hot, but this part of the world kept its shine deep into evening.

Rhianne collapsed to her knees. Ants scurried from her pack as it hit the soil. It thrashed and rolled, every muscle desperate to tear Jackie's encased world apart. One twist opened a seam in the cloth, exposing light-brown skin surrounding a pale yellow eye.

Chelsea dove into the dirt and tucked the fabric over Jackie's face. "You're safe, sweetie," she said, hugging the bundle tight. "I promise."

If her mothers were hot in their tanks and khaki shorts, Jackie had to be roasting all bundled like this for the climb. Her outrage blasted in a cacophony of ear-splitting shrieks, angry car horns, and mid-'90s earworms that she'd picked up from one of Rhianne's playlists, now cranked up to eleven. The world's worst soundtrack drilled into Chelsea's skull. Rhianne's, too—her arms twitched, an instinctual urge to cover her ears.

No good. This terrible music played just for them.

"Soon, sweetie," Chelsea said, fighting herself not

to shout. Could Jackie hear or understand during these twilight fits? Rhianne soon wrapped herself around Jackie and Chelsea, a battle they fought as a family to keep Jackie from rolling over the cliff to her death.

Or from breaking free of her hood and murdering her mothers.

Chelsea had been napping after one such murder attempt back in Massachusetts, her ribs aching, when the idea of the island entered their home. Sedatives couldn't stop Jackie's overactive mind at dusk and dawn. Every time, her mothers had to ride it out, and Chelsea thought she would die of exhaustion first when she awoke to Rhianne chatting with someone downstairs.

The conversation was wrapping up when Chelsea descended. She found Rhianne nestled into the living room love seat, hands folded on her lap, and the lanky-limbed Yellow Hat Man seated across on the sofa, dressed in a canary-yellow rain slicker and matching floppy rain hat. At seeing Chelsea, he stood and said he had to be going, but he hoped he'd brought good news.

What was his name again? Rhianne had mentioned it, but Chelsea had already dubbed him the Yellow Hat Man. Whether he was Benjamin Something became chalk on stone, and there was plenty of rain in her thoughts to wash that away.

Rhianne summarized his proposal—that an Indonesian island summit with strange magnetism would calm overactive parts of the brain—Jackie wasn't the first. "He told me she'll find her peace out there," Rhianne said after, rubbing nervous arms so hard that her skin began to scale.

"You trust him?" Chelsea had asked, as if the Yellow Hat Man were conspiring a reenactment of Abraham dragging Isaac up a mountain, albeit without angelic intervention.

Rhianne's desperate eyes gave her only answer—what choice did they have left?

A half-hour after the sun finally dipped behind the jungle, Jackie's thrashing eased into limp-fished surrender. Twinkling stars winked their own celestial Morse code: You made it another day.

Rhianne's gentle fingers unpacked Jackie from her bundle. The hood covered her head down to her lips. "Unwrapping the best Christmas present, every morning and night," Rhianne whispered, flashing a warm smile that Jackie couldn't see.

Chelsea let herself breathe and then built a small fire. No cooking—they traveled light, settling for protein bars, granola mix, dried apple slivers, and a few fruit snack pouches for Jackie. Rhianne fed Jackie by hand. Since her condition had worsened, she'd stopped using her limbs, and her mothers wouldn't risk taking off her hood so that she could feed herself through her newfound power.

Chelsea tore off a chunk of her protein bar and offered it, but Rhianne waved a hand, fingers pinching a fruit snack piece. "I got her."

Before Chelsea could argue, Jackie asked, "What color's the next one?"

"It's red," Rhianne said. "Or, orange?"

"I want to see," Jackie said, but limp limbs kept her from pawing at her hood. Her world stayed dark. Firelight danced over a narrow chin, so different from Rhianne's rounded jaw. Chelsea wondered sometimes what Jackie's father looked like, and how much of him she wore on what remained of her face.

Would he cringe if he could see how much her features had changed?

Rhianne slid the squishy fruit-shaped chunk between Jackie's lips. "Just eat your snack, Jackie-girl. Tell me what color it is from flavor."

Jackie chewed a moment. "Red."

"What kind? Watermelon, cherry, strawberry?"

"Red-berry." That set them both giggling.

Rhianne's laughter was a blessing, but Jackie's melodious eight-year-old tittering cut cold down Chelsea's spine. Behind that merciful hood, the twilight outbursts, and the bruises and broken bones Jackie had inflicted on doctors and family alike, she was still a little girl.

"She needs the loo," Rhianne said, drawing Jackie to standing.

"I can take her," Chelsea said, but Rhianne led Jackie toward the jungle, a mini-flashlight in hand. Chelsea wasn't to help with anything anymore, it seemed, as if

Jackie's condition were her fault. "Watch for monkeys!" she called after, which sent Jackie giggling again.

Another spinal shiver. Being this nervous, maybe Rhianne was right to keep Chelsea at arm's length. But how couldn't she worry? Hard to believe that near dawn, their sweet angel would again fill their heads with nightmare songs while she struggled to escape her hood. If freed, she would kill her mothers and then afterward, when she came to her senses, she would cry for them.

What would her father do? Doubtful he was worth a damn, otherwise Rhianne wouldn't have ditched him in London and scurried across the Atlantic, Jackie in tow. They wouldn't have appeared in the children's section of the Janesway Library in Massachusetts where Chelsea worked. Jackie had already been sliding bits of regional accent into her native British in an adorable clash, and Rhianne's smile brought both the warmth and clouds of a sun shower. Chelsea felt the connection by that day's end.

Rhianne must have felt it, too, and that mattered. She'd left Jackie's father and later chosen Chelsea, a change-up that wouldn't have happened unless Chelsea would make a decent parent. Jackie's father couldn't have done better. He was the type to make Rhianne toss and turn in her sleep, haunted by memories and unwilling to share his name. Jackie didn't seem to think about him in the slightest.

But now, while alone, he consumed Chelsea's mind. Was Jackie's condition hereditary? A symptom of missing him?

Or maybe for all of Jackie's non-thought toward him, her father thought plenty about her. Hard, obsessive thought, his focus drilling a hole out his skull, across the fabric of the universe, and into her brain. Maybe he had infected her with thought and overturned forbidden mind stones, now revealing dangerous secrets that were scratched into their undersides.

Father's fault or not, he was two oceans away and couldn't help if he wanted.

Chelsea could. If she wasn't allowed to caretake in typical motherly ways, she would think real hard at Jackie and try to flip those mind stones right side up. One at a time, thought pouring out every minute if that's what it took.

She set the tent before the others' return. They planned to make the summit tomorrow, camp there, camp again coming back, and reach dockside the day after. Two more nights at worst, and if the Yellow Hat Man had it right, Jackie would have her mind back, maybe even control of her strange new gifts.

Chelsea tried to dream of that uneventful return journey, first to Jakarta, and then home to Massachusetts.

She awoke at dawn's edge to Jackie's evil song blasting in her head, a harsher wake-up than any alarm clock. Jackie thrashed for two hours in her mothers' arms, an act as habitual as brushing her teeth.

Was she hurting? The spasms rocked her body worse than seizures. Chelsea wondered if the cacophony slammed

Jackie first, that she chose to share it with the people she loved in a twilight cry for help. If it lightened her burden, then the noise was worth the pain. Every song ended, even the bad ones, and as the early morning lit the island's climbing slopes, Jackie settled into daytime lethargy.

Chelsea helped bundle her again for another day's hike. Rhianne shrugged the pack on, but standing up sent her lurching. The island's easy part lay behind; the slopes only steepened ahead. No sheer cliffs of the kind that dropped to the beach, but within an hour, Rhianne was huffing and puffing. She would blow herself over before noon. Slowdown would cost another day stuck on this narrow upward path.

"I can carry her a bit," Chelsea said. "We'll swap. My pack's lighter."

Rhianne didn't look back. "Thanks, love, but we're—" Her breath cut off with a grunt. She forced herself up another ridge and began to pant. Sweat scurried down her shoulders, her skin crying in the heat.

Chelsea clambered beside her and gave a cold stare. "She's my daughter, too. 'We're to make this work, she's got to be your own.' Remember?" Chelsea paraphrased in a terrible imitation of Rhianne's accent. "And what did I say?"

Rhianne turned around. "That she's yours because I'm yours. Right, I remember." Her sigh fought the wind as she knelt down. "Fine, we'll swap, but only a couple of hours."

Chelsea tried not to glow, but that couldn't be helped with the sun glittering off the Pacific waves. She slathered on another layer of sunblock and made the switch. Swaddled Jackie weighed heavier than expected, the pack's straps eating into Chelsea's shoulders. Raucous monkeys and birds mocked her for trying, but if her discomfort could lighten the burden, she'd shrug her shoulders and take the lead.

A couple of hours dragged longer. Even after their noon break, Rhianne didn't look ready to carry Jackie again, and Chelsea still had her strength. She let Rhianne pack up and started toward another slope.

Hours of ascent meant leaving the island's green hell behind, its noisiness drowned out by high winds and the ever-present hiss of waves just before they crashed on the shore. They sounded so close that Chelsea could believe the island might sink into the brine. Anything to stop them, right? Anything to teach them that they didn't belong here.

According to what Rhianne had repeated from online research, the island used to welcome wild goose chases, an ex-hotspot for spiritualistic yuppie tourists in search of enlightenment. They, too, came seeking peace at the summit, but no word on whether they ever found it. Those visits ended years back. Few approached the island now except on the Yellow Hat Man's recommendation.

Magnetic properties impacting the brain sounded as outlandish as psychic powers. The summit was a Hail Mary play—was that the phrase? Geology and sports weren't Chelsea's areas of expertise.

Neither was Jackie anymore. This condition wrapped

her in mystery, and her pain splintered Chelsea's heart. If the island's summit couldn't help, what then? Surely the Yellow Hat Man wouldn't be back with new solutions.

The next rise curved at its cliffside, offering an unhindered view of the beach below. Waves formed lines of white froth that broke against seaweed-coated sand in a soothing rhythm. If anything calmed the mind on this island, it was that natural song. Chelsea paused to enjoy it, long enough to realize that she wasn't looking at seaweed clumps in the faraway sand.

Yesterday's odd sighting felt like forever ago. She and Rhianne had climbed so far since then that she doubted she could've made out a solitary beach-thing like before.

But now several beach-things draped the shoreline. Seafoam burst across their backs, wet scales glistening in the sun. They had to be large fish, dredged up and tide-washed against the sand. Had there been a mass stranding?

The sight chilled her skin as if she'd plunged into those waves. The beach-things had to be dead. An uneasy thought slithered down the back of her mind. Much as she and her family didn't belong on this island, the beach-things did. They might not be dead, only waiting below, patient as more of them gathered for... what?

"Eyes ahead!" Rhianne called cheerily from behind. "You can't go dozing when you carry her."

Chelsea shrugged against the straps and kept moving. She wouldn't bring up the beach-things; that would only convince Rhianne to take Jackie again, as if Chelsea couldn't do it. She was already playing this disappointment game with herself. What would she mess up next?

When Rhianne's office promoted her to higher pay and longer hours, Chelsea had taken up getting Jackie ready for school in the morning. Disastrous—she took weeks learning the skills to do Jackie's hair alone and had never felt such parental ineptitude. Now she couldn't possibly feed, escort, or carry Jackie, right? That hair milestone mattered, but it felt distant.

Especially when Jackie no longer grew hair. Her scalp had turned bald and sandpapery, and her beautiful brown eyes now dipped into that angry pale yellow. Worse changes followed.

Chelsea felt them at the next rise. Sky bright, sun shining, but against all hope, this hemisphere again turned toward dusk. Jackie's bundle thrashed backward, dragging Chelsea from the slope and toward a freefall.

Rhianne shouted something unintelligible from downhill, lost in the wind.

Chelsea clawed at hard earth. A fingernail split down the middle. Screams and car horns filled her head and sent her teeth clenching, but she scrambled up over the ridge.

One final slope stole Chelsea's attention. It stood a few feet ahead, the flat summit awaiting above. They'd made it.

Rhianne clambered over the rise a moment too late. "Jackie-girl, don't—"

Jackie leaned her body left and then threw herself right, a roll that yanked her straps off Chelsea's shoulders and tore them both to the soil. Pebbles scratched Chelsea's skin. She lifted her head and saw what draped the dirt, realization sinking deep into her guts—a crumpled puddle of black fabric.

Jackie's hood.

She writhed until she'd sat up, still swaddled from the neck down, but her head was free. Weeks had passed since her naked scalp had last seen daylight. From lips down, her features resembled old Jackie. Chelsea could almost forget the changes while hidden beneath the hood, but not now.

Jackie's nose curled into her face as if the cartilage had melted; same for her ears. Flesh hugged her skull around yellowed eyes and turned pale as it climbed her skull. Every coil of hair had fallen out, and now jagged, shark-like scales coated her scalp down to the nape of her neck. Dull-red protuberances wormed between scales like writhing antennae for Jackie's brain. They only stood at dawn and dusk, ready for every twilight fit. The hood didn't stop thought projection, that music blaring no matter what, but covering her eyes kept her from knowing her surroundings.

From manipulating them.

Chelsea belly-crawled toward the hood. Rhianne couldn't have seen it lying there or else she wouldn't have charged desperately at her daughter to hold her, to tug her from the cliff's edge, and maybe splay hands over her eyes.

For one moment, she stopped being a mother and became a soft toy, easily thrown by Jackie's invisible force. Rhianne crashed into the forward slope, and one leg gave a wet crack.

Chelsea slung the hood over Jackie's head, whipping right and left, and wrapped her limbs around the bundle. Across the ridge, Rhianne curled into a ball. She would have a hard time climbing now. Shins weren't supposed to dent inward like that.

"It's OK," Chelsea whispered, lips to Jackie's hood. "Everyone's OK. A couple hours, you'll settle down, and I'll take you. Listen to the water. Peaceful, isn't it?"

Jackie writhed while Chelsea turned her head cliffside and tried not to think how much pain Rhianne had to be feeling. The tide was coming in, waves beating their rhythm. Chelsea counted them as light ebbed from the horizon and a headache dug its heels into her skull. The sky slid from pale blue to thick orange.

A white-green glow replaced the sunlit glittering reflection on the water. Chelsea lifted her head for a better look. Was that moonlight?

The ungentle luminance grabbed her thoughts first and dragged them screaming down as if she'd thrown her mind over the cliff.

Images flashed—shallows, sand, windswept greenery—coalescing with Jackie's projections to make a nightmarish music video. Chelsea's vision filled with beach-things in the sand, no longer lying in wait, but active and vibrant, their black silhouettes standing on two legs beneath the ripple of a reddening sky. Scales coated their bodies, densest at the scalp. Fleshly worms writhed from too-human heads, the same protuberances that grew from Jackie's infected brain.

No, these beach-things were different. She was an ordinary girl with a condition. Why would her thought sickness leak into fish creatures? They were nothing like her.

But then, maybe they were. Deep down in the genes, hadn't every human bloodline begun in lizards, and before that, in fish? Ancestral memory passed trauma down generations. Chelsea remembered reading that widespread arachnophobia spun its web from millions of years ago when everyone's great-grandmother to the umpteenth power was a fun-sized lizard, hunted by spiders the size of a sedan. No reason to think other traits hadn't descended that scaly lineage.

Just how old were those stones that Jackie's father may have overturned in her mind? Lizard-old? Fish-old? Older? Were the beach-things' eyes bright and yellow? Those protuberances said yes. They said, Come to us.

A pebble clattered over the cliff, a shortcut drop to the beach. Scattered pebbles followed, and then a lumpy rock as large as Chelsea's hand began to quake. Hairs stood from her limbs, likewise tugged.

The beach-things could project thought; they'd shown

that. With eyes uncovered, they could manipulate the world. Like called to like.

To Jackie.

Chelsea scrambled back, clutching Jackie tight. "They want her," she hissed.

Rhianne rested against the foot of the summit, one hand clasping her injured leg. Only her eyes answered, tired as when the Yellow Hat Man had come and gone from their home.

"The beach-things," Chelsea said. She lugged Jackie under one arm to the final slope and began climbing one-handed. "She's calling them. Or they're calling her." Or worse, both.

Rhianne looked ready to argue. What did Chelsea know? How could she understand? But then Rhianne threw her head back and wailed, likely a taste of beach-thing images flooding her mind.

"Why's this happening?" she shrieked.

Chelsea kept climbing. "Maybe they know Jackie's special. Why wouldn't they call to her?" And think at her, same as her father might have.

Rhianne clasped her head in her free hand. "Go."

Chelsea obeyed. Every hard-earned upward inch put a little more distance between Jackie and the beach-things, but their thoughts hooked Chelsea's mind. A rock gave beneath her hand, and she nearly tumbled after it. She could have a nice leap, dash her head far below. No more music, no more visions. Easier than climbing.

Easier than motherhood. She could keep trying, sure, but wouldn't it be a shame, after all this time since meeting Rhianne and Jackie in that library, to find out her fear of inadequacy was completely justified?

She grasped another, firmer rock and pushed her thoughts against the beach-things. Love for Jackie and Rhianne. Recipes to cook fish with lemon pepper and olive oil, and how good that tasted, and how good the beach-things might taste, too. She demanded explanations—if they were so strong, why not climb after her? Why suffer ships and garbage to intrude on their seas?

Answers came in flashes. Gathered plastic, harvested trash. Oh, they liked the mess, could twist its shapes, build cities of telekinetic, telepathic gill-folk, the mythical Atlantis made manifest in polymerized crude oil.

If they'd meant to stop the climb, they seemed too distracted projecting thoughts. Chelsea clambered to the next ledge as the sky purpled over. Her palm patted flat earth.

The summit.

She slung Jackie up first, crawled after, and hauled her toward the center, one hand clutching the hood in place. They'd made it at last.

Now what?

Visions, noise, and blood surged through Chelsea's aching head. Jackie didn't seem peaceful, either. She writhed harder, her once-dormant limbs now remembering they could punch and kick. Maybe the gill-folk had reminded her. If this magnetism meant to heal her, it needed to work before she fought her way out of the swaddling and tossed Chelsea like she'd tossed Rhianne.

What were they supposed to do? If the Yellow Hat Man had given Rhianne clear instructions, she would have shared them. No mystical shrine stood here; there were no stones to signal that Earth's magnetic properties might give a damn about Jackie.

"Sweetie, please," Chelsea pleaded, clutching the bundle tighter. The mental song grew ravenous, gnashing teeth and scraping nails having joined the traffic-meets-pop song cacophony.

Beneath that, Rhianne belted out a rough scream.

Chelsea glanced down the slope and made out Rhianne through scant light, her fingers clinging to soil, an invisible giant's hand tugging her legs into the air. The beach-things had a far reach.

It had to be almost night, time for Jackie to calm into her old self. Chelsea laid her down, told her to stay put, and scrambled down from the summit. Her hands cupped under Rhianne's armpits and dragged backward against the beach-things' thought-grasp, toward the opposite cliff. Without jungle to brace them, they put their backs to another ledge, the shore below dark and quiet. No beach-things for that beach—only the frothing tide.

"Jackie?" Rhianne sputtered. Her leg looked twisted. "Is she better now?"

Anxiety filled Chelsea's veins as Jackie descended the summit, having broken through her swaddling and torn off her hood for the last time. The shore's eerie glow silhouetted her scaly scalp and its wormy antennae. Yellow irises glowed in the dark. She wasn't climbing down hand and foot.

She floated gently on invisible hands.

"Jackie-girl?" Rhianne struggled up from Chelsea's grasp. "Jackie-girl, it's Mummy. Do you hear?"

Jackie's feet aimed at the soil, but she didn't land. Her head cocked at her mothers and then turned to the other cliffside overlooking the beach-things. If she could float from summit to ridge, she could probably make the beach.

Chelsea let go of Rhianne and charged, trying the hands-over-eyes trick again. Inadequate mother or not, she made as good a toy as Rhianne, easy for Jackie to throw. Her invisible shove sent Chelsea sprawling across soil and over the cliff. She clawed at the ledge, and the sudden jerking halt sent a crack through one forearm. Pain screamed from wrist to shoulder.

She almost released her grip. Easier than motherhood.

Jackie loomed over the edge. The beach's glow lit her skin, and she hovered out into the open air.

"No, Jackie-girl!" Rhianne shrieked. She came hissing under her breath at a frantic lump, and then she collapsed to one side. Jackie's invisible hands pressed her to the soil, the air turning heavy. "Baby, please!"

Jackie floated close enough to touch, if only Chelsea had the spare strength to reach for her. "Sweetie, we don't belong here," Chelsea said through clenched teeth. A plea for Jackie to stop, maybe use her power to help, to forgive her mothers; they had the best intentions.

Jackie's eyes looked calm. Dusk couldn't have ended yet, but her fit had settled. Her head tilted, heavy with new thoughts, and then those thoughts filled her body like stones in pockets. She sank down the cliffside through humid, muddy air.

Rhianne snapped free from the ground and dove for the cliff in a wordless shriek. She might have gone sailing off, but Chelsea dangled at her feet, desperately clinging to the ledge by her good arm. Jackie could float; her mothers could only plummet.

The beach opened to her, a bioluminescent wave washing her skin. The beach-things must have upturned another mind stone and showed her a new talent. She glowed with them, a paper lantern floating to shore.

Bright light filled the ocean to greet her, much like Chelsea had seen in her beach-thing visions. Now she saw more—their city, an enormous undersea metropolis thrashed together with plastic and refuse. Every scrap that human land-things tossed away found new purpose at sea, the gill-folk using it to build, and learn, and become more than whatever they used to be.

They would even take the land-things' children.

Chelsea's arm began to slip from the ledge, her body drawn to follow her thoughts. Sweat-soaked hands grabbed her bicep and hauled her into Rhianne's arms. Rhianne's throat danced between screams and sobs. She shuddered hard, a drowning victim on dry land. Her lungs couldn't find the air.

Chelsea clutched her tight. "You have to breathe," she said. She thought hard against the beach-things' projections, as if that was still the worst battle waging in her wife's head.

Rhianne's chest went from heaving to shaking. She pressed against Chelsea's shoulder, guilt heavier than the island's mountain, and quit screaming, committed to sobs. Tears ran hot down Chelsea's cheeks as she stared at the ocean.

Jackie became indistinguishable from the beach-things as her lantern melted into their foaming light. The tide surged and crashed as their city absorbed them beneath the waves. It shined brighter at their return, and Chelsea made out colossal white-green walls and shrines and tunnels, a mesmerizing network that's light harmonized with the ocean waves in a deep-sea heartbeat.

Angry music slipped from Chelsea's mind. Without speech, the gill-folk would pass a new song to Jackie, maybe as peaceful as had been promised on the island.

Nothing like her twilight fits, but it probably couldn't match her melodious laughter either. All her thoughts and sounds now sank into the depths. Every song ended, even the good ones.

Questions pounded through Chelsea's head to their own rhythm as she clutched shuddering Rhianne. Had she been present for the Yellow Hat Man's proposal, would she have felt a music of his making? He had carefully led them to Indonesia with promises and fairy tales, would have said anything to send them to the island. When he'd told Rhianne that Jackie would find her peace here, he'd had the beach-things in mind. The two-day climb had only kept the family around long enough to draw the gill-folk's full attention.

How many people had their city swallowed up? What transformation might the Yellow Hat Man have been hiding beneath that rain hat? How many kids were growing this condition around the world, reading thoughts, projecting them, and tossing their parents like ragdolls?

And just what did Jackie's father really look like?

The undersea city's luminance soon faded as it abandoned shore, thrusting against the tide, as much submarine as metropolis. It shrank first to a blinking star, muddled by waves, and then to darkness, leaving the island warm and black. The gill-folk had better places to be.

And Jackie with them.

LAAL ANDHI

USMAN T. MALIK

*"Whenever a laal andhi rises,
understand that an innocent has been murdered."*

PAKISTANI PROVERB

July 2008: While threading through heat-drowsed traffic near Bhatta Chowk, I nearly ran over a pedestrian dashing across the road. Tall, lanky, bearded, the man wore a prayer cap, dusky shalwar kameez, and a navy-blue sweater bulging around his chest. (A sweater in July?) He didn't flinch when the wheels screeched and the bumper lurched to a halt inches from his torso—just cocked his head, leapt across the manhole by the sidewalk, and disappeared in the crowd.

Panting, I shouted at his back and clutched the steering with knuckles that had turned white. I was in my thirties then and had a nervous disposition, and this brush with a certain fatality left me shaken. Eventually I murmured my thanks to Allah, jerked the gearshift forward, and drove on to my uncle's jewelry shop near Delhi Gate in the walled Old City. All day I fingered gold chains, pearl necklaces, lapis lazuli earrings, diamond wedding sets—and I couldn't get the incident out of my head. Something about the man, his profile, the way he ran, head tilted as if with torticollis, one arm still and dangling like an ape's, kept returning to me. In bed that evening I tossed and turned, wondering why the stranger's memory wouldn't leave me alone.

Two days later when a grainy black-and-white photo showed up on Geo, Samaa, Dawn News, and other channels, I knew.

I sat quietly as winter shadows gathered amidst the peepal and sukhchain trees in our backyard. My wife brought my favorite meal—sarson-ka-saag and makai-ki-roti—for dinner, my favorite meal, and I was trembling, she said later. She put the tray down, touched my forehead, and I was burning up, I had a fever, oh God could it be malaria, she will call the doctor right now.

That night I had drenching sweats. I slept and jerked awake, dozed and dreamed; and in my dream, Lahore was enveloped in red dust that shrieked and blew across the city in crimson funnels. The vegetable market, Mall road, the intersections where countless had died, glimmered and faded in the mouth of the laal andhi. The evening newscaster stood swathed in shadow, flecks of red plastered to her eyelashes. Two children among twenty dead, she said, her bright, clear eyes staring at my numb, terror-shaped face, even as her camera panned on three bloodstained teeth lying like pearls in the alley's gutter.

My wife was shaking me awake. She held my flailing arms and hugged me as I whispered over and over again, Nearly killed him again. Killed him twice. It was a dark and very long night. Not even the fajr azaan from the neighborhood mosque could soothe my fears.

◈

The summer of '82, and Lahore lay like a dying fish, belly up, as we struggled to grow up inside it. Its scales still bloodied from the riots of the seventies, arteries exposed and twitching in a concrete gut blackened with hegemonic fear, the city oozed a human plasma that coagulated within its core.

It was a blistering, dry hell of a season filled with scorching lu winds that swept up from the plains and left not a drop of unvaporized water in their wake. A summer of sunstrokes and floggings and midnight kidnappings. Of bloody hockeys and roaming thugs and rumors about Russia and Amreeka's Cold War drifting in from the north. The Great White Helper, we were told, had sent our Afghani brothers powerful weapons to fight the good fight. Anti-aircrafts and Kalashnikovs and Stinger missiles would weave the tapestry of resistance. General Zia's state machinery ran nationalist jingles on TV and radio. The Queen o' Melody Noor Jehan made appearances, singing tributes to the Pak Army's heroism in '65, while a dull-faced woman in a headscarf assured us that our brothers across the border would win, for wasn't their cause just and righteous?

'82, and it was the summer we were still young and untouched. Four teenage boys who lived in the same neighborhood and went to the same school and were equally short of money to buy sweet shakarkandi, peanuts, or roasted bhutta. Once or twice, we stole sugarcane ganderi and apples from vendors fanning themselves with old newspaper outside the school, but after I heard the maulvi sahib deliver a thunderous Friday sermon about theft and its hellfire consequences I refused to participate again. (Wasif just laughed and, slipping his feet into some unfortunate's new shoes from the mosque rack, left his sandals behind.)

It was the year we discovered magazines with women baring all. Buxom girls with never-ending legs wearing nothing but tall heels, cowboy hats, and fake silver crosses groped themselves and squeezed breasts with pink nipples, brown nipples, black nipples. You could find these totay behind the counters of certain shops in Urdu Bazaar. The proprietor had a secret signal for customers like us, passed on by word of mouth: If you kept staring at him during a regular purchase (the latest A. Hameed, or an Imran series novel by Ibn-e-Safi) he would glance at you and knock thrice against the plywood wall with his knuckles.

If you reached over and rang the brass bell sitting on the countertop, he would smile broadly and ask if you needed "something else." Wasif and Ali Malik were experts at the sport. Me, I always blushed and mumbled, and they'd push me away rudely and step forward to negotiate.

Saleem, Wasif, Ali Malik, and I. Always the four of us banded together against the uncertainties of a city running on trepidation. In this season of yoking and yearning, of bereavement and besetment, we started doing the thing we did, for with fear and death and sulfur in the air who would stop us? Who would point and say, Watch it, children, you must survive your age. Must get through one hell to enter another.

'82 was the year of army generals and feudal lords touring their fiefdoms grandly while the populace died thrashing in gutters from torture or heat or Hadood Law floggings. Of VIP villas and ruined shanties, bright-tiled façades and haunted houses, police encounters and prison suicides, and sectarian attacks.

Most of all, though, it was the summer we went to Bad Bricks during a laal andhi.

༺❧༻

I might have suggested the game, true, but Wasif took it to its awful conclusion. This I'd swear before any jury, judge, or qazi.

The graveyard was three kilometers from our muhallah.

Five acres of crumbling headstones, weeds, and overgrown grass. We used to sit in the shade of the banyan grove close to my grandfather's grave, and that was where Wasif came up with the final twist.

It was Grandfather who told me many stories. He was an unsmiling tall man, browned by years of tending crops on the family farmland in the country. Sitting with his arms around my pale-faced grandmother, he spoke to me of terrible legends honed in the villages far from Lahore. Tales told by braziers not yet replaced with heaters; in the heart of pitch-black nights not slashed open by gleaming airplanes.

So it went that these stories made their way to my lips and I spoke—first hesitantly, then emphatically—of the hellish game I had designed.

It was simple. We would congregate at a place where the vagaries of death had swooped—bomb blasts, sectarian shootings, suicides, homicides. At each crossing where human limbs had flopped and turned rigid, we stopped and paid our respects. We lamented the departed with elegies and dark fables. Tales of terror, torture and turpitude that we filled with the presence of those passed. We imagined their lives of our own making. We prayed for the victims with mantras of madness.

We read to the dead.

Of course, it was stupid and dangerous, but really, how could we have known? We were kids. How could we have understood? We found it enthralling to give meaning to their slaughter, and the game was taken up ecstatically by the boys.

Wasif suggested the initial reading by Grandfather's grave (later we moved our mecca around, but returned to the cemetery every few months). Once a week we gathered to read our stories. The whispering breeze, the gentle rustling of hallowed dust as it curtained and showered over old graves; the smell of flowers bloomed from such dust; the flexing and twitching hag-fingers of branches beckoning us close; and the two skulls we found half-buried by a grave and dug out, cleaned, and preserved—they consummated the unholy process.

On this particular Thursday evening (night of souls, night of saints) we sat in the graveyard with a furious red sky above us, and a heavy, grit-filled wind beginning to blow. It was Saleem's turn that day, simple Saleem, gentle Saleem, fourteen years old, the youngest of us. It was his turn to read, his pledge to the dead. Saleem was shuffling the pages of his notebook. Ali Malik smoked a cheap Capstan, his back against a headstone, and I dug into the moist earth with a twig.

"Well?" Wasif said.

"Well, what?" I said, not looking up. The twig wedged on a pebble. I yanked and it broke. I threw the sharp end away and glanced at the sky. An angry red, the horizon throbbed with coiled clouds, blood glories unfurling. Dead leaves spun in the air and blew against my lips.

I spat on the ground.

"I said, a laal andhi is starting up, man. Who knows if it will rain after." Wasif looked around, his lips peeled back, a shred of lunch chicken tucked in the web of his mustache. He was tall, dark, and the first of us to sprout a man-beard. He slapped my back. "Why don't we get away from this graveyard, these dog-pissed streets, today?"

"And go where?" said Ali Malik in my stead. "Forget the muhallah, and last time we read behind the tobacco-and-paan shop, someone told my dad I was smoking and he beat the living shit out of me. I'm not chancing that again. I've got to have my smokes when we read, but Dad's fucking everywhere."

Wasif looked at Ali as if he were a particularly nasty malaria-laden mosquito. "Grow a pair of balls. Buy 'em from the eunuchs." He scratched his head. "Well, lemme think. I'm sure I will…"

A smile cracked his face, a sideways grin that spilled his teeth into the sun. I knew that grin. Usually, it meant trouble.

I turned and gazed at the sky, listened to the softly murmuring laal andhi.

The crimson storm.

Backwoods folk, country folk scoff at our city notions, my grandfather often said. You can't talk to them about Richter scales and earthquakes and monsoon winds. They hold on to their dark worries, dismissing scientific explanations of red dust blowing from the mountains, howling across vast plains, carpeting cities in its wake.

Country folk believe in other things.

Grandfather had heard their stories and when he spoke of them, he had that stark-red look in his eyes, a cultivated respect for the unknown.

"Raza baita," he said licking his lips. "The crimson storm is not like any other storm. It's a vast, moving veil, it is. Evil things slip out from behind it. Jinns, Dyos, alien and terrible, smear blood all over their naked melting bodies and scrrech in the heart of the storm until the earth gags and gives up its tenants. Solemnly these raise their heads and take off their masks of passing.

"The storm's wind itself is rotten, you understand? It turns people, it makes things happen. Don't you ever go out in a laal andhi, you hear me, son? You stay in the safety of the house."

But Grandfather was dead, sunk below the dark waters of oblivion. Worms and rodents swam over him now, nibbled on his face.

I shivered.

"Bad Bricks!" Wasif was beaming. "Didn't I say I had the perfect place this time?"

His words hung in the air for a moment, splintered, and faded away. The wind gusted, and the headstone Ali was leaning on toppled and crashed, taking him down with it.

"Motherfucker." He grunted and heaved himself up with his elbows. Wasif sniggered.

Saleem said quietly, "You're talking about the reporter's house." He raised his head and looked at Wasif.

"There is a cellar under the stairs," said Wasif. "I saw it once with Fareed people when we scaled the boundary wall to smoke joints. It's perfect for your story. The ambience, boy, I can totally see it now: the candles in the skulls, the shadows, the rotten cellar smell."

Saleem was silent. I was silent. He was pale, his full, almost feminine lips colorless as grave-slabs. He had been chewing them again: the lower one was torn, a shimmer of pink visible in the shades of gray. He is scared, I thought. He is terrified. Why?

Saleem's face turned blank. "Sure," he said. "Sure."

'82 was the year of my father's affair with Auntie Nasreen from four streets down. Each evening Father would return from the 7-Up factory, his white half-sleeve shirt bobbing like a flag in the alley, and walk right past our house. Spitting and hacking (he had pneumonia as a child and his lungs were scarred), he returned home only when it was time for dinner. Mother would never say a word, but she slammed steel bowls on the dinner mat and broke a china plate, and once at night I heard her crying.

It was the year of the Hadood grounds near Lahore Railway Station. Scores of prisoners were brought there blindfolded, hands tied behind their back, tethered to bamboo posts, and lashed. Rarely, a public hanging followed.

It was also the summer Saleem's father went missing. This happened two months before the laal andhi and the incident at the reporter's house. His father had been leading a pro-Bhutto rally near Kalima Chowk one evening, chanting slogans against the dictatorship. On his way back someone shot at his bicycle fifteen times, puncturing the wheels, winging the side mirrors, and knocking the bell off. His white skullcap was bloodstained and lying near the axle when they found it. Wasif's mother and uncle begged lawyers, judges, and journalists to take the case national. Every police station in the city was scoured and draped with his photographs, but no news was to come of him.

⋙∗⋘

The sky was a blood-soaked mantel as we trudged down the streets. A steadily building wind clutched newspapers, dubbed them red, and hurled them away. Plastic shopping bags spun, the burning air visible through their flesh, and rolled away like heads. Sprinkles of vermilion dust blew in my face, crawled into my eyes, scrabbled up my nose, as the gale shook a bloody fist at us. The crimson storm was gathering strength.

Then we saw it from afar.

The place Lahoris had named Bad Bricks stood like a weed amid the cheerful homes under Sherpao Bridge. The neighborhood was great, suburban to the core: two-story walled villas filled with gleaming Toyota Coronas and Mitsubishi Pajeros. Short flagstone driveways coursed parallel to manicured lawns and residents parked their cars below hanging terraces. Snug, welcoming often redbrick houses.

Not Bad Bricks.

The house was dead. Weary, stunted trees leaned against its rain-bleached boundary walls. Paint was gouged off its sides, like skin off a maimed beast. Rusted black iron gates that must have gleamed once now hung open like mouths frozen in agony, twisting in the wind.

We stood and gazed at the cracked driveway winding in, lapping at the front door. I glanced at Wasif once, and stepped inside.

We sometimes played cricket in these streets. Someone would score a six and the ball would rise, spinning in the air, arc above the boundary walls, and bounce across the lawn. The older kids would have to climb them to retrieve it. The house's reputation made it an ominous task.

The lawn was a jungle now. Weeds sprouted all over. Undergrowth sprawled over cracked gardening pots stirred—with wind or life, who could tell? The absence of animal droppings puzzled me. Dried bird-shit and turds from strays should be everywhere. Garbage from the neighbors too. Yet I saw no rotting banana skins, orange rinds, or gnawed chicken bones. Just pebbles, broken ceramic, and shattered brick.

"Lovely," Wasif said. The storm moaned, ripped leaves from the frantic lawn, and flung them over us. Dead petals plastered against my skin. Brick and storm dust mingled and whirled away.

And then we stood by the entrance, a splintered wooden door with hinges choked by termite, swinging slowly back and forth.

The last inhabitants of Bad Bricks left in '79. It had stayed empty since. The first owner was a retired army colonel who gifted the house to his son, a crime reporter, in '74. I knew these dates because Uncle Dara, a friend of Father's, was a realtor and told stories of for-sale houses whenever he came over. The reporter was an eccentric man (batshit crazy, Uncle Dara said), who was digging up skeletons in the land-grabbing mafia's backyard. He had plans to write a book. To scoop out the corruption of the army brigadiers and generals who'd long been in cahoots with the land-grabbers.

Until one night unknown men came for him.

So it goes that the maid enters the house. It's cold and feels empty. She's come to dust the windows and scrub the floors, and his red-white eyeballs are staring at her from the soup bowl on the dinner table. She screams, and her fifteen-year-old grandson stops sweeping the patio and comes running. He sees his grandma wheel, try to run, trip on something and go down. When she does, she's lying next to the dead reporter, his arm extended out from under the sofa. The holes that were his eyes are crawling with ants. Grandma has an epileptic attack—she tends to miss her pill sometimes—and starts seizing. The terrified boy runs to her, but now grandma's turning color. Her head bangs against the dead man's *wham! wham! wham!* and the child backpedals, lets out a shriek, and flees from the house. By the time paramedics and police get there, the old maid is dead from aspiration, face engorged and blue, arms wrapped around the murdered reporter.

A few months later the colonel dies of a heart attack. He has no other family and never got around to making a will, and so the house is empty for a while, until Lahore Development Authority claims the property. Eventually a newly married couple takes it—low rent and all—and, in the middle of the night, rush out the front door in their night clothes, screaming and gibbering. They jump into their Suzuki Alto, race away at eighty kilometers per hour, collide with a brick truck, fishtail, and go up in flames.

Not much left to tell. The house is baptized Bad Bricks. Neighbors whisper it is haunted. Something shuffles inside the place at twilight. Rumors of visitations, of faces at windows, of moonlight congealing like blood on the iron gates, and the LDA gives up. It leaves the house to smolder like a pile of litter.

Now there we were in front of the entrance. Four brave souls in search of the holy dead.

Above us thunder screamed. Lightning ripped the clouds open, spewing their slippery guts forth. Storm-reddened rain began to hiss around us. Silver-brown lines of water snaked down the driveway, curling around our shadows. The storm began to whirl and dance.

Ali Malik was the first to step forward. He reached for the door and grasped the rusted handle. Perhaps I was the only one who saw the hesitation, that tremor in his fingers as they gripped the metal tight. He yanked the handle down and flung open the door. Oil-hungry hinges creaked. Dust rose, moved forward with gentle arms to embrace us, and dissipated.

Sunlight had died in the heart of the storm and we gazed at absolute dark. Red shadows hung from twisted vines and branches by the swollen black throat that was the doorway, and without a light Saleem could never read his story in there. We didn't have to enter. We didn't have to move into the beyond. I was ecstatic, relieved, damn the house, fuck bravado, and I turned to say so.

Wasif had a flashlight in his hands. In the tatters of daylight, the bulb glimmered, and woke up as he flicked the switch. A knob of light shot at the rain, expanded into a vortex, and cut through the cavernous gloom.

We stepped inside the house.

※

This one I can't be certain of, but my heart tells me it's true: '82 was the spring Saleem and I found the Rampuri chakoo knife at the foot of the banyan tree.

We were returning from school. Saleem was beaming. His grandfather, a clerk at National Bank, had visited that weekend and given him a crackling five-rupee note. We frequently pooled our allowance and my share of this treasure was secure. Visions of samosas and keema pakoras danced before our eyes. I suggested we take a detour along Kabootar Purah where most vendors sat.

From WAPDA bus stop, a dirt track led through a grove of peepal, keshu, and villayati shisham, curved around an abandoned construction site, and ended at the market. Swinging an old shoe on a plastic string, giggling, we dashed between the trees. It was early March, Saleem's father's disappearance was two months away, and the keshu and shisham had blossomed. Blazing orange and gentle lilac flowers lined the branches like tiny birds. Their sweet perfume, coupled with jasmine growing in clumps and thickets by the main road, overwhelmed the diesel fumes left behind by roaring trucks and school vans.

I would've missed it had its face not caught sunlight at an odd angle and burst into reds. It looked like a shower of blood in the corner of my vision, and when I jerked my head, the illusion dissipated. I nudged Saleem and we walked to it warily.

The trees made a bower here, hemming in the grove from the road. The grass, though dense, was short and pushed back by roots. Five feet from an old bunyan's trunk the knife was driven point first into the ground, a gilt carbon-steel blade about sixteen inches long. The handle, shaped like a leg with a boot heel on the bottom, was hand-chased and depicted flowers with a rat curled among them.

"What the..." Saleem crouched and touched the rivets close to the pommel with awe. "This is real, Raza. By God, this is a real slip-joint."

"What?"

"Slip-joint. This is a folding Rampuri chakoo." He grabbed the handle and wrenched the knife out of the ground. In the afternoon light the face glittered even though it was pitted and covered with a patchy dark membrane from point to guard.

"Now watch." Saleem pressed his thumb on the blade's spine, forced it down and backward until it clicked into a groove at the bottom of the handle. "See, how easy that was. Uncle Hamid, who lives in Sargodha, sells chakoos. Hunting knives, switchblades, slip-joints. He showed me one just like this when we were there last year. Said this kind used to be made in Rampur, India. Town was famous for them. Real expensive, too." Grinning, he tossed it from one hand to another. "Wasif is going to leak shit when I show him this."

He scratched the blade with his nails and rust-colored flakes fell off it.

"I want a look." I made a grab for the chakoo, but he was quick and leapt away. We chased each other around the tree trunks. A fat white slug dropped off the banyan.

Before it could scurry under a root Saleem stepped on it and squashed it.

"Bastard, give it up," I yelled, panting and laughing.

"Come and get it, faggot." When I feinted a lunge, he stepped back, tripped on a root, and crashed to the ground. I dove at him at once, but before I could tackle him, he had cocked his arm back and heaved the knife.

Up it went spinning, arcing over the banyan branches. It caught the light, flared like a lamp, and came down twenty feet away in a tangle of wildflowers and grass.

I grunted and rolled off Saleem. "Asshole. What if you broke it?"

Saleem said nothing. His gaze was riveted on something overhead, his eyes large.

"Raza," he whispered. "What is that?"

We were in the tree's shadow and when I tilted my head up, a shaft of sunlight blinded me. I shaded my eyes, rose to my feet, and there above us something dangled from the banyan.

I walked until I stood directly below it—a massive, heavy-looking gunnysack hung from the fattest branch. When the wind picked up, the tethering rope stirred and the sack turned gently. Its bottom was black at the center.

I dropped my gaze and what I saw chilled me. The grass below my feet was crisp and red-black. I bent and touched it. The blood was still sticky. I was stooping in a puddle of it.

Speaking softly, enunciating each word, Saleem said,

"What the sisterfuck is that?" Our gazes met. Somewhere above us, a golden oriole whistled.

Saleem licked his lips. He had almond-shaped eyes, black as oil puddles, and something swam in them.

I think he figured it out before I did.

"I don't know," I said. "Saleem, fuck the chakoo. Let's get out of here." I backed away from the blood. On my left, the knife gleamed amid dandelions and jasmine, the blade still folded in its gilded handle.

"Wait." Saleem bent and rummaged through the underbrush, found a rock, lifted it.

"What are you doing?"

He aimed the rock, pulled his arm back, and launched it. He had a good throwing arm and the rock sped like a bullet and hit the sack right in the blackened center.

"Aaaaand score!" yelled Saleem, arms high above his head. His voice was hoarse, filled with more than a touch of hysteria, and the golden oriole along with a dozen sparrows and starlings took wing. The grove echoed with their squaws and trills. "That's how you do it."

I stared at him, watched the smile on his face vanish and his eyes widen. His arms dropped and dangled like pendulums.

New sounds cut through the avian scolding. A gurgling from above followed by intermittent choking.

"Ya Allah." Saleem staggered back, and fell to the ground. "Ya Allah."

I didn't want to look up. I could feel my heart beat in every inch of my body. It should've filled my ears, my head, but the sound wouldn't let it. Hissing and whispering that ebbed and rose. I raised my head and the sack was twitching. It swung and shook as if its contents were having a grand mal seizure. It gurgled. Fresh red bloomed at the bottom and began to spread.

Saleem moaned and dug his heels into the grass as he scrambled. I followed him and we both fled through the trees, out the grove past the deserted construction site with its monstrous yellow digger trapped in a ditch.

We ran home and told our parents. The police were called and a squadron sent to the grove immediately. The Rampuri chakoo was found and confiscated. (An official-looking man with a sweetmeat belly came to Saleem's house a week later, applied blue ink to his fingers and asked him to place both hands on a shining white cardboard carefully. Frightened of the man's blank face, Saleem refused at first, but his father slapped him and told him to do exactly as the officer said.) I was grounded for a week and Saleem for a month.

They never told us what was in the sack or who had put it there, but for months I had bad dreams. I'd be back in the grove with the sack twisting and gurgling above me. It would be dusk. The birds hung limply in the sky as if staked to the night itself, and the knife driven into the grass would quiver as if the earth were pulsating. The mouth of the sack would open and a river of black lice-infested hair stream out and pour across the foliage, rotting everything in its path. The jasmines would wilt, their smell that of spoiled meat, the dandelions crumble into dust beneath my feet, as I fled through the darkening, whispering grove. But the path would not open, not open before me, and the gurgling would not stop.

It would not stop.

꧁꧂

Back in Bad Bricks, four teenagers were piled in front of the cellar. The door was open, swaying back and forth above an abyss.

For a moment, all those old fears burrowed out of my heart and sat on its stony ground, watching me with dull black eyes. In the shadows a gunnysack flapped and twitched with the moaning thing inside it, the bloodied nightmare that wore body bags.

Ah, you're back, aren't you? the gunnysack whispered. My sweet child. Know then that evil children, devilish children who celebrate the dead, cannot escape. I come for them, I spill for them, and they smell me. Smell my skin, smell my hair. Been looking for me, have you? I know. I know. So come smell me, rub your face in my clotted fabric. Come you little brat COME...

The hair on my arms stood on end. I shuddered and tore my gaze away from the hole of the doorway. The blackness was a tattered thing, ancient evil grew in its belly, and all at once I was sick of this stupid, twisted game. I wanted to get through Saleem's reading and get the fuck out of this terrible house where awful memories slept, coiled in their graves.

We began to descend the wooden stairs.

Wasif's flashlight threw a wobbling circle of light across the dusty stone wall. A carpet of filth, spider silk, and frayed rope dangled from the metal rail on my right. Threadbare coal sacks lay draped over its edge. Some were curled up at the bottom when we reached it, bits and chips of coal spilling out their mouth. I smelled the damp in the sacks, an odorous disease eating through the fibers, but I also smelled something else. Dank, termite-pored wood, and dead rats.

(...come smell me, smell death, smell the grave, and devilishhh children are sacrificed to the Devil...)

Wasif and Ali began to clear a corner. Saleem shivered. He wrapped his cashmere shawl tight around himself. I could only see his eyes now, white and glittering, suspended in the air.

I placed the skulls on the floor. Took the wrapped shopper out of my pocket. Unfolded it, brought the matchbox out. Flick. The flame touched the candlewicks one after the other. In their trembling light the skulls began to grin.

Saleem drew a circle on the floor with blue chalk, arranged the skulls on opposite ends so that the light would just fall on his notebook, leaving gashes of darkness around him. We settled cross-legged inside the circle. Wasif turned the flashlight off and the night lunged closer and crouched beside us. Saleem's face was swallowed by the gloom, but his eyes glowed, particles of yellow dancing in them.

He began to read.

Now, years later, I clearly remember that magic circle we made, the skulls staked by the candles, the air in that cellar frozen with dread—but, try as I might, I can't remember the story Saleem read to us that horrible storm-lashed evening. When I strain memory, strange words rattle in my head; a few sentences, etched in eternal red, that glisten in a fog of forgetfulness:

"'Thus I see Your Crimson Servant snuff out heaven's stars.

"'So I hear the dead pawing at my door.

"'From Pataal's earth shall explode an army of dust crows.'

"As Hashim turned the pages of Kitab-al-khabaith, he learned these lessons and more. The meaning stripped the skin off his bones, turned him inside out. Finally, he understood what altar the Red City gazed at, unblinking..."

That is all I remember. Granted that half-words and phrases flit about my mind, like restless bats. Kitab-al-khabaith comes to me again and again. The crawling thin-men flapping in the wind. Natasha's fingers that wiggle in a storm's skein. The knife that cuts a thousand worldthroats.

Of the plot I remember nothing—only that it petrified me, like it did us all. We were plunged into a coma of listening to a story about the worldskin melting away, a moaning, juddering melt. About effervescing in death and rising like blood vapor. Truth be told, we were induced into a near-death state ourselves, a rigor mortis that left as quickly as it had come, once Saleem stopped speaking.

The candles were sagged deep inside the skulls. We started and quivered, a ripple to melt the death grip. Saleem had lowered the notebook to his lap. The candle flame danced in his eyes.

Ali coughed. I flexed and stretched my back. Wasif threw his head back, juddering. But Saleem just sat there, silent, unmoving. Perhaps he was waiting for applause, a standing ovation to the masterpiece he had written and performed. He knew perfectly well that no one would best that story, its elegant, haunting prose, the powerful narrative; and I opened my mouth to congratulate him.

The candle flame writhed in Saleem's eyes, a serpent thrashing out its death dance. It was strange, I thought, very strange that the flame would do that. The candles were sunken inside the skulls and they were behind him.

With palsied hands I pulled away his shawl.

The empty jute sack sank to the floor, an avalanche of black coals tumbling out of its mouth. Two glowing, smoldering embers rose from where Saleem's eyes had been and began to swim lazily in the air.

Wasif shouted. Ali moaned, a sound that raised the hair on my neck, and the candles in the skulls went out.

I lunged at the flashlight, switched it on, and I was screaming too. From the darkest corner, which the light's glow had never reached, came a low humming. A familiar childhood tune. Maybe One, Two, Three—The Old Sawbone's Machine. A terrible sound, a haunting lullaby that made my flesh crawl. The humming changed, ebbed into a muffled growl, and finally a gurgling sound that filled my heart with so much terror I could do nothing but clap my hands over my ears.

Something moved in the corner. The coals sacks stirred.

Wasif broke into a run, leaving everything behind. Ali followed, his eyes bone-white, mouth gaping. I ran too. We clattered up the steps. *Thud! Thump! Thud!* A nightmare memory fretted and laughed inside my head. A darkening grove with no way out. Wasif and Ali fled to the hole of light at the top. They burst out the doorway, dusty hands flopping at their side, and I leapt after them. Last step, and my foot punched through the rotten wood.

I yanked at my leg frantically, eyes bulging, fingers clawing at the edge of the doorway. Below me, behind me, the stairs creaked, snorted, and began to scream as something made its way toward me. Wood splinters dug into my flesh and blood began to ooze.

(Raza, my son, the Crimson Storm is a bloodstorm. In its eye the dead raise their fermented, lolling heads from the well of death. Stay home, child. Stay.)

I didn't want to—how could I?—but I looked back, I had to look, and I saw.

A shadow that crawled up on all fours. A face that flashed in a quick loop of light, features muffled, a black cowl spilling onto its singed forehead. Was it the reporter with his eyes scooped out; or the epileptic maid, eyes sewn together by the undertaker, strands of thread hanging over swollen cheeks, lips drawn back in seizure, foam curdling and bubbling at the corner?

...And if devilishhh children are caught doing evil, they will hear the dead knock at their door with a loud hammering. Natasha's fingers will wiggle, and the Knife that cuts a Thousand Worldthroats will chop their feet, their stinking fucking feet OFF...

Was that spit glistening on those yellow teeth? Spiders hanging from her hair, his hair, my hair; pouring out from the caverns of our cheeks, dropping down, scuttling away? Were those hands twisting into claws, elbows bent at impossible angles, as if in catatonic seizure, as if in rigor mortis?

Was it a gunnysack that twitched its way toward me, a tangle of lice-squirming hair spilling from its mouth?

I was screaming and screaming, and the steps were laughing and laughing. The cellar echoed and throbbed with it all. I smelled filth, the city's menstrual blood, unwashed pubic hair, maggot-slick meat. I yanked my leg, one last powerful jerk, for surely that was all the strength left in me, and my foot slipped out of the shoe and I bounded across the last step.

Something black and frayed wavered in the corner of my eyes, then vanished.

Through the pursuing, hollering, tugging crimson storm I fled. Wasif and Ali were long gone, and after I had raced past the lawn out the gates to the end of the street, I turned my head helplessly to look at Bad Bricks one last time.

On the edge of the boundary wall stood a figure. It was no taller than Saleem. It wore a gunnysack and its arms were outspread as if embracing the city's bloody sky. The laal andhi whorled around it, shrieking, lifting the ends of the sack, but it stood motionless, even as rain pelted it and turned it black from head to toe.

The figure never moved.

It will keep its watch forever.

⁂

After each storm, Lahore is peaceful for a few days. People visit their doctors and hakims, complaining of styes and grit-itch in their eyes. Fallen trees are cleared away, power pylons pulled upright, gleaming electric cords duct-taped and snapped back into place. Slowly the city emerges from the hurt. Thugs and dissidents, the military and the militants, subdued briefly by the storm, slip into routine again. Sectarian violence, lathi charges, homicides, executions. Railway Station, Data Sahib's shrine, a girls' school. It's a matter of time.

It was a matter of time before Saleem staggered home that night. His eyes were cracked marbles, his hair completely white. He shivered uncontrollably, head cocked to one side as if in torticollis. His fingers snapped and pinched as if trying to grasp the corner of some cloth. And he stank. Of musty jute sacks, dead insects, rotting meat, and jasmine.

We never told anyone what happened that night and Saleem could not anymore. He stared into a deep intimate distance, where no one could reach him, and spoke in whispers. To whom? I'd never know.

Once when I went to see him, he muttered, "That black hair, all that tangled black hair. It's his smell, yes. His smell."

After that, I didn't visit Saleem. Sometime later, Father moved us to a neighborhood in Defence (something to do with Aunty Nasreen from four streets down and my mother's vow that she'd cut her own wrists if we didn't move away), and our paths didn't cross for fifteen years until that hot summer day in 2008 when I nearly ran him over.

Hours later, at the gate of a children's Montessori, my childhood friend Saleem blew himself up.

I don't know why he did it. His mother and younger brother were taken in by the military for interrogation. Some feared they would go "missing," but when reporters from as far as Amreeka and England took notice, the two were let go. What could they have told anyone anyway? What could they say? That his father didn't return home one summer many years ago? That for months Saleem had been wandering the streets at night, scratching and pissing himself, like a senile dog way past his expiration date?

I remember what his mother said to the TV people who showed up at her door. This one guy, an asshole cameraman with a dense mustache and a mole on his upper lip, kept pushing her as to why her son would commit such an atrocity, until she finally screamed, "Leave me alone! Blood seeks blood. My son died a long time ago. He was killed by your city. He was a good boy. He was good. And you turned him. Leave me alooonnneee."

That was all I could take. I stopped watching the news altogether.

※

When my wife asked me again, I told her everything that happened that spring and summer of '82. The gunnysack, the crimson storm, Bad Bricks. She didn't believe me, not really. She asked what happened to Wasif and Ali Malik. She had never heard me mention them before.

Wasif moved away, I told her, a pale shell drifting in his

own cloud of guilt and misery. Ali smoked his smokes and ended up in his dad's workshop, hammering metal pipes and replacing car parts. Last I heard he took up heroin, breathing in the whispering vapors from old Coke bottles with a straw. Chasing the dragon, is what they call it.

Me, I nodded right along with my beloved city. I went to work at my uncle's jewelry shop and dutifully I returned home every night. What if I sometimes dreamed and woke up trembling? We go through one hell to get to another. We walk in the midst of the dead and the dying—gold-red explosions, dust clouds, acid flings. Uncle Dara the realtor once told me that the crime reporter, that batshit-crazy dude, wanted to write a book. Maybe sometime memories can be written in the restlessness of the grave. Maybe sometimes we come back to read our words aloud, just to feel them tremble in a membrane of life. Maybe sometimes old maids die, unwanted, unloved. Hell, what do I know? Maybe sometimes children grow up in a limbo filled with body bags hanging from trees, like slaughtered goats, a nightmare that never flickers, never recedes from us.

So it went that Lahore breathed, quiet in its slumber, and waited for another laal andhi.

I did too.

THE WOODS

ERIKA T. WURTH

The hotel lights glowed lurid and green in the dark. I sighed. Though I was happy to let Tim drive, it had been pouring so savagely, for so long, it was like we were living underwater. I could tell Tim was tiring, the wheels correcting sharply to the left or right, making me wonder if we were going to get through this alive.

"Tim." I tapped at the windshield.

"What?" he answered, his voice weighed down with irritation.

I pointed. He squinted through the dark, a sound coming from him like he'd entered a good, long restful dream.

"A hotel." I peered harder into the black.

"Yes," he whispered. "Thank God." His pale, freckled hands tightened on the wheel.

A few minutes later the words appeared out of the deluge as if we were surfacing for breath: The Woods—A Hotel.

"Wow," Tim said, pulling in. "This looks nice. Especially for the wilds of Tennessee."

I nodded. I'd been thinking the same. The lettering was block, like it had been manufactured for a fancy eatery in Brooklyn, a destination that right now, seemed impossibly far.

Tim parked, yanked our suitcases out of the back of the beamer. We ran as fast as we could through the rain, my hoodie nearly soaked by the time Tim's hand hit the handle, opening the door for me.

Inside was a marvel. The front desk looked like the base of a tree, black cherrywood, cords winding up and around the walls, the limbs dark and glistening. At first glance, I could've sworn they were breathing. There were two forest green chairs across from it, and large, ornate, black mirrors covering the walls. I turned to Tim to comment, but his back was to me. He was already charging up as if our surroundings were no more exceptional than a Motel 6.

The man at the front desk looked waxen, an automaton waiting eternally for guests to appear out of the water. He stood, unblinking, a pleasant smile on his face, his dark hair perfectly coifed—conked even—as if someone had packed him in cotton around 1942, and recently realized there was a use for him after all.

"Checking in?" he asked, cocking his head sharply to the left, adding to that android-ish, surreal quality he'd given me upon first glance.

"We are." I stepped up and pulled my hood down. I ran one hand through my long, dark, and now thoroughly wet hair.

"Wonderful," he said, typing at his computer and pausing. "First visit to The Woods?" He looked at me sharply, eyes mirroring the darkness of my own.

"We don't get to rural Tennessee much," Tim said, a sophisticated little chuckle following.

"Well, I do," I said, narrowing my eyes.

"When, Lushanya?" Tim asked, wiping at his jacket with quick, incensed little jabs.

"We were just at an exhibition in Memphis." I stared at the side of his head, willing him to meet my gaze.

"Your family's from Texas," he said. "And you were born in Brooklyn. Where we live."

The concierge's pupils seemed to dilate, almost with pleasure at listening to our argument. "You'll love The Woods," he said, turning his computer around and pointing. "Every room is different. Every room is exceptional."

"As long as it has a shower and a blow dryer, I'm in," Tim said, exhausted. "Hell, even if it doesn't."

I kept my mouth shut, but I could feel the rage boiling in my brain, waiting to spill out. How many times did we have to go through this? His family was a mélange of whiteness, generations of whom had settled in different parts of New York, yet the topic of his heritage was never the subject of our arguments.

The concierge pushed an old-fashioned key across. I shot a hand out quickly to retrieve it, but Tim was faster. He pulled it up and dangled it questioningly in front of him. "No key card?"

"It's easy," the concierge answered pleasantly. "Just hold it up to the door and it'll open. Like magic." A slow smile spread across his face.

Tim rolled his eyes, pushed the key into his pocket and whipped around, moving towards the hallway.

"Tim?"

He turned back.

"Just being the man here. Isn't that what you want?"

"Do you want to hear about our restaurant? Bar?" the concierge asked.

Tim merely flipped one hand behind him and kept going.

"I do," I said, "and I'd like a second key."

⁂

In the room, I sat down on the bed. Tim was already on it, prone. He began caressing my back. I wanted to take the fancy, gold letter opener that matched the ornate mirrors—that seemed to be a theme here, mirrors—and stab it into his hand.

Instead, I got up and started putting my clothing away. I knew we'd only be here for one night, but it was habit. Tim's suitcase was lying on the floor, open, his clothing strewn across the entrance to the bathroom. I kicked it as I went in to tidy my toiletries.

"Hey," he said, and I kicked again, this time at the door, which slammed shut with a satisfying clap.

"Lushanya," Tim called from the room, running the "a" long.

The bathroom was equally as beautiful as the room, the entire hotel—also covered in thick, black wooden vines, as if the whole place were sitting on a massive, ancestral tree. I threw my bag on the toilet and began noisily putting my toothbrush, brush, and other accoutrements on the sink, taking as much room as possible.

The TV switched on. I ran the brush through my hair and re-did my eyeliner, smoothed my favorite pink lipstick onto my lips, popping them as I finished. I turned my head a bit to the left, then to the right and sighed, hard. I'd wanted to have a good time on this trip.

Behind me, reflected in the mirror, one of the vines moved.

I screamed.

Tim was up and pounding on the door. "What's happening? Unlock the door!"

I blinked and looked again. The vine was still. I opened the door slowly.

Tim put his hands on my shoulders. "Jesus, you OK? I thought you cut yourself. Or that someone was in there. Did you cut yourself?" His blue eyes roved over my body, the bathroom.

"No, I... look. I thought I saw something in the mirror." I pushed past him and tugged my shirt off, opened the dresser for a dry one. I took a white T-shirt out and pulled it over my head.

He was silent, but I could see through the scrim of my T-shirt that his mouth was open, his hands moving nervously through his red hair. Ever since the miscarriage, he'd been like this.

I pulled my key off the dresser, ripped my bag off the bed, opened the door and started down the hallway. I needed a break. I needed a drink. And that bar the concierge had described sounded fun.

I didn't hear the door open behind me.

The hallway was dark, the same vines running along the walls here too. With the light flickering in old brass sconces, it looked as if they were moving along with me as I walked.

⁕

The door to the bar was black and ornate, covered in carvings of berries and corn, packs of wolves, a lone panther.

"Interesting," I murmured, pushing in.

There were a few couples, scattered throughout. I didn't see any families. There was a Black couple near the window, watching the rain pour, her hand over the glass, his hand on her knee. I nodded, and they nodded back. I settled at the bar, opening the menu the bartender handed to me without looking up.

"I'll have a—" I started, then stopped. "Oh. You, again. You run this whole place?"

The bartender cocked his head. "Excuse me?"

I laughed, folded the menu. "You checked me in… and my boyfriend, you know, the guy with the red hair?" I said, pointing stupidly to my own extremely dark, slightly wavy hair. "Like, fifteen minutes ago?" I smiled.

"Red hair?" he repeated.

"You changed fast, though." My laugh became a nervous titter.

"No, I've been here," he said. "Have you had a chance to check into your room?"

"I…"

"Every room is special. Every room is unique," he said. His pupils dilated the way they had when he checked us in. I had no idea why he was playing coy.

"Yeah, you mentioned that." I shook my head. I didn't care what this guy's thing was. I just wanted a drink. "Martini," I said. "Extra dirty."

"Right away," he said, smiling and turning from me.

I pulled my phone out of my pocket, wanting to see if the pictures of my mural at the exhibition had gotten any likes. I'd worked hard on that piece, for months and months. I glanced up. It was not unlike this hotel's décor. A giant tree. In my case, distorted. But with butterflies flying out of the top, carrying seeds in their wings. It had gathered quite a few likes, which made me happy.

"Your martini, ma'am." The bartender was back.

"Thanks," I said, accepting the drink as he scooted it delicately my way.

"Cheers," he said, staring at me.

"Right," I responded, staring back.

After a moment, he blinked, and walked away.

What a strange guy, I thought, taking a large sip. I turned around. In the middle of the bar was a gigantic tree with large black branches reaching all the way to the top. There were red berries growing in between little frosty green leaves. I leaned in. I could've sworn that it hadn't been there when I'd first stepped in. I had been distracted, sure. I was pissed—still was pissed—at Tim. But this thing was enormous. I sipped again, the taste bitter in my mouth. It almost looked like an oak tree, but the colors were off. I thought I heard laughter coming from the trunk and drew back.

I drank the rest of my martini and looked at my phone. Tim, I guess, had given up on me. I closed my eyes and thought of him then, as if he weren't in the hotel. As if he was someone I'd known long ago. His long-fingered hands. His freckled face. His pink lips tipping up toward mine in bed. I turned away from the image and ordered another drink, this time, a glass of red wine.

The music in the bar was strange. Dark and dreamy, as if piped in from another world. It fit the ambience well. I began to feel sleepy but fought it off. I didn't want to go back to the room. I wanted to wait until Tim was asleep.

What was the point of arguing? Tim would complain that I was moody. I would tell him that he was the moody one. He'd bring back past hurts. Then I would. It would climax in insults, and then I'd cry, something I tried never to do but always did with Tim. And the next day, we'd get in the car, and drive back to New York.

I blinked. I felt warm. Extremely warm, my face flushed. I pulled myself out of my reverie. It had grown dark in the bar, the patrons now missing, the only source of light wild and orange. Was that… was there… a fire at the base of the tree?

I stood up, my legs feeling leaden, my brain strange and milky. It wasn't just that it had grown dark, or that everyone had left. The bar had disappeared, and I was in the middle of a lush, southeastern forest. The trees surrounded me, white-purple woodland phlox covering the ground, bluebells, chokeberry dotting the landscape.

"What the fuck?" I said, looking down at my glass of wine, which still appeared to be in my hand. It rippled, like I was underwater.

The fire in front of me grew, and instead of destroying the tree, it fed it somehow, the great black glossy roots undulating and almost sucking at the flames. I heard the singing I thought I'd heard earlier grow louder, and then, through the smoke and the haze, I could see people around the tree. They were dancing, moving around the fire like a great, strange bough. A man pulled out of the spinning circle of dancers and my heart caught in my throat, my hand at my heart.

"Julian?" I said, my voice breaking.

He smiled and moved back into the circle.

"No," I said, my mind breaking into chaos.

I ran for where I remembered the door to the bar being, the fire at my back, burning. Following me. Burning so hot I could feel sparks at my neck, smell my own charred skin. I screamed. The door was there. I went through.

In the hallway, all was quiet. It was as if I'd never seen a giant tree in the middle of a bar. Never seen strangers dancing around a fire. Never seen my dead brother, Julian. My back was clear. The glass in my hand still. I turned around, but the door I'd gone through was latched. I pulled. It was locked.

Sweat broke out on my brow, and I felt, for a moment, like I was going to pass out. I set the glass down on the floor near a door, closed my eyes, and put one hand on the wall to steady myself. I took several deep breaths. There had to be a logical explanation for what I'd just experienced.

My eyes snapped open. *That asshole put something in my drink*, I thought, picking the glass back up and turning it over, and then lifting it to my nose to sniff. There was a faint, unfamiliar, maybe even acidic odor to the sediment left over in the glass. But it wasn't as if I'd been roofied before, so I had no idea if it smelled like anything at all. And the odd part was, at that moment, I felt fine.

Maybe that's just how it works? I wondered. The lights in the hallway seemed to flicker in response. God, this place was strange.

My anger at Tim gone, I stalked down the hallway purposefully, letting myself into our room with the old-fashioned looking metal key. Tim was on the bed, one arm behind his back, the other lazily resting on the remote. The TV was blaring an old episode of *SVU*.

"Oh, you've deigned to join me?" he asked, not even looking up. "Sorry I can't provide the abundantly superior company your brother could." His lips trembled.

I closed my eyes.

"Tim, listen," I said.

He turned to me listlessly, one finger pushing down on the remote.

"Turn. That. Off!"

He looked like I'd slapped him. "God, *fine*," he said. "You're so violent."

I knew a baited statement when I heard one, but instead of taking it, I explained what I'd experienced. At first, he stared at me as if he'd been sedated. But after I told him I thought my drink had been drugged, his eyes went wide. He sat up. He threw himself off the bed.

"We need to call the cops," he said, pulling his shoes on.

"What? No, I—"

He stopped. Stared. "Lushanya? Someone drugged you. Someone at this hotel, fucking *drugged you*," he repeated, punctuating each word with a karate chop to his hand.

"I'm not even sure that's what happened," I said, my hands on my hips. "Chill out. Not everything has to be a five-alarm fucking emergency."

He stared at me for second, then shook his head, picked his key up, and strode past me, turning in time to grip my arm. "Let's go."

I squinched my lips up in frustration, not wanting to cause a fuss, worried about whatever the cops in rural Tennessee, where one set of my ancestors had been "escorted" out of, another set had fled, would think of me, and my complaint, but decided fighting Tim would take more energy than giving a lackluster weird account of what happened to me to the cops.

⁂

"Did you hear me?" Tim was beating one fist down on the table, the man who'd checked us in earlier staring at him like he was a feral animal.

"Call the cops! My girlfriend was drugged."

The concierge blinked as if Tim wasn't speaking a language he understood. "Very well." He turned, disappearing behind a little door, the faint sounds of laughter, much like what I thought I'd heard in the bar floating out behind him before the door shut.

"Can you believe that guy?" Tim asked, his eyes rimmed with red.

"No," I said.

Tim huffed, shuffled over to a chair, and with a hard plunk, sat down. He pulled his phone out and began scrolling, his masculine duties satisfied.

I leaned against the wall.

Ten minutes passed. Then fifteen. Tim got up as if startled at the fifteen-minute mark, and walking over to the desk, looked around. "Where is that guy? Do you even think he called the cops?"

I shrugged, frustrated and tired.

"Real helpful, Lushanya."

"Look, maybe I was wrong..."

Tim stalked around to the other side of the desk, to the strangely small door the concierge exited from. It was as if the door was growing smaller, the more I looked at it.

Tim pulled at the handle. Locked.

He knocked. "Hello!" he screamed, "Hello! Hello!"

"Tim, calm down," I said, embarrassed even though there was no one around to witness his behavior.

Finally, as if the door were making a conscious decision, it swung open with a rusty sounding creak.

"Well, looky here," Tim said, walking through slowly.

"Tim, I'm not sure—" I said.

He turned to me. "Wait here."

"Tim," I said, standing up.

But he was through, and the door shut, the big black snake-like branches around the frame pulsing.

I went over, tried the door myself, afraid. It was locked once more.

"What the...?"

I had to find someone.

In the hallway, I wandered, the lights still flickering, the branches glistening, the sounds of laughter growing stronger. I passed doorway after doorway, TVs blaring, a couple arguing, children banging things around. The cracks under the doorways were black. Except for one.

I could hear the laughter behind it. I want to say it was gentle, but it wasn't. It wasn't even human. The door eased open on its own.

Behind it, I found a little house, the brown wooden walls like the inside of a giant tree, complete with rings, the furniture made of forest things, black wood tables and chairs hand-hewn from bark, berries and other foods lining the top of the table, little people sitting not only at the table but on forest moss couches, the rugs underneath them also made of moss, lichen. They didn't smile, they didn't gesture, but I could tell they were beckoning me in.

"Have you seen my boyfriend?" I asked.

They stared, their tiny black eyes implacable.

I sat.

They watched me, and it felt as if I was surrounded by people, if I could call them that, that were impossibly old, though I wasn't sure if they were wise.

I wondered if I hadn't been drugged, if I was not

still dreaming, whether maybe I was dying instead. Had already died. Was in the car somewhere on the road. We'd skittered off in the rain, we'd hit something, my head had shattered against the windshield, my brains spilling like black-eyed peas, my spirit drifting, dreaming of all this to comfort itself as it slid into nothingness.

I ate.

It was a test, I could see now, whether I was alive or not, and I had to pass the judgment of these tiny ancestors, or I wouldn't just die, I'd go somewhere dark and cold and without the love of anyone I'd ever known.

I ate berries the color of blood, my mouth lining with their juice. The little men and women watched, silent except for the occasional titter, and I thought about the stories my mom used to tell me, that her mom told her, that her mom told her when something was lost, missing. The hidden people, who liked to hunt, who liked to play, who had knowledge of medicine.

Julian had needed medicine.

Someone began beating at the door. The room whooshed around me, and I felt, for the second time that night, as if I was going to pass out. I closed my eyes.

When I opened them, I was back in my own room, Tim still on the bed.

I shook my head. I knew I'd been drugged for sure now.

"Did you... did we?" I started but couldn't finish.

"Couldn't find the guy," Tim said, shaking his head.

He'd seemed so worried, so urgent before. What was going on?

"How did I even end up here? How did you?"

"What are you talking about?" Tim asked, changing the channel.

Why was he being so blasé?

"Tim. We need to leave. Now."

Tim looked at me with his eyebrows knit. "You're crazy, you know that?"

"Don't be a dick," I spat.

He leapt off the bed. "Dick? Dick? Why don't you find another *dick*, cheat on me again, won't you!" He stood over me, expression a mixture of triumph and misery.

I closed my eyes. "You know why I did that," I said. "We both know why."

"Because I wasn't enough for you?"

"Because I wanted a child. And you didn't."

He opened his mouth, then shut it.

"You never did before," he said. "That's what we talked about when we first got together. We agreed."

"I changed. People change. Why are we arguing about this now?"

"You didn't change. You just got fucked up when Julian died."

He was right about that. Julian was who I called when I was sad, when I was happy, when I wanted to celebrate, when I'd been passed over for a gig, when a stranger stroked my hair again in a bar. Tim had been jealous of my brother.

And now Julian was gone.

"You would've hated the responsibility," Tim said.

"Speak for yourself," I replied, then, to dig the knife in, because I was tired, because I couldn't believe after all these years Tim couldn't understand, "and yeah, it *was* bigger than yours."

Tim's face went beet red. Then he started crying.

I left.

In the hallway, the lights seemed not just to flicker now, but shimmer, the air around me holding a kind of strange, still magic. The mood felt hushed, expectant.

Determined, I made my way back down the hallway, mind swimming with confusion. Behind the doors I was passing, I could hear wild, childlike laughter again.

I squinted. The exit was receding. I shook my head. I knew that was wrong. I stopped. Closed my eyes.

When I opened them, I froze in terror.

At the end of the hallway was a person. But not just any person.

"Julian," I whispered.

He looked angry.

I wanted, then, to go back. Back to my safe, albeit static, life.

I couldn't. Julian wasn't going to let me.

The lights began to go out, first behind me, then above,

then in front, and I knew eventually, in just a few seconds, I would be left alone, in the dark, with my dead brother.

The last light went out.

I thought, in that blink of a moment, of the child I conceived with another man, the child who had grown inside me until it hadn't, and then, without warning, fled this earth, following my most beloved, my twin brother, my Julian. How alone I'd felt.

I felt hands wrapping around my neck in the dark.

I began to scream.

"Hush," Julian said, his tone just like our mother's, "hush." And I realized in that moment how wrong I'd been. He had not wanted to choke me, to kill me, his embrace simply started there, at my neck, the way it always had. He had been my first child in a way, younger than me, vulnerable. He loved to hang at my neck and swing up and into my arms.

I wondered, then, who I was holding, who was holding me, was it Julian? My own child, come to life in this hotel that seemed to hold such strange, ancestral magic? Were the little people who'd fed me the same folk my mother spoke about in her stories? Had the ancestors brought me here to teach me? To punish me?

"What is this place, Julian?" I whispered, frightened. "Why am I here?"

Julian hushed me again, laid me down on the rich, mossy carpet. Fibers curled around my head, my body, and as they did, a flash of my latest mural entered my head. An ancestral tree, beautiful and whole. I wanted, as I grew sleepy, to ask Julian if he blamed me for his death. If the miscarriage was my fault. But he continued to rock me to sleep, and I knew, if I ever woke up from this dream, this nightmare, this wild known and unknown place, that though I might never have all the answers, I had never been alone, and I would never be.

UNSEWN

AI JIANG

For all the women in my family who I am both mad at and mad for, who didn't know any better, who knew better but couldn't say otherwise, and who thought "no" could not be a part of their vocabulary.

※

At eight years of age, before Ma sent me away, she held me by my shoulder as we sat at the edge of our wooden mattress-less bed. A single, tall red candle cast our shadows onto the sheer mosquito tent around us. We looked like monsters waiting to consume caught prey. Her hands rested, wrinkled and calloused like an old rag stretched over bones, against my moth-eaten plain cloth pajamas that did little to protect the young flesh beneath—taut rather than supple. There was not enough food to go around, and certainly much less for the daughters, even as they pulled us into the fields and told us we had to work like the men but longer, but stronger, on less.

Even in the rain, when there weren't enough cloaks for everyone.

If you want to survive, you show them, you show them you're more than—show them you're worth feeding and keeping. At least, that was what Ma said at first.

Yet, Ma took those words back as quick as she swiped her meal tickets from the unforgiving hands of the government and spat new, contradicting words back at me the way she'd spit into the ground at the backs of those she despised most. Yes. This included Ba. Sometimes he would catch her doing so, and sometimes he would not care. Sometimes.

"When you're older, when you marry, you must have a son. You must. You cannot be like me, haizi. Do *not* be like me." Her spittle splattered across my dirt-streaked cheeks after the day's work in the rice paddies.

It was so sudden, all of it, the way she clutched me and whispered in my ears. She had never held me, hugged me, never—not since when I was first birthed, not that I remember. But I understood, inside, these were the things she had always held back because we all knew that one day I would no longer be of this family, whether it was because I would be given away or my hand would be in marriage.

Back then, no one told me that the sex of a child was

not a thing chosen by the body of women but by the seed of men, and yet, we were blamed again and again for not producing a son to carry on the family's name.

"Why can the child not carry my name? Why can daughters not carry the family name?" I asked, utterly convinced of my logic, picking at the dirt between my fingernails and resisted the urge to suck on each digit due to hunger.

Ma looked as though she wanted to slap me, then she stared at her raised hand, blood seeping from her cheeks, down to her neck, disappearing, leaving her a flimsy white sheet. Then, she looked as though she wanted to slap herself. And I'm sure she does, even if not physically.

"This is how things are. Never, never mention what you said to your future husband. Do you understand?" I nodded, and she shook me again, eyes unfocused. "Tell me. Tell me, do you understand?"

"Yes, Ma, yes," I stuttered, remembering how Ma would occasionally mutter about the ringing in her ears after her last argument with Ba. She no longer complained, though I suspected it was not because Ba had done any less shouting, but because she had little hearing left to process it. Or maybe she did not want to or have the energy to any longer.

Ma stood, stumbled away, hands knocking her wedding photo from the table next to the wooden bed we shared. Nothing shattered, because glass was for the rich. The black-and-white photo collected specs of dust from the ground. Ma blew out the candle.

She felt her way back to the bed, its hard surface barely covered by a stretch of stained floral-patterned lace fabric. The fabric was cheap, but it was still the most expensive thing in the house—a gift from Ba's family to Ma when they married.

That night would be the last time we shared the bed.

With her body facing the wall, Ma trembled. I picked up the photo from the ground and set it back in place against the extinguished candle, its red wax dried in drips down the length of its body like blood stalled in time, like the way it had from the cut on my knee, the dribble down my shins, that I did not dare ruin my clothing to wipe while helping Ba in the fields.

Sometimes I wondered if I'd been pushed down on purpose, just to see if I'd cry like he expected me to. I didn't. And somehow, that had disappointed Ba more, as though he didn't have any further excuse to get rid of me if I pulled my weight.

I climbed into bed, pressed against Ma's back.

She turned.

I slept, close to suffocation, in Ma's clutches at night. Her bony elbows dug into my back; her knees drove into my ankles. Next to my ear, her words became her breaths, rhythmic, sometimes stuttering but never halting completely.

You must have a son. Do you understand? Do you understand? You must have a son.

I was unsure of when she fell asleep, but when the

sun came up, her chest was damp with my spittle and the remnants of my answer.

Yes. I will. Yes, yes. I will. Yes.

But of course, I did not have a son. At least, not until the end.

When I left Ma on the bed to prepare breakfast for Ba in her stead, she was caressing her stomach.

I had a sister the next year, and then I didn't.

⁂

There was a legend about a marriage that lasted many reincarnations, of a marriage bound by fate, by threads, rather than vows—a marriage unbreakable, even if such fate is forced. More times than not, the forced fate is one women enter into willingly, for they have no other choice but to adorn themselves in red, wait for their veils to be lifted, and smile without teeth, without spite, without desire for anything more than what they are given, even if what they are given is little to nothing. And if they are showered in rice and meat and gold and silks so fresh the scent of worms and leaves still linger beneath the floral essence rubbed on, well, how dare they ever complain?

In some versions of such legends, these threads of fate are not spiritual, metaphorical, invisible things binding the soul, but real, tangible, and physical weavings that strike skin, pierce flesh, bringing two bodies together—inseparable.

⁂

Pick her. She seems strong, having worked in the fields. It has made her less womanly, less feminine, but she will surely have healthy and strong children. Sons. Of course, she would. Of course, she will.

He picked me up from my old family home that had long since sat empty except for my ghostly presence at night, during the hours I was not labouring in the fields.

The plague that swept through our villages left few. Those who remained stayed behind, holding on to what had already been long lost.

We tended to the graves up the mountains, swept them until they were cleaner than all our homes. Yet everyone left, one by one, eventually, whether it was by passing or because they were whisked away by the hopes of greater prospects and opportunities in a nearby city growing as rapidly as we were shrinking.

He was from one of the remaining villages, and his parents were kind, until they weren't.

❦

Donned in red with shimmering golden accents, we married in the home of his parents. His family had little, but I had nothing. And I supposed that was the only reason his parents forwent the dowry, and I supposed that was the same reason I accepted a meagre bride-wealth. I wondered if Ma would have been glad to see that though we had nothing material, we at least had some semblance of love, even if it was mostly bound by duty.

We bowed to the sky, bowed to the earth, bowed to our parents—*his* parents—and bowed to each other.

Our parents wasted no time in bringing us to the fortune teller, a friend of theirs for more than three decades. *She has never been wrong!* they insisted.

And she wasn't, until she was.

With trembling hands, she read our palms, our pulses, our faces, and told us we would be with child in less than a year, *a son*, in a dialect impaired by her crooked teeth and kind yet sharp smile.

༺༻

We planned, we prayed. Hope swelled. He was their only son, and I was the only one remaining from my family.

Indeed, we were with child within the year.

When she grew within us, we had a daughter.

Once our daughter arrived and had been confirmed that she indeed was a daughter, it was no longer *our* daughter, it became *your* daughter.

"What do you mean? It's *your* daughter. Not mine. *Yours*," was what my husband said, and from that moment, that, too, became what I believed, as I stepped outside of myself, unable to cope with your cruelty.

Then, it became all I ever heard—you, you, *you*—and that was exactly what I became.

You.

That sliver, that semblance, of love you so desperately

clung to severed within seconds after everyone gathered and looked at the naked, screaming child in your arms, covered in your blood, then your tears, then the spiteful and disappointed glares of all those around.

The fortune teller told your fortune thrice more. She was right, until she was wrong—thrice more.

By the second time, your parents, *his* parents, had stopped accompanying you.

By the third time, your husband had stopped accompanying you, too.

As hope waned, you decided to visit the fortune teller once more, a final time. But her home was empty when you trod across the village and knocked on her door until your knuckles bloodied and continued knocking even though you knew she had gone, fled, in fear others would call her a hack even though such whispers had already been floating across the village, poisoning the ears of those who had their faith in her most.

※

In the legends, the woman cut her fate threads again and again and again, but in every life, she met the same man, and in every life, she had the same family who tried to make things better but only made things worse, and in the same life she had daughters and daughters and daughters, and then—

She prayed to the gods, she prayed to the deities, the immortals, anyone who she thought might listen. But when she became pregnant once more, swelling with her belly was the desire that her prayers had been answered. Instead, she brought into the world another daughter who she tried to rid, who she had been told to rid.

This angered those who she had prayed to, and with the same fate thread that bound her to reincarnations of pain, the gods and deities and immortals sewed each daughter she had, both dead and alive, to her body, to every limb, every exposed piece of flesh.

※

You gave away your daughters, one by one, whether it was to families looking for a girl to be their son's brides so they may grow up together, families looking for extra helping hands, families without children, or to death themself, in hopes of severing your fates the moment you severed your umbilical cords from their bodies, even as much as guilt threatened to rip your newly closed wounds, plunge and further fester the infections still standing, shadow more so the darkness growing within your mind, and gouge out the heart you'd already been losing piece by piece to each daughter you swore not to grow attached to.

You needed a son. That was what you had been told growing up. That was what you were being told now.

※

One was sold to the Huangs as the bride of their son. She was a one-year-old, and their son was already twelve.

Two was handed off to Auntie Li and Uncle Chen, plagued with infertility. Neither would admit who it was of the pair that people called barren, though more than enough rumours had gone around. Two was pampered by them, as they were comparatively well off, but passed of illness when she turned two.

Your last visit to the fortune teller before she left was just before you had miscarried Three. "Laogong," you had said, clutching on to your husband's hand tight. Yours was clammy, his chafed like rust on the cold iron of abandoned rickshaws in the dead of winter, before you left for the fortune teller's house on your own.

When you had arrived at her house, her raspy voice floated from the entrance, stale and scratchy like sand to taste as your mouth had opened and closed like a dying fish, wanting to refute her but also not knowing how.

Her voice went through one ear then out the other as you dug into your growing belly with your gold and jade wedding ring. The same ring your husband wore but with a slimmer band, larger, darker jade, the size of an olive pit. The same ring you had seen your husband stare at when he believed you'd already gone to sleep, with a torn expression, a warring within the mind in which you knew you were amid.

"You are cursed with daughters. Cursed." The fortune teller had abandoned her composed nature, whispered to you with a shaking finger. Neither you nor she nor anyone else seemed to be able to will a daughter from your womb.

At the local herbal doctor, you asked for a concoction, one that twisted your stomach, made you bleed for days, made it seem as though everything bound within you boiled and melted and struggled against the confines of your flesh to escape or so implode. You refused to bring Three into the world.

But without anyone to tell you about Four, you allowed her to enter the world, grasping desperation that this was the son everyone had hoped for. She was not, but still you allowed her to remain in the household the same way your mother had, even though she had been told time and time again to let you go, to give you away. She didn't until the end, until she had to, had no choice but to. You wanted to give Four the choice you never had the chance to make. And stay Four did, until she herself decided she wanted to remain no longer, running away from home at the age of six after discovering the fate of her sisters.

And you let her because you yourself could not run.

You wanted to leave. Oh, so desperately you wanted to leave. But you were cursed to try again, and again, and again. Sometimes, at night, you found your mind following Four out of the village, and that was as far as any kind of liberty went.

At least, for you.

You caught the fortune teller sneaking back into the village, having forgotten something from her home. She had her back turned, cursing as she fiddled with the lock of her door, when your voice drew a yelp from the elder. This time, your husband came. A gut feeling, he'd said. This time, surely, this time.

Then you had a son.

Then, it became *we* had a son.

Then, it became *he* had a son.

And you were left alone after they cooed at the golden egg, and when that same egg cracked, stopped breathing several hours later, you continued to coo, to mimic *them*, at his body, hoping that it might somehow bring him back to life.

※

In another legend, the woman was said to have drowned in a well, and fortune tellers speculated whether she threw herself in or if it was her husband. She took all her daughters with her, and even their only son, and the husband also threw himself in. Or perhaps the woman had risen and pulled him in with her.

※

The boy died.

The boy looked like your husband, the faces of your husband's parents, your own parents.

But you pretended Five was alive.

He was Five to you, but he was One to everyone else. To some, he was the *only* one.

You returned to your empty village, a day's walk away, to your parents' old home. A thin blanket of snow resting on the grounds.

Bundled on your back was the half-sewn quilt for Five, enough food for a week, and, tucked next to your supply, Five's body, as pale and translucent as the flesh of longyan, and soon, as blue as the ink on china you could never afford. Within the womb-like quilt, Five's small hands clutched a loose thread, a replacement for your umbilical cord, a fate thread he dared not let go of, as though willing your destiny to remain connected even though it had been already severed.

When Five began to rot, legends and realities no longer held boundaries within your mind.

That was when you could no longer stand yourself, your husband, your family, the thought of any or all of your children, and yet, you couldn't let go of the only identities you had left—a mother, a wife.

❦

As the Mother, you took him apart.

The Mother went to collect her daughters, in the form of ghosts, hovering by their graves, in the form of shadows stepping out from The Mother's own because she never looked back to notice, in the form of the bride who had passed early from childbirth, in the form of the runaway daughter who never made it through her first winter gone.

To each of her daughters, she handed a part of their brother and asked them to deliver to those who asked for him, the son, One.

Four daughters—legs, arms, body, head.

With the same needle The Mother had sewn her quilt for her son, she sewed Five to One, to Two, to Three, to Four.

The Mother herself took one thing only.

⁂

In that same legend, the husband's body was fished out of the well, bloated, with scratch marks, but whole. But what the villagers do not know is that his soul is gone, kept imprisoned by the ghosts of his wife and daughters whose bodies have disappeared from the well, leaving rotting water that cannot quench thirst and floating flesh that cannot sate hunger.

The son unalive yet undead, rises from the waters, walks back to the village as though he had never gone, and carried on, because that is what is expected of him.

⁂

The Wife left her empty village, empty house, behind and returned to her husband's doorsteps.

In a half-sewn quilt, she held a cold, un-beating heart out to her husband. Stunned, he remained unmoving as he asked, "Whose heart is that?"

"This is your child. Can't you tell?" The Wife asked.

When her husband refused to accept the heart, she asked, "Is it a boy or a girl?"

But of course, her husband could not answer.

All hearts look the same.

And all hearts suffer the same pain, and all hearts die when they stop.

Legends, or stories, or real accounts, no one could tell the difference, but the women in these tales continue to exist, as the living, as the dead, as the haunting, as spite itself. As hearts that had been born, that had beat, that had been beaten, that had begged and bargained, that had been betrothed, that had been bereaved, that had been besieged and betrayed, that had bled, and that had seethed, simmered, and stilled.

TO FORGET AND BE FORGOTTEN

ADAM NEVILL

Even in the most populous cities on earth a multitude of people exist in solitude. And yet, after a sufficient period of time has been endured while feeling awkward, or being neglected socially and professionally, it is my experience that individuals can yet make themselves moderately comfortable in the role of the excluded, or the barely tolerated.

I was never really cast out, but manoeuvred toward the edges of human affairs by the herd. And it was only after considerable experience within this role of the outcast that I finally accepted my own fate. It was liberating.

I considered myself a true outsider, because my loneliness itself became a purpose. My new vocation was to avoid all of those things that drew people together and could be termed a shared experience, for I developed a desire to create a silence and stillness around myself, and a space within my head, in which to think and to read. For the rarest aspiration for any individual to pursue, in this solipsistic age of me, is to be ordinary. Just ordinary. Unexceptional and invisible. And this was a goal that I would take to the mountain.

I would take the last seat at the back of a tram and remain so still as not to attract scrutiny; I would stand in shadow at the edge of a crowd if a crowd could not be avoided; I would not court fad or fashion; I suppressed any feature or attribute that could be termed distinguishing; I lived in unremarkable lodgings without cohabitants in unfashionable districts; I took no part in any community or subculture; I never stuck my hand up, or spoke out loud. I shuffled away from the party and breathed a sigh of relief. I would be courteous and civil if contact was unavoidable, but if it could be avoided then it would be. Every time.

And I began to come to life in a way that few could imagine, because much can be seen and understood when the mind is not clamouring for attention and approval or acceptance from those around it.

Fade to grey. It became my motto, my release, my peace. And my mission led me to Dulle Griet Huis in Zurenborg, Antwerp.

The very idea of work is an incongruous proposition for the self-excluded who want no truck with team players or professional advancement. But funds for the basic needs of lodging and food were still required. A modicum of security was necessary because I did not want my new mental space troubled by gnawing financial anxiety. And what was required, I realised quickly, was an occupation as opposed to a career, and an occupation that could be performed alone. Such positions without colleagues and supervision do exist. In fact, there are plenty of openings available because few want to fill them.

Where I was going to commit myself, even the poorest imagination could envisage a profound isolation, a lack of opportunity for progress, inhuman working hours and a slide down a slippery slope that could remove me so far from society that I might never find my way back. "When do I start?" I said to the agency manager who had interviewed me for the job of nightwatchman. "Sounds perfect." My new job title was the fastest track in Antwerp to nowhere, and I stepped onto it with glee.

The only qualifications required were a clean criminal record, the ability to be punctual and the willingness to stay awake for twelve hours. My duties were described as "light" by the agency that employed such odd individuals as myself, by placing us in the old but well-maintained apartment buildings in Antwerp's chi-chi zones.

I would relieve a concierge at 6 p.m., and he would then relieve me at 6 a.m. the following day. I would work four nights in a row, and then take four nights off. While on duty,

I was required to monitor the monitors that monitored the nine-storey exterior of Dulle Griet Huis, patrol the internal communal areas every four hours, and assist the residents when required. The rest of the twelve-hour shift was my own.

The last duty on my job description did set off bells and buzzers, as I imagined perpetual interaction with the affluent residents and their guests, going on through the night as they entertained and swaggered and brayed as the privileged seem keen to do. But not so, according to Pieter, who ran the employment agency. There were only forty flats in Dulle Griet Huis and most of them were empty; all owned by overseas companies, or belonging to private residents who lived abroad and hardly ever used their properties. The building had a strictly enforced rule that forbade children under the age of fourteen, so there were no families, and the only permanent residents were very elderly and rarely left their apartments. At night, in Pieter's own words, "It's dead. You'll never see them. So I'm afraid you'll have to amuse yourself."

"Not a problem," I assured him, and could barely contain my elation at what sounded like a bespoke position for a gentleman of absence like myself. "Is it OK to read?" I asked. "I like to read."

Pieter nodded quickly, as if he was as pleased at filling the post as I was at taking it. "Of course. I have a lot of students working nights, so they can get some work done without distractions."

"And who can blame them? This sounds ideal, Pieter."

"It might well be. Terry, your predecessor, worked that building for thirty-five years."

"Thirty-five years?"

Pieter nodded.

I will confess, that detail alarmed me, as if by taking the job I was signing a guarantee that I would stay for an indefinite period of service, and it felt akin to making a final decision about something that would change my life, and there would be no going back.

Pieter closed our interview quickly by handing me a background-check form and reminded me, "Take a look at the monitors now and again."

I quelled my last vague doubts and left the agency whistling. And I could not remember being more excited about starting a job. In fact, I could not remember being excited about beginning any job before, because I never had been. I dreaded them all. But now, at last, I would finally be free of the manipulative, and so far beyond the hunting grounds of the pathological who delight in a colleague's downfall in conventional employment, that they would never pick up my scent again. I would have no colleagues at Dulle Griet Huis who could deride, contradict, undermine, or discredit me. And no one would ever take ownership of another one of my ideas, because this was no place for ideas, or competition, or ambition. It was no place for anyone but me. I didn't even have a supervisor. My employers were the residents, who left the business of paying me to an offsite management company. Finally, I could forget and be forgotten.

⁂

Dulle Griet Huis cast a long shadow through the back streets of Zurenborg and instilled a strange hush on the square below. Looking up at the ten floors of imperious red brick and white stone balcony from the street, the first time I saw the building I was tempted to lower my eyes, and even to bow my head in deference to the aura of exclusivity that the building projected. Run along, my good man. Nothing for you here.

The interior had been renovated in the 1920s and not since. It had the eerie grandeur of a luxury passenger liner. There were antique elevators panelled in brass and mahogany, stairwells and corridors papered with silk, and ornamental light fittings of patterned glass that created a brownish haze in the communal areas. I even imagined myself wearing a top hat and tails and roaming between decks on some giant floating ballroom. And the entire interior had that peculiar smell of traditional importance. Not quite ecclesiastic, but not far from it: a scent of old things preserved and of poor ventilation, of wood and metal polish.

On each floor a square landing contained the elevator entrance and two veneered front doors, with brass knockers, which led into penthouse apartments. Ornate marble radiator covers, reminiscent of late-nineteenth-century tombs for children, stood beneath the gigantic gilt-framed mirrors, fitted at eye level opposite the elevator doors. Between each floor, a staircase turned once.

Manuel, the day porter, was so tired each morning when he arrived to relieve me, and so eager to get out of the building at the end of each day shift, that contact between us was minimal. And we both liked it that way. No gossip, no intrigue, no Machiavellian tactics, just a nod and we were out of each other's space. We changed our little guard without fuss or spectacle.

The front desk was quaint and efficiently positioned opposite the elevator doors in the ground-floor reception. Below the top of the desk were six tiny monitors showing greenish exterior views of Dulle Griet Huis, as if the square outside the building were at the bottom of some silty ocean.

The remainder of the reception sparkled. It was all very quiet and civilised. Not a bad little environment in which to pass twelve hours while reading the great books under a good overhead light in a comfortable leather chair that could be reclined. The three nightly patrols could be done in fifteen minutes each, and who was watching to say that I even did them? Though it was always my intention to complete the patrols; it would be good to stretch my legs after sitting still for hours, and it was also one of my duties, and what little I was being paid to do, I would do. I am a recluse, but that is no screen for laziness.

And during my first four weeks, I often eased backwards in the recliner and congratulated myself on discovering a successful escape route from life and its responsibilities. I had pulled it off. I was actually free, at last, of them. Free to reverse my absolute ignorance of most subjects too, because I had created an opportunity to re-educate myself with what I thought significant. I began reading the historians, the philosophers, the popular scientists. I made lists of all the things that I wanted to know. I spent my days, between shifts, in bookshops and public libraries, making careful choices. I took a broadsheet newspaper in with me each night and subscribed to two literary journals as insurance. And if I liked, which I often did, I would just sit and stare into the rain. A much derided and underrated pastime, though one that must be meted out or the mind can turn against itself.

My new position was showing so much promise that I even began to prefer a night shift to the days that I spent in my dim lodgings. Though only until my second month, when Dulle Griet Huis decided to show its true self to me.

At first the alterations within the building were barely perceptible: minor alterations in temperature and lighting that I easily shrugged off. But these atmospheric changes soon intensified to command my full attention and discourage me from making the second patrol at 2 a.m., when the activity reached its peak.

I began to feel uncomfortable using the staircases. And it took time to define exactly what was making me feel peculiar. But I reduced it to an unaccountable manifestation of enclosure. After midnight, when a silence fell over the world outside, my chest would tighten from more than exertion, the air would feel unnaturally cold about me, and I would struggle to catch my breath, while all the time something pushed at my thoughts. Squeezed them into sudden frenzies of recollection and paranoia and fear that seemed unaccountable when I returned to my desk downstairs.

The sudden claustrophobic feeling was accompanied by shadows. In every case, at the edge of my sight, I would catch sudden flits of movement. Movement loaded with the expectation of an appearance behind it. Only no one ever came into view. The shadows seemed to come down the stairs after me, as if their owners were closely following my descent to the ground. Or at times, as I walked to a lower floor, a shadow, that was not my own, would rush around a corner on the stairwell ahead of me.

A few times I even called out, "Hello there?" But no one answered or showed themselves. When I stood still and applied a steady and careful scrutiny to my surroundings there was no longer any evidence of these moving shadows at all. But the lights on the walls, and the ceiling lights on each landing, would dim. It gave me the impression that either my sight was failing or the environment in which I stood was gradually disappearing into darkness.

Or did the lights dim? Was all this merely a result of my tired eyes? These were only vague and peripheral hallucinations and I was unaccustomed to night work. I was not, after all, a nocturnal animal and was only becoming one by design. Who could say how it would affect me? So I passed the phenomenon off as the early signs of sleep deprivation, as it always happened at around two in the morning when my need for rest was at its peak.

The noises were more alarming because of their unaccountability. They came after the beginning of the shadows. Joined them, in fact. And I knew after checking the duty roster that the sounds were originating from inside empty apartments.

It was as if a tremendous wind could gust through an open window on the outside of the building and narrow its way through the rooms and corridors of the penthouse apartments, before striking the front doors, from the inside, with terrific force. A blow that made the doors bang, then shake in their frames.

Perhaps, I'd thought, this might have been caused by strong air currents, or updrafts from the air-risers. I knew nothing of the physics of air circulation in these old buildings and there was, of course, no one to ask. But the sudden boom and tremble of a door beside me, at the precise moment of my passing across the landing, began to do strange things to my nerves, and to my imagination. I suffered the unsettling notion that someone had thrown their full weight against the inner surface of a front door, as a disturbed guard dog will hurl its body at a door at the sound of a postman. My increasing paranoia suggested that something inside the empty apartments was demanding my attention.

"Excuse me?" I would say to the closed doors. "It's me. Jack. The nightwatchman. Everything OK?" But there was never an answer and I realised there was no one to answer because, when I checked the desk ledger, the affected flats were clearly marked VACANT. But the noises occurred even if it was a windless and calm night. And on both sides of the building too.

Still, this was a dream job and by the middle of my third month I convinced myself that I could live with the malfunctioning lights, the strange inner winds and the odd mental side-effects of working nights. But no sooner had I renewed my vow to stay than my tolerance of Dulle Griet Huis was challenged again, though by a more tangible threat.

What began to introduce itself to me from the occupied apartments was more alarming than any tricks that the lights or air currents were playing on my senses. And I had never seen such a collection of the aged assembled under one roof. A community at the height of dysfunction and eccentricity too, and one that had kept itself completely hidden from me for the first ten weeks of my employment. I suspected that it was my stubborn presence within the building that had awoken them.

The first residents that I saw were the Al Farez Hussein sisters, of number twenty-two, who were both over one hundred years of age. Or so Manuel told me once the sisters began to make an occasional appearance during my shift. And I had no reason to disbelieve him.

Upon entering the building (though Manuel had no recollection of them leaving during his day shift), they would walk at an impossibly slow pace across reception, as if they were performing an odd Regency dance that had been slowed down to such a degree that they didn't appear to move anywhere but slowly up and down, from one foot to the other.

After offering a customary smile and wave, I would return my eyes to my book, only to then be fooled by the illusion of the sisters making quicker progress across reception. And their speedier movements, glimpsed in my peripheral vision, were aided by them dropping to all fours and scurrying.

Impossible and no doubt another strange quirk of sleep deprivation. Because the two figures, swaddled in robes, one in white and the other in black, were so shrunken and hunched that it would have been impossible for them to move with any rapidity, let alone ease.

They never spoke a word to me in any language, but their eyes were always fixed upon me as they made their way to the elevator doors. One small face, treacle-brown and wrinkled like a raisin, would turn to me, so that the two small glints of obsidian within the collapsed flesh of the eye sockets could study me. The other wore a mask. A golden beaked mask, attached to her face by a series of chains that disappeared inside her burka. I believe it was supposed to represent the face of a hawk.

But there were unappealing curiosities within that building far graver than the sisters.

The first thing I noticed about Mrs Goldstein from number thirty was her extraordinary hairstyle: a perfect bulb of silver wisps. But completely transparent from any angle. And through the illusory lustre of this spherical creation, her birdlike skull, bleached between the liver spots, would present itself horribly. Her nose was a papery blade, while the flesh of her avian features was as transparent as boiled chicken skin in the places where her make-up had rubbed away. At the age of ninety-eight her body had also wizened to such an extent that the top of her head only reached the bottom of my ribcage. But she moved quickly, in a spidery manner, from the front entrance to the lift doors in reception, aided by two black sticks that moved like quick chopsticks. I never saw her wear anything but high heels and the ancient black suits that her maid, Olive, hung from her skeletal body. She made me think of a marionette with a papier mâché devil face. She was no sight for the faint-hearted, certainly not at night.

Mrs Goldstein and Olive resided in a palatial three-bedroom penthouse. And Mrs Goldstein did not care for me at all, Olive told me. Whispered it to me with a smile as her round Filipino face passed my desk one evening. "She think you too young to be porter. Not married. No children. 'He up to no good,' she say." Olive soon became fond of reporting to me all of her mistress's disparaging remarks about me.

I began to see the pair once each night at eight. Olive would bring her mistress downstairs for a short walk around the square outside the front of the building. Or so they said. Again, as with the Hussein sisters, I was stricken with the uncomfortable notion that they had only come inside reception to stare at me.

According to the desk ledger, all of the other permanent residents were female too, but bedridden so I never saw them. Though I would sometimes hear their nurses talking in the stairwells.

But it was number eighteen on the eighth floor that housed not only the building's longest-standing resident but also its most sinister occupants: Mrs Van den Bergh and her full-time nurse, Helma.

༺༻

My first brush with Helma and Mrs Van den Bergh created such a powerful impression upon me that I suffered a nightmare the following day while I slept at home. A long, random and tortuous dream scenario in which I was wed to ancient Mrs Van den Bergh in a meadow, while my parents and two sisters were slaughtered with halal knives in a pen nearby to the accompanying sound of clapping children and excited young women; a crowd that I was unable to see clearly, but which circled the corral in a strange slow dance.

Inexplicable, or, after all that has happened since, perhaps not.

Mrs Van den Bergh was a long, skeletal individual who bore little resemblance to the living, and was confined to a wheelchair as ancient as its occupant. The first time we were introduced, I was reminded of the minor royal of an Egyptian dynasty who had been unwrapped and displayed in a case in the British Museum, in London, where I had once seen it as a teenager during a school trip. Mrs Van den Bergh's skin was so mottled with liverish discolourations she appeared brown-skinned in any light. Her gender was indistinguishable too, and the black capillaries visible beneath the translucent skin of her bald head and her hands reminded me of the baby birds that fall from nests and that I sometimes found as a child.

Always dressed in a leisure suit, faded like a candlewick bedspread in a Schipperskwartier squat and stained down the front, the heiress was contained in her chair by canvas ankle and wrist straps as if she were a danger to the public. And yet her eyes were as clear and blue as the arctic waters that lap around an iceberg.

Despite her shocking appearance, Mrs Van den Bergh had once been a great beauty, in possession of a brilliant mind. She had laid waste to three husbands and was worth over one hundred million euros from property ownership. She had also been a notorious high-society nymphomaniac. "A tart! Dreadful!" Helma told me, with one of her conspiratorial asides, on our very first meeting. Mrs Van den Bergh then apparently entered a kleptomaniac phase before finally becoming a pyromaniac. In short, a maniac. "She brought the dark man here."

Helma's comment about the "dark man" confused me — was this a racial slur? — and when I tried to question her about it, Helma only smiled enigmatically. Helma would never answer any direct questions; Helma liked to talk at me. I was only there to listen; it was the role that she had assigned to me. But she could tell that I was curious about her ward and she would occasionally elaborate when I frowned at some provocative remark or suggestive detail.

According to Helma, a trauma in the 1930s had transformed Mrs Van den Bergh into a deeply disturbed young woman. It was the birth of her "gaga child" that caused the breakdown; an incident she never recovered from. "Gaga child" was an infantile expression that I had never heard before, but Helma was referring to children born with both mental and physical disabilities that were unacceptable in high society, or as heirs. Children that were shipped off and contained within a private sanatorium in Carlsbad, along with several Habsburg princes of which the world still knows nothing, according to Helma.

It was an odd revelation to confide in the uniformed security guard, and as a result it was a story that I disbelieved.

Apparently, Mrs Van den Bergh's two equally glittering and talented sisters then spent the next seventy years containing their damaged and errant elder sister at Dulle Griet Huis. Having spent small fortunes both on hush money to extinguish scandals and for treatment at the best Swiss facilities, it seemed they had finally settled on an expensive method of security combined with sedation that Helma excelled at. Though Helma never presented the treatment to me in that way.

In this part of the world, I also quickly learned that it was not unusual for an employee, with a live-in position, to make themselves indispensable to an elderly resident who had hired them, or for whom they were recruited as guardians by trustees. It was grotesque in the tradition of the Gothic, and redolent of the age when hysterical wives were secured in locked attics. If people had seen how Mrs Van den Bergh had lived under the occupation of Helma, they would have taken their chances in a Romanian nursing home.

Helma was a garrulous, paranoid and profoundly manipulative woman in her fifties, but still almost half a century younger than her patient. In my third month, the frequency of Helma's visitations to my desk increased to at least once each night that I was on duty. Sometimes, to my chagrin, she would stay an hour and talk at me.

Helma also slipped into the habit of wheeling Mrs Van den Bergh down to reception and leaving her beside my desk, while she "popped out" to fetch knick-knacks from the store open late on Kleine Hondstraat. Why these items were not procured during the day remained a mystery, but I began to suspect that Helma wanted me and the heiress to become acquainted. Though how we would form a connection was doubly mystifying.

Mrs Van den Bergh's mind was long gone. During these short but uncomfortable periods when she sat beside my desk, there were odd moments of lucidity from her, in which an impeccable voice would rise from the chair and wish me "Good morning". But most of the time, there were only streams of gibberish about someone called "Florine", before Helma returned to the building and reclaimed her ward from beside my desk.

It wasn't until my fifteenth week as the nightwatchman of Dulle Griet Huis that I was reluctantly drawn across the threshold of their penthouse and plunged into the insane world that the apartment enclosed.

During my second patrol, at midnight, one Sunday evening, the front door to flat eighteen was open before I completed the final set of stairs to the landing of the eighth floor. And Helma was waiting for me, wearing a pair of Jimmy Choo shoes, silk fishnet tights, a pink Chanel suit and more make-up than a drag queen's eyelids could support. "Oh, Jack. I need to ask you a big favour. Would you watch Mrs Van den Bergh for an hour? I have to pop out. Something's come up and it's very important. An emergency."

Emergency, my ass, I had thought. "Afraid I can't. I have to watch the cameras downstairs."

Helma's eyes both brightened and hardened and they held me still. This was not a woman who would be defied. "It'll be all right for a little while. Now, she's been fed and had her medicine, so she won't be any trouble at all. This is for you." Helma's lacquered claws stuffed two twenty-euro notes into one of my hands, and then squashed my fingers shut over my paper-filled palm.

I tried again to refuse, then attempted to give the money back, but I found myself swiftly "shoo-shoo'd", as if Helma were talking to a house cat, and then manoeuvred inside the flat. Upon entrance, I wondered if I was now on some kind of illegal payroll and complicit in the imprisonment and extortion of Dulle Griet Huis's equivalent of Howard Hughes.

Then, from the living room, before I could get my bearings in the dingy hallway of the penthouse, a familiar voice began to shriek. "Florine! Florine! Florine! Let them out! Please God, let them out! Florine!" It was Mrs Van den Bergh, and no doubt disturbed from some drugged nap by the volume of Helma's voice in the hallway as she ushered me deeper into the dark and cluttered interior of the apartment. Helma had been guiding me towards the kitchen, but stopped to shout through an open door on the right-hand side of the hallway. "Stop it! You're just showing off because Jack's here! You only want attention!"

It didn't sound like showing off to me, and I cringed inside my skin at the awkwardness of the whole situation. I had come to Dulle Griet Huis to avoid interaction with other people, as well as the predictable conflicts that would result.

"Florine! Florine! Florine! She's hitting me!" from Mrs Van den Bergh.

"Enough! Enough of that!" Helma screamed.

From the hall, I peered into the living room while Helma and Mrs Van den Bergh screeched at each other like two vultures in a nest fighting over a vole.

Around the room, sealed boxes marked FRAGILE competed for space with sloping heaps of documents and printed receipts. Letters piled up in drifts against mimsy porcelain figures and silver utensils. It looked like someone was running a business, or a racket. Every other door in the hall was secured by a deadlock. I never found out why, though; after what Helma and Mrs Van den Bergh revealed to me, any further curiosity about their living arrangements was short-lived.

Among the debris, Mrs Van den Bergh and her chair

were walled into a corner by a large television set. Her hairless, shrieking head looked ghastly when lit up by the greens and whites of the flickering screen.

"Now, darling! Now, now, sugar plum! Shush, shush, darling!" Helma shouted at Mrs Van den Bergh to calm the outbursts.

My eyes then moved to the enormous oil painting hanging between the balcony doors and the dining table. It was a full-length portrait of Mrs Van den Bergh in her prime. An intolerably beautiful, regal face stared down, unimpressed with the detritus and disgrace inflicted upon her final years. Ice-blonde hair was pulled back beneath a diamond tiara; the forehead was porcelain-smooth; the nose perfect beneath the thin arches of haughty brows; full red lips smiled, faintly; white satin gloves shone to the elbows; a glittering necklace pulled my stare to the princess's neck; below the jewellery, a long white dress hugged her embraceable lines and curves. But it was the astonishing arctic eyes that really enchanted and also withered me. It hurt to look into those eyes, but it was impossible not to. They possessed an expression of piercing curiosity, and they revealed the fevered thoughts of the inspired, and the vulnerability of the passionate.

But the sense of impending doom in the painting, the tragedy of these qualities that were soon to flounder into madness, stopped my breath. It was as if the painter had been commissioned, just in time, to capture the last of the subject's allure, before she became something else entirely.

A lump formed in my throat. *She had been an angel*, I remember thinking. An angel. As close as anyone would ever come to being an angel.

Mrs Van den Bergh and Helma fell silent too, and they had turned to stare at me. From her chair, Mrs Van den Bergh smiled as she acknowledged her admirer.

And then the spell was broken. The moment had upstaged Helma. On her clattering pink heels, she muscled across the stage to obscure the great beauty once more. "She gets so disturbed! It's the new medication! The doctors are useless! Four hundred euros for a call-out and they're useless!" Now she was talking about money, and reasserting herself as a dreadful painted parody of her mistress's beauty that she might have long despised. Helma vulgarised the very space in which that picture hung.

I felt sick and longed to get back downstairs to my chair. Especially as Helma was now eyeing me with a combination of suspicion and bemusement, a look peculiar in my experience to those who were fond of underestimating me. Helma then brushed passed me on her way to the front door, and slid one hand across my chest, provocatively. "Goodbye, darling!" she called out to Mrs Van den Bergh.

"Florine! Florine! Florine!" the ancient creature cried out from the wheelchair.

"But... but what do I do?" I implored Helma, following her.

"Just watch her."

"But what if she needs something? The toilet?"

"You don't need to worry about that. She'll just watch her programmes."

"She could fall."

"How? She hasn't walked in twenty years. You took the money easily enough, and I'm not asking you for much. You can keep your eyes open, can't you? Vaarwel, my love!" She closed the front door on her way out and was gone.

Alone with Mrs Van den Bergh, I hid myself inside the kitchen, directly across the hall from the living room. Surrounded by soiled dishes and cutlery, old newspapers and plastic carrier bags that were filled with yellowing catalogues and rubbish, I decided to wait out my sentence. If there were any sounds of distress, I could look in on Mrs Van den Bergh. Otherwise I would stay outside her line of sight, because the moment she caught a glimpse of me – and she was always looking for me from her chair – she would begin that dreadful shrieking for Florine.

In the dim brownish pall of the apartment, I then suffered the unhealthiest thoughts about age and ageing. These black impressions and notions extended to my own life and to all of humanity. I felt that despair and immobility were the only natural outcomes of the miserable struggle that is life. At one point I even buried my face in my hands. I desperately wanted to weep, but somehow held that back, though I don't think it did me any good.

In the distance I could hear the chatter of the television, a whooshing sound of what could have been fireworks, and the clang of bells. It was some appalling quiz show that she had been sitting before. A programme that produced whitish flashes that briefly illumined the living room.

It seemed my dream-life of seclusion and contemplation was coming to an end. Even here, at night, while the world slept, there were still parts of it, these obscure quarters, that would give me no peace. Places that would seek me out and torment me in the same insidious manner that caused my former misery working for a corporation, where I was overrun by the will-to-power of baboons with silver tongues.

Was it so much to ask for? To be just left alone?

I thought the world mad. Desperate and cruel and stupid, endlessly repeating the same mistakes with terrible consequences. The world's refusal to leave me out of its activities made me consider its destruction. Bring on the wave. Please, the asteroid. Anything. Just take it away. And then Mrs Van den Bergh stood up. And she ran from the living room on those long brownish bones that served her for legs.

She appeared at the corner of my sight, impossibly tall and thin with that little dry skull grinning above her narrow shoulders. I turned, at once shocked out of my morbid stupor. And I watched her flee, bandy-legged, with both chicken-bone arms thrown upwards at the ceiling.

Her hands had looked strangely masculine, atop wrists as thin as woodwind instruments. Her long feet had slapped down the hallway toward the front door.

"No," I said. Or I whispered it. Perhaps it was just a thought that never made it out of my mind. But I moved into the hallway, unsteadily, where the amber lights were caged within such dirty glass that they gave me the impression that I was trapped inside an old photograph. But I could still make out the figure of Mrs Van den Bergh scrabbling at the latch of the door, and a keening sound issued from her mottled head. The noise transformed into a growl, before it broke into a bellow. "Florine! Florine! Dear God, let them out! Florine! I can hear them!"

I approached her, but I made it no further than the threadbare mat in the hall before she had the front door open and was out. Outside. Suddenly. On the landing, under brighter lights, naked, and racing across the landing at speed and on limbs so spindly the sight of them striding like that made me want to crouch in a dark corner and never move again. And as she skittered at the top of the stairs before making her rickety descent, my eyes locked on to something even more dreadful. Folded flat against her prominent scapulae were two brown flaps. Like wings, but hairless, and shrivelled in the manner of dried fish.

What could I do but follow? Below me in the building, I heard Mrs Van den Bergh shouting as she fled from floor to floor, "Florine! I can hear them! Florine! Florine!"

Though whether she was crying out with elation or with grief, it was impossible for me to decide.

I leaped three stairs at a time. My tie flapped about my face. My hand clutched at the brass railings as I pursued the sounds of her flight.

Somewhere below, a door opened quickly. Followed by another, and another.

The other residents must have been disturbed. What would they think, coming to their doors in nightwear, only to see the emaciated form of Mrs Van den Bergh racing past, shrieking for Florine? Had she not looked such a fright, I might have been tempted to add my own hysterical laughter to the commotion. The entire episode was as absurd as it was disturbing. And my reason tried desperately to assert itself, telling me that all of this was not possible: the woman was over a hundred years of age and had not walked in twenty, allegedly. But then maybe Helma was behind this. Helma must have known this would happen. She had deliberately left her ward unsecured in that chair and I had been set up. And now it was my task to catch an infirm and half-crazed resident. Oh, how they would all laugh: Mrs Goldstein, those mute Husseins, little Manuel and half-smiling Olive. I would be reported. I would be fired.

But so be it; I wasn't being paid enough for this. Any of it. It was not in my job description either to enter flat seventeen, flat fifteen, or flat fourteen. I was not to enter any of the apartments unaccompanied by the owners. But the doors to these apartments were now gaping. Wide open.

I saw the open doorways as soon as I staggered off the stairs on the relevant floors. So why were they open, as if they had so recently released occupants into the communal areas? Had I been misinformed? Was the information in the desk ledger not up to date? I then thought of the desperate winds and the bangs from inside these dark and empty spaces, and for a few seconds I wondered if this was now my last chance to flee the building and to never return.

I called out for Mrs Van den Bergh, my voice disappearing into the darkness of every open flat I passed. But I received no answer.

Flat twelve on the fifth floor, where I came to a stop, was also supposed to be a sealed and empty property. The other flats with open doors were unlit and they issued an air of vacancy, but not flat twelve. That one was different.

Hovering on the threshold, biting my bottom lip until it bled, my chest rising and falling too quickly, I could hear them inside. Them? Mrs Van den Bergh perhaps. And others. I heard a muffled voice, or voices, over the sound of weeping, coming out of the dark hallway, and from somewhere deep inside the apartment. Yes, there was a thin light seeping under a door at the end of the hallway. The master bedroom, if this floor plan followed the graphic in the desk ledger of how these apartments were arranged on this side of the building. But why then were the remainder of the lights out in the apartment?

I dithered. I vacillated. I did not want to see, or to know, where I was being led. It was as if my involvement in this madness had somehow been assumed. But out of some deluded sense of duty I went down to that bruised orange light, faintly washing from under the door at the far end of the hall. And as I went down, I turned on the ancient lights in the hallway by flicking down the heavy porcelain switches in fixtures the size of butter dishes. It was like walking through a museum, with its telephone table, coat-rack made from antlers, and the dusty oil paintings of peasants and beggars engaged in what appeared to be odd and unpleasant gatherings. I glanced into the kitchen and saw enamelled appliances and yellow lino that could not have been changed since the Second World War, and wooden cupboards painted buttercup yellow with little glass doors that protected thin china sets. The dining room was mostly draped in white sheets tarnished with dust, but the chandelier, above a table fit for a boardroom, glittered in what little light seeped inside from the hallway. This place had not been lived in for decades; I knew that at once. Though part of it was occupied that night.

I listened outside the far door. Heard the low murmur of voices again, and something else. Something rhythmic. Like clapping. Gently clapping hands. There were several people inside the room. People who were also cooing in the way that adults make noises around infants. I cleared my throat. I knocked.

No one answered. Was I trespassing? About to intrude on some strange but private gathering that had nothing to do with my search for Mrs Van den Bergh? I feared I was, and experienced far more anxiety than curiosity about what was on the other side of the door.

I turned around and began to creep back down the hallway in a way that made my every footstep resemble the absurd mime of a man trying to withdraw quietly.

"Florine! Florine! Florine!"

After that, there was no mistaking the presence of Mrs Van den Bergh within that room of dirty light and soft clapping and the incongruous cooing. And her utterances suggested that she was in a state of excitement not yet matched in my experience of her. I was instantly tempted to believe that Florine herself had made an appearance within that room.

"Enough of this," I said. It could not go on. I had to remove the resident from this place and take her back to her chair and strap her in. Without another thought, I acted. I opened the door.

※

Round and round they went in the large bedroom. In the slow up and down dance, one foot after the other, the residents staggered in their ungainly circle.

I did not know where to look at first, and saw everything in a jittering panorama because my eyes would not allow themselves to settle for long on any single detail. Not on the diminutive Hussein sisters, naked as cadavers and shrivelled as figs; or the worm-white Mrs Goldstein prancing with those sticks, her hair extending wildly from her scalp as if she had been hit by a gale, and her empty paps with black nipples flapping; or the long and dry Mrs Van den Bergh, with her eyes rolled back white, and the gurgling from her stringy throat and the big hands thrown up to the ceiling. I didn't look long at the others either, whom I had never seen before, but immediately understood them to be the bedridden residents who had somehow made it down here for this occasion. Some thing with skin like a plucked bird went up and down, up and down, from heel to toe, heel to toe, and shook its wisps of hair about in delirium. Others tottered like undraped wooden puppets with their strings cut, or the fossils of birds suddenly reanimated out of stone, and they must have been even older than the figures that I recognised. But all did their very best to hop and teeter in that circle. And all of them carried the shrunken flaps behind their shoulders with the skin that looked like the salted cod, rolled into sheets, that I had once seen in Norway. Flightless birds, I thought. Not extinct, but nearly.

And it was an elegant drinks trolley that the bony procession was moving about in this grotesque whirlpool of brittle limbs and gargles and skin like the parchment of dusty scrolls. And upon the top tier of the old and highly polished silver trolley was arranged a set of pickling jars, made from thick glass, with heavy wooden plugs rammed into the necks to keep the occupants safe from exposure to the air. The small figures inside the jars were adrift in a thick but semi-transparent fluid. Their limbs were as pale and delicate as cartilage, but their heads were enlarged and bulbous, thin as eggshell, with tiny faces at rest. On the back of one small body I saw appendages no bigger than thumbs, or unformed wings.

A second sedentary circle had formed around the skipping residents. It was the nurses and carers, and they were responsible for the clapping and the cooing sounds. They wore little crowns of golden paper on their heads and had all dressed in their finest clothes for the occasion. And they encouraged their wards to hop and stagger like that, round and round and round.

No one even looked at me, agape in that doorway. Though I thought at one point that Mrs Goldstein hissed at me from the side of her mouth, as she skittered past.

The first one to break ranks was Helma. Shaking with excitement, she ran to the head of the room, and then padded her hands along the wall until she reached the middle. It was not a wall, but a wooden screen. I had seen the same arrangement in a studio flat, and also in a hotel; an attempt to give one room the potential of becoming two, for privacy. Something I thought odd on every occasion, including this one.

I was sure, with every molecule in my being, that I did not want to see what was on the other side of the screen. But before I could wrench myself away, Helma had the screen opening along its ancient brass runners, the wooden panels folding flat like a concertina.

In my strengthless delirium of disgust and fear and shock, I then stared across the bobbing of the stained skulls and the thin arms of the prancing circle, and I caught a glimpse of the father of this extended family. Bedridden, mercifully, but still keen enough to raise his great horned head from the enormous bed, in order to smile on what must have been his wives, their staff and the bottled offspring who would bear him no heirs.

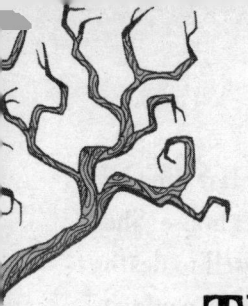

THE VETERAN

V. CASTRO

Carlos slumped against a cement tube that also served as his bed and stared at the frayed rope hanging from a tree branch. The late afternoon light filtered through the leaves and cast ghoulish shadows on a pile of empty bottles and beer cans at the base of the tree. He knew it was over because he lacked the energy to wander far enough to find more booze. He loved and resented those bottles and cans. In life, in a lot of folks' lives, you could count your wins on one, maybe two hands. Every sip, every drink a guaranteed win. Alcohol didn't criticize or reject. A finished drink was like a pat on the back, or a hug. And didn't that feel good, acceptance? Tall boys didn't have eyes to show their disappointment. It broke his heart when his sister Christina rushed to the hospital for the third time in a month because he drank too much outside the H-E-B and passed out with the paper bag still in hand. Someone called an ambulance and there he was in the hospital. That was the last time he saw her, because after, she kicked him out of her house. She couldn't take the pain of seeing him drink himself to death or all her forks get tossed in the trash because he couldn't see straight when throwing away his takeaway cartons. She couldn't cut off his money. As a veteran he received a check every month in his credit union bank account. He got even more after he was beaten up sleeping rough in a park one night. A bunch of rowdy kids cracked his jaw and a few ribs. To think the only reason he joined the military was to escape doing what his grandparents did, farm work. Brown folks, at least those without money, had few options for employment. It felt like those options could be counted on one hand, just like their wins. Fight and maybe die for a country that wants your life but despises your presence. Feed a population that wants your cheap labor but treats you like you don't exist at all.

Some might say Carlos was lucky. He survived this long on his own because of his time in the military and the years after he'd spent homeless (when not staying with Christina). Sometimes he picked up day-labor work with guys who mostly only spoke Spanish, who were generous with beer after a long day and the food they brought from home. He didn't need much and asked for less. If he died, he didn't care. That's why he'd made the noose. Everyone who might miss him was dead. Not even the beer would miss him. He sure as hell wouldn't miss the thirst for it, the thing that took everything away before the creatures did. His desire for it above love, family, health, always there, like a hungry chupacabra salivating in the dark.

He groaned as he rose to his feet. Next to him, his salvaged candy and pile of books. His favorite were the dark writers. The stories of hauntings, ghosts, and devils. Those beaten-up paperbacks, and the booze, had seen him this far, constant companions. It was the books that got him teased in school before he dropped out and after, during basic.

It was time to say goodbye to his two loves, his only loves.

As he approached the overturned bucket to stand on, there was a rustle in the bushes. Carlos turned. Probably a deer or stray dog. Didn't matter. He turned back. The sound came again. This time he jumped. It had been months since he'd seen another person.

And now he faced a brown child carrying thin pieces of wood in one hand.

"Help, señor?"

Carlos stared at the boy. His dark eyes were large and bright even if his face was dirty. His little shoes were duct-taped together. The arms of his shirt stopped just above the wrists, yet his jeans were too baggy.

"Do *you* need help? I don't need help," said Carlos.

The boy stared at him for a moment then ran off again. Carlos looked at the noose. The heat of shame rose from his neck to his cheeks. What if that tiny boy had found his body? Hadn't he seen enough horror in his young life? Moments later Carlos could hear footfalls, rustling. He quickly untied the rope from the branch.

"Hello there."

He turned with rope in hand. It was a woman, in her late sixties maybe, white hair pulled back with a braid that trailed to the middle of her back. She wore military fatigue pants and cowboy boots with a plain blue sweatshirt. Clothes that were probably not her own by the way they fit, except maybe the boots. You can tell when a pair of boots are a perfect fit.

"Hi." He didn't know what else to say. He let the rope slip from his hand to the ground, still feeling ashamed.

The woman gave him a pleasant smile. The little boy held her hand, stared at the books and candy where Carlos had been sitting before.

Carlos' eyes followed his gaze. "You want them?"

The boy nodded. Carlos reached down and picked up the bag of sweets that had long expired but tasted fine. God bless processed food.

"Here. Take them. But don't eat them all at once. You'll end up looking like me." He grinned, showing two missing upper teeth.

The little boy giggled and took the bag. "Thank you." He began eating the treats, smacking his lips with joy. For the first time in a long time, Carlos felt good about himself.

"I didn't think I would see anyone. It's been so long. You headed anywhere particular?"

The old woman gave him a warm smile. "Funny you should ask that. We are. How about you?"

"Nah, just camped here. I like sleeping under the stars. Feels more natural to me. Where would I even go?"

Her face turned serious. "You don't know about the salt water?"

"No, but..." he glanced back at the cans and bottles. Until recently he blacked out most of the time, avoiding survivors. That's why he wanted to end his life. A permanent blackout.

She picked up the conversation, so he didn't have to.

"We are headed to Corpus Christi."

"Salt water?" His curiosity was piqued.

She paused before answering. Her gaze didn't gravitate towards the bottle, his bed or the rope. She looked him in the eyes, studied his face. The only sound was the crunch of the candy the little boy ate. "Would you like to join us for supper? You look like you need a hot meal. It won't be long until the sun goes down."

"I..." He glanced at his few belongings.

"We are not that far. We stopped at the gas station through those trees."

Carlos knew there wasn't any booze there. He checked weeks ago. Maybe longer. Time ceased to exist except for night and day. Probably a good thing it was empty. The withdrawal symptoms were subsiding as his desire to no longer live grew stronger.

"A hot meal sounds good."

He grabbed his backpack, shoved his few clothes and the books inside. There wasn't anything else of value.

The little boy took his hand, led the way to the gas station.

※

When they arrived a small hole with all the makings for a fire had already been prepared. The boy scampered off, dropping his thin pieces of wood next to the pit then running into the station. He brought out a plastic bag filled with cans and pots.

"Should I make the fire for you?" Carlos asked.

"That would be wonderful. Thank you… by the way I am Itzel, and he is Raul."

"Carlos." He kneeled next to the pit and began to light the kindling. Itzel and the boy prepared the canned food they would warm over the fire.

They ate in silence, all of them hungry. He hadn't shared a meal with anyone in a long time, even before the plague hit. His heart ached as much as his malnourished belly. He wondered if he should make conversation. What did people talk about when there was nothing to talk about? No TV shows, politics, sports. He continued to eat, absorbing the sensation of feeling full until there was nothing left. The boy also finished and lay next to Itzel. The food made him drowsy.

"Who were you? What was your life like before this?" Carlos asked.

Itzel touched Raul's head. "No one anyone noticed except those in my neighborhood... But I was a curandera and full-time grandmother. Mostly egg limpias and platicas. My faith and my belief kept me going after seeing my children and grandchildren die."

"I see. One of those... I don't believe in folk magic."

"Magic? Not magic. Touching the energy that always surrounds us. It's greater than magic. Curanderas have guided women during birth, blessed the dead, helped injured soldiers during wars. It is physical as well as spiritual healing."

"And the boy?"

"He doesn't say much. His English isn't fluent. We met on the road."

"Good of you to take care of him."

"It was the right and only thing to do. Surviving children must be protected at all costs. We must give them the tools to carry on with what we learned from our victories and mistakes. And you?"

"I was a marine. Spent a lot of time traveling. Had to go to war. But all I ever wanted to do was read. Listen to music. Was never much of a soldier. Didn't like the idea of picking strawberries either. But what does anyone know at seventeen? I did what I could."

Itzel watched Carlos fidget with the handle of his backpack, his eyes darting toward the shop.

"Hand me your water."

"Why?"

Carlos passed her his water bottle with the cap off. Her hands shifted around the inside of her bag and emerged with her thumb and index finger pinching something. Itzel released her fingers, rubbing them together to get all of whatever was on them off into the bottle. He could see her lips moving as she mumbled in Spanish and grabbed the bottle, swirling it around. With her eyes closed she continued to whisper. The fire seemed to burn brighter as the darkness of night cloaked the sky. She inhaled, exhaled, then handed the bottle back while opening her eyes.

"It is time to wake up, Carlos."

He sniffed the bottle, took a large gulp. There were bits in the water that tasted like whatever it was had been stored in a damp closet or basement. But he drank it all.

"Funny time to wake up."

"I'm sorry life left you so disappointed. You lost your way. Many have. You are not alone. Why don't you stay with us?"

"Are you sure? How do you know I'm not a bad guy. Both of you are…"

"I know. I believe we met for a reason. In this desolate journey, what are the odds?"

Carlos looked at the boy again. He didn't like the idea

of the pair being out here alone, even inside the gas station. The empty bottles and cans didn't need him. "I will stay. Thank you."

That night he was up every few hours to urinate. The strange water seemed to be flushing him out. As he stood at the edge of the property barely illuminated by a half-moon, he thought he saw something move in the shadows. At the base of the tree, a white shape appeared and disappeared. A plastic bag, blown by the wind? Garbage was everywhere as the weather shifted and scattered the remnants of society. But if that stuff made him pee nonstop maybe it also messed with his vision. He walked back into the gas station to get a few more hours of rest. He stared out the glass door as he waited to fall asleep to see if anything, or anyone else passed. He didn't like the feeling he had. He hadn't seen one of the creatures in a long time, or another human with one attached to it.

But that didn't mean they didn't still exist.

Her mind was a kaleidoscope of fractured thoughts and visions. Horrid smoky masks of various demons mouthed words to her, but she couldn't hear what they said. It began when the slimy grayish head attached to the base of her skull. There were human thoughts, then theirs. Sometimes they blurred and created a reality she couldn't understand. But what she did know was that sacrificing that child might calm them down. Let them know she was on their side. One of them.

What better an offering than a child?

She first saw the boy and old woman two days before, as they passed the cemetery she'd been sleeping in. From behind the gravestones, she watched them, slinking across the dirt as they sang a song in Spanish. Neither noticed her. A whisper in her ear said, *follow*.

She began sleeping in cemeteries since living with this thing feeding off her body. It made her feel less alone. She knew she was part of this reality yet felt detached from it. The stronger the visions, the more she was convinced the unseen world was colliding with this one. A few times she dug up the graves of small children. She used their little bones to create a circular barrier between herself and the dark, then slept inside of it. Their tiny skulls were a reminder of the children she lost. They had done nothing wrong in this life, but she had. Her husband of fifteen years thought all four were his when in fact they were not. Every day she had woken up living a lie, thinking it was the day he would find out. The shame of not being perfect, of others knowing the truth, ate at her the way she starved herself regularly. Slowly she grew to resent the children. It was their fault. She hated them. If she could have rid herself of them and not get caught, she would have. And then they died, and she lived. She got her wish in the end. She had to live with her hate and deceit, both in the physical wasteland of the world, and in her own mind. She also had to answer for it. She was alone with no adoration. The worst fate she could imagine, because she was her only audience. Knowing there was a place with others gave her the motivation she needed to keep going and do whatever it took to get there.

One of the bones she dug up was the femur of a four-year-old child. She sharpened one end and attached it to the old belt she wore over her favorite white summer dress. The belt belonged to her husband. He would have done anything for her. He begged her not to leave him. He begged her for sex. All she could give him in return were children, not his own. Once she picked up the phone in the other room while he spoke to his mother.

"Why do you stay with her? She isn't nice to you!"

He paused. "Who else would want me now at this age, with four kids and no money because it all goes to child support?"

There was another pause before his mother spoke again. "Sometimes I think those kids..."

"Don't, Mom. Just don't."

His mother tutted.

"One day she will have to answer for it all."

She had put down the phone and sat on the bed looking at the crystal bowl holding a few pieces of jewelry he had given her as gifts over the years. She kept some of it there to make him think she put it on from time to time. But the reality was, she didn't care about anyone or anything.

She could smell the fire at the gas station. Her plan was to snatch the boy after dark. The old woman was weak and would be easy to kill. To her surprise, however, they picked up a man. As if he was sent at the exact moment to derail her victory or test her worthiness for a new life.

***

Carlos woke inside the gas station feeling great after whatever Itzel put into his water. He felt free. It calmed a part of his brain, closed that gaping wound inside that he'd tried to fill with alcohol. Itzel and Raul were still asleep. The boy clutched the bag of candy in his small hand. The sight made Carlos' belly ache like the warm food had. He looked at them, wondering what would happen now. Should he slip out, or wait? Boulder was still a good distance away by foot. Maybe he could find a car that worked, could get enough gas for the journey, save them time. Before he made a move, Raul opened his eyes. The boy smiled at Carlos.

"Hey, buddy."

Itzel woke on hearing Carlos' voice. She lifted herself up with a groan. He could see the pain in her face from sleeping on the hard floor. It reminded him of the stories of his grandparents sleeping on the side of the road when they traveled from farm to farm. How could he forget the tales of how hard the desert floor felt when they came to this country? The midday thirst none of them forgot. He wondered if that was where he inherited his thirst from. Stored trauma, lurking in his DNA. The chupacabra.

"You like coffee, Carlos?"

The idea of coffee, hot coffee, made him hungry. It was like his mind and body were coming back to life.

"I do."

"Good. Let's get that fire going again. I want to make good time on the road today."

"I wanted to talk to you about that."

Itzel held on to a chair as she rose to her feet. "I won't make you feel bad for not coming with us, but I would very much like it if you did."

Raul jumped to his feet and ran through the station looking for food and leftover odds and ends to take with them.

"I will go with you as far as Corpus. No promises after that."

"Fair enough."

Carlos rose to his feet. "I'll get that fire started. Coffee sounds real good this morning."

⁂

After coffee and a light breakfast of tinned salmon on crackers, the three set off toward Boulder. Itzel took Carlos' bottle and gave it another pinch of whatever was in her bag. His brain calmed and focused. Walking with the pair gave him a renewed sense of purpose to see these two make it to their destination safely. The pace was slow with quite a few breaks. Sometimes he carried Raul on his shoulders. It had been a while since he had taken a clear-headed journey like this. His military training seemed to snap back into his mind, sharper than ever. He observed everything. While he waited for Itzel and Raul to return from a bathroom break, he looked toward the abandoned buildings of a small town. The only sounds were birds and the wind. He had a sense of being watched. The unease felt like storm clouds gathering in the distance. He took a swig of his musty water. There were too many empty places to hide. Less so on the open road. This would be the last time they traveled on the smaller roads and would hereafter stick to the highway straight into Boulder. It was only convenient for breaks for Raul and Itzel and looking for supplies.

When Itzel and Raul returned, they headed down the main road through the town. Carlos turned to Itzel.

"I think we are being watched. Just a feeling… but also when we camped last night, I thought I saw something white in the distance. Probably a plastic bag or trash blown around."

"I hope it wasn't La Llorona," teased Itzel.

He chuckled. "God, my grandmother used to tell me about her at dinner. She broke her back in the fields all day then would take care of us kids at night. She was incredible."

He glanced back to see if there was any more unusual movement as they walked. Nothing.

"But serious. What is it you're putting into my water? Could that cause me to be seeing things, feeling strange?"

"No. It's not enough. You are simply open to the world around you now, with a tiny dose of plant medicine. The medicine of our ancestors. To help you ease yourself away from the other stuff that blocked the world out."

"I suppose. I'm dreaming too. The first night it was just shadows, garbled voices. Some I knew. My dad. A buddy of mine who died of AIDS. They comforted me. Told me to keep going and listen."

"Good. When we pass on, we are given the larger picture. The panorama we can't understand in this form. That is why ancestral veneration can be useful. Ever think you wish you knew then, what you know now? They do that for us. Blood knowledge. And I *do* feel a presence. We will have to wait and see. Just like I knew I had to wait and see when I prayed for a guardian. Then we met you."

"I don't even know what a 'presence' is. And I am no guardian."

"Well, look at us. We are wearing these clothes that are odd fitting. They hang this way and that way, not a perfect fit for our bodies, what's inside the clothing. It's the same for us, and other entities. Our souls reside in suits of flesh that don't always match. We are conscious of them to our detriment. Other dark entities don't care. They just want a vehicle for their destruction. Either by influence or habitation."

Carlos watched Raul skip ahead. He was a good kid.

He wondered what type of father he would have made if he ever let anyone close enough to have a family.

They walked until late afternoon so by sunset they could have another camp prepared. Raul fell asleep straight after eating. The pace and distance of their travels exhausted him. It was the same for Itzel. Carlos pulled out a paperback he had read multiple times about a haunted hotel in the mountains. He loved it. The boy in the story made him think of Raul.

Carlos read until the fire was low and he could feel himself finally drifting to sleep. The weather was pleasant enough to have only a sleeping bag without feeling too cold. Soon he was in a deep sleep floating toward dreams. He soared above the mountains with the view from the eyes of an eagle. Little Raul played below. Then fell on his hands and knees. Carlos swooped down to help him. Raul looked to the sky but he had no eyes. Blood poured from his mouth. Carlos' throat let out a bird-of-prey cry. *Don't abandon your post, soldier,* said a voice that was his dad's. Another eagle joined him in the sky.

Carlos snapped his eyes open.

On the other side of the fire, he could see the bottom of a dirty white dress. A woman stood next to Itzel, ready to strike with a sharpened bone. Carlos' hand went to the inside of his backpack beside him. He jumped to his feet.

"Get away from them!"

The woman's head whipped towards him as Itzel and

Raul woke. Itzel grabbed Raul and moved away from the woman, whose attention was now on Carlos.

"Give me the boy. He will be my offering. Give him to me now!"

The woman shrieked. Four tentacles capped with sharp bony barbs emerged from the base of her skull. Her eyes were as black as the hem of her once white dress.

"Innocence will be preserved, La Llorona! You can't have him!" cried Itzel, holding the trembling boy tight.

"They want a sacrifice!"

Carlos walked towards Itzel and Raul. "Then it will be you."

Her eyes narrowed. Red lipstick-smeared lips curled to a sinister smile. "How long has it been since you had a woman? You can't be getting anything from that old bruja. Or you like the boy…"

Her vile insinuation made Carlos shake with rage. "I am not afraid to kill you. I have killed before. Too many times to count. And I am fucking good at it."

That was the first time he'd said that out loud. It was almost a relief. He raised the gun he'd pulled out of his backpack and hid in the back of his jeans before confronting her.

The weapon aimed at her chest.

"You won't dare. You're too weak. Fucking drunk."

With expert aim he shot her in the right kneecap, then the shoulder. The woman shrieked in an inhuman voice, louder than before, tumbling to the ground as exposed bone could be seen through the blood. Her head jerked from side to side, seeming to follow something only she could see and hear.

The tentacles began to stab her with a violent rage.

"No! I haven't failed. Go away! Stop!" Her arms thrashed, swatting at the air.

In the dirt she tore at her eyes. Jagged nails caked in mud clawed one out. She screamed in agony as blood oozed from the now empty socket, staining her filthy dress.

"Go away! I don't want to see you!"

Raul, crying, had his head buried in Itzel's neck.

"Let's go. She will destroy herself. Whatever she is fighting will be enough."

They turned away from the miserable woman clawing at herself and cursing the darkness. Carlos couldn't be sure, didn't want it to be real, but the blackness surrounding her appeared thick, solid. Like a bramble of obsidian thorns. It made his blood run cold.

The longer they walked in the night, the less they could hear her. Carlos carried Raul who trembled and cried. He had never spent so much time with a kid. It made him think of his dad, how he did his best beginning his life as a migrant worker.

"Will you join us? I think you were meant to find us, protect us. Start a new life. One you want, and not what anyone, certainly not a dead society, tells you to be."

"You really think we can rebuild? The world is so broken. So many gone. Those things are still out there. They want kids."

"I have to hope."

Itzel's sun-weathered brown skin looked youthful in the light. She reminded Carlos of his grandmother. For the first time he believed in the concept of the soul. Whatever was inside of Itzel, it was bright, glorious as full sunlight on the ocean. Blinding like truth. Goodness. Something that could not be lost. That is what the world needed. A brightness that could not be stifled or snuffed out. It would meet the darkness head on, one surviving soul at a time.

Dedicated to Carlos David Castro 3.18.62–5.21.23
Rest in power, beloved soldier.
May you have a never-ending pile of books on the other side.

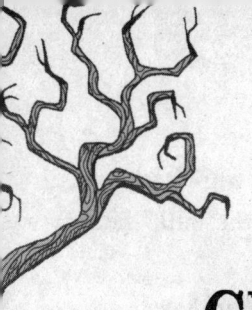

CHALK BONES

SARAH DEACON

There is a single old tree, on a mound, on a hill, on the land my grandad farms. I know not to play there.

The story goes that the mound is a fairy palace, that fairies are not pretty with wings and bells but sharp and jealous, and that a long time ago they lured a boy into their palace and he was never seen again.

The story goes that there are tunnels with hidden entrances to forgotten places and that once a girl crawled in, got lost, and was never seen again.

The story goes that alien craft land here, that strange lights are seen in the skies, strange patterns in the fields, and that not so long ago another boy went to watch for them and was never seen again.

Grandad says it's all nonsense, but he does remember a child going missing up there, back when he was a young man.

"Is that why I'm not allowed there on my own?" I ask.

"You're not allowed up there because of the bull," he says.

"I can't imagine losing a child like that," Mum says.

She gives my back a brisk rub, like she's making sure I'm still solid. I twist out of the way. "I'm not a child," I say, "I'm a teenager." The cards from my thirteenth birthday are still on the shelf on the dresser.

Later, when I'm in bed, I remember Grandad telling me about the stories of fairies, tunnels, and aliens and I drift away thinking of the missing children, maybe a crowd of them up on the hill, watching us sleep.

※

The hill rises up out of nowhere, an island of chalk and grass in a sea of wheat turning green to gold. In the summer it stills with the murmur of insects and high-above skylark song; in winter it catches the frost before everywhere else, cocooned in white, the old tree a black silhouette of tangled branches. On the rare occasions Grandad or Mum take me up there it's like climbing out of the ordinary and into somewhere different, somewhere separate. It's on the boundary between counties, on the edge of the village, and people give directions by it. When we're driving home after a trip away it's the point where Mum always says, *home again*. You can see it from almost every room in Grandad's house, but from my place, on the other side of the village where half the houses are now empty, forcibly sold, boarded up windows pasted with *Stop the Bypass* signs, I can only see the hill from my bedroom window if I sit on the sill and press my cheek hard against the cold glass. But I know it's there.

The mound on top is called a barrow, where Bronze Age people buried their dead. We did a big project on the history of the village in my last year at primary school; I asked Grandad who he thought was buried there and he told me he didn't remember that far back. He thought he was being funny. But then he said our family name is on the oldest stones in the churchyard. I took that back to my teacher and she told me it's possible for archaeologists to DNA test old bones. She said they analyse the chemical and mineral make-up of a skeleton to find out where that person grew up, because the chemicals and minerals of the land are built into our bones through the food we eat and the water we drink; from every blackberry I've picked and every potato I've had from the garden. It made me feel the chalk under the fields and footpaths differently when I walked on it after that, knowing it had built me; grown me; it made me feel like there was no gap between me and it, that when I raised a foot to step, the chalk rose with me.

Strangers go up the hill sometimes; no one from the village. They go for the old festivals, Halloween or solstice, and with my cheek against the window on those nights I can sometimes make out the fireflies of their lights, high up in the black. Grandad mutters about them, but as long as they keep to the field edges he lets them be. He goes up the day after to check the fences, clear up any rubbish.

This year, the day after the summer solstice, he takes me with him.

He parks his truck at the road and we walk down the old greenway, two cows wide when they go shoulder to shoulder, earth banks knotted with roots of hawthorn and ash that lean over, heavy with chattering sparrows and great tits, wrens talking over our heads, robins calling their *tick-tick* alarm at the sight of people here. Last night's footprints lie where the ground is still soft from recent rain. The greenway turns into a narrow-fenced track between flats of wheat, where a few years back a great pattern was swirled into the crop, spiralled and circular, laying every plant uniformly flat in curving sweeps of gold. Grandad was cross at the loss of money, but Mum brought me up to look. You couldn't see it from down in the village, you had to be almost at the top of the hill. It wasn't meant for people down here.

We check the gate and the fence that runs around the foot of the hill, keeps the farmed land out, wild pasture in; we circle with it, spiralling up like the pattern in the crop, like a pilgrimage, denying ourselves the top until we've earned it. Then even Grandad stops for a breath. We can see for miles from up here, rippling, ripening fields with wandering boundaries of dark hedgerows between, farms and houses dotted about where people have rooted. We can see the whole village, the corner that the bypass will shave away; my house. We can see the roadbuilders crawling towards us in the distance, the new bypass a scar bleeding yellow diggers and trucks at its fresh end. We can see the protest camp, a smudge of colour and waving flags.

Up here, a skylark is singing.

On the top of the barrow, under the tree, the people from last night have laid out flowers and a pomegranate. They've tied ribbons to the lowest branches. There's the remains of a fire, which annoys Grandad. He kicks through the flowers, spreading the ashes, making sure nothing smoulders. It feels wrong for him to do that. When the flowers scatter something stirs beneath my feet.

Rabbits have dug a burrow into one side of the mound. I take a look while Grandad checks other things. I always look into rabbit holes, little windows into the ground, and here it's as though, if I could only reach in far enough, I could touch the bones of my buried ancestors. I get on my knees, face right up to the entrance so I can smell the tang of topsoil and the softness of chalk, half expecting to see the fluffy bum of a rabbit inside, half expecting to see the face of a missing child looking back. It's just dark. So I close my eyes, hands flat on the rise of the mound, and let myself feel the land throb up though my veins, my knees sinking deeper than the grass; I can feel the chalk cloaking up around me, a recognition of family, a welcome.

It's bright when I open my eyes again. It makes me squint and it's the squint that lets me spot the shape of something as dirty white-yellow as the dirty white-yellow of weathered chalk. I pick it out of the rabbit hole to look properly. It's a tooth. A human tooth, I'm sure. Big, like an adult's. I think it might be a front tooth because it's flat like a spade at one end, stretched long into its pointed root, like a fang the wrong way around. The rabbits must have dug it out from the centre of the barrow, from the person buried there. The thought of that stings me with an electrical charge where the tooth sits in the palm of my hand. I look for more but there's nothing else. Just one tooth. Just one part of a person from thousands of years ago. Just like a piece of chalk.

※

We move in with Grandad a week later, so they can pull down our house. The protesters sing and chant at the end of our road the whole time we're packing up the truck. We're one of the last families out. It feels like we're being celebrated and mourned at the same time. There are kids in the protest camp and they've all been brought to watch. They're here so often I've gotten to know a few of them. A four-year-old called Elsie always runs to see me when I walk past the camp on my way home from the school bus. She waves at me now, grinning. She has no idea what's going on.

※

I don't sleep very well at Grandad's house. My new room is too small, old and gloomy. When I doze off I feel like the walls are closer. I imagine I can smell the tang of topsoil and the softness of chalk. I imagine there are children in the room with me, in the dark.

There's someone on the hill.

The certainty of it wakes me up.

From the window I can see a light where I know the mound and the tree are; big, bright, flickering. I can hear the repeating thump of music.

Grandad goes straight out in the truck. Mum calls Clive from the farm over the way to meet him, so he won't face them alone. "It's probably kids," she tells me, but her face worries that this isn't like the usual people on the hill.

The thump of music stops.

We wait.

I hold the tooth tight in my hand.

When Mum's phone goes we both jump. Grandad tells Mum it was a group of lads, already scattering when he and Clive got there, trampling in panic through the wheat. They'd set a fire too close to the tree and the tree had caught. Grandad and Clive managed to put it out with irrigation water, running up and down the steep slope of the mound until both could barely stand on their legs anymore. The fire is out but the tree is badly damaged, too old to recover. It'll have to come down before it falls and takes half the mound with its roots, he says. When I cry Mum says, "Better to let the bugs feast on its dead wood, let its stump rot back into the earth it grew from."

The tooth has imprinted its shape into my palm.

※

On the day the tree comes down the village goes silent, like we're muffled. The air around us is thick with the ache of it. It's an amputation. It's part of us hacked away. We feel it more keenly than when the bulldozers razed a quarter of our homes to the ground; demolished the house I grew up in; disfigured the shape of us. The hill is bare, the mound vulnerable. They won't let me go up to see, so I carry the tooth with me everywhere, part of it, part of me, a kernel of a thought, until I finally manage to sneak out.

It takes ages to walk all the way. I have to be careful I'm not seen. Once out of the greenway I keep low through the fields and climb the hill on the steep opposite side to the farm. The top is exposed now so I stay close to the ground, crawl to the barrow, hands and knees and belly right down among the crickets and seeding grasses, until I reach the felled tree. It's lying head down on the side of the mound; a murdered carcass, butchered in the field. The limbs splay unnaturally, a million small, brittle branches, twigs and leaves jumbled and tumbled out as though the fall has uncovered guts and veins and strewn them like offal over the grass. It's a giant; it used to fit in the sky. It's not supposed to be down here. Out of place. Out of element. Left to rot.

I stay with it for longer than I should, to keep it company. The wind pushes deeper and deeper into my ear until it's sore and I can hear the whispers; I can sense the throb of the chalk; I can feel the missing children.

The first thing that goes wrong is the tractor. I wouldn't usually pay much attention, something is always breaking on the farm, but whatever's wrong is going to be expensive to fix and means Grandad can't help Mum with money for us to rent a new house. Mum says it's fine, but I know it isn't.

Now I've been up the hill on my own once, it's like I've broken the taboo. The cows up there are young, there's no bull, there's no reason for me to stay away. But Grandad has always kept that rule absolute, so I go in secret. School has finished for the summer. Mum and Grandad work all day and trust me on my own a lot, so it's easy enough. I climb out of the world and lie on the mound and feel the chalk beneath me. The ancestors are a whisper I sense more than hear. I try to listen. I try to cut out all other sound, the skylarks, the drone of distant traffic, planes passing far overhead. The whispers are telling me something. Sometimes I concentrate so hard I feel like I'm inside the mound with them, in the cold and dark and calm; then I don't have to block the sounds outside because everything goes away apart from the black. And sometimes I feel a small hand slide cautiously onto my bare arm or leg, and it makes me jump back into noise and sunlight. There's never anybody there.

※

A burst water main sends a torrent through the oldest part of the village that the bypass hasn't touched, flooding houses, even washing a car down into the river before it's stopped. Nobody has water for two days; we have to go to the village hall to collect bottles rationed out by the water company.

The tree is now truly dead, leaves browning and skeleton laid out, shock tremors still rippling outward. The rabbit hole where I found the tooth looks bigger; maybe it's not a rabbit hole, maybe it's a fox den. I lie on the mound and talk to my ancestors and they whisper things to me that I can't quite catch. I ask them to help. Sometimes I think they ask what I need help with, and I don't know how to answer. The children whisper too; they get in the way when I'm trying to hear my ancestors. There are more children than I thought, one every generation, going back so far that the oldest ones are very faint and far away; the more recent ones clearer, louder. Most are younger than me; one is only four. They like to play here.

※

There's an incident at the protest camp. The bulldozers that demolished our house are vandalised and security guards from the bypass try and break up the camp in retaliation. Some of the protesters are hurt, others arrested, including four-year-old Elsie's mum. Elsie is taken in by someone else in the camp. Anger at the incident lifts the muffle. We all wait for the next bad thing. People in the village mention that it all began with the tree. Then Grandad finds yellow rust on the wheat, spreading so rapidly it's already halfway across the fields before he sees it. He'll lose part of the crop. I catch him looking up at the hill, at the bare top where the tree used to guard the mound beneath, part of it, grown from it. "It wasn't your fault," I tell him, "It wasn't you who killed it."

"It doesn't matter," he says. "Something was taken, we have to put something back."

I squeeze the tooth in my pocket and the chalk thrums through my arm.

―――

From the top of the hill I can see the bypass crawling closer. The children watch it with me. The skylarks sing. The reason the bypass cuts right into our village is because of the river and the floodplain, something about the geology being a problem elsewhere. They've promised to build new houses on this side, not far from the farm. A whole new estate, they say. But it doesn't work like that;

you can't build something new and think it's the same. The sapling Grandad's planning to plant on the mound won't replace the old tree that grew here, not for centuries. If you're going to give something back, it has to be something that matters the same amount.

The hole in the side of the mound is even bigger now, as though a badger has been excavating, only there's no debris of fresh earth and chalk kicked out. It's almost big enough for a small child to crawl in. Or out. I think about putting the tooth back. I ask the ancestors if it's the tooth or the tree that has made them angry, but I can't hear what they answer. The whispers of the children get in the way, clearer and more insistent. I need to go deeper to hear the ancestors, so I put my whole head into the hole and listen, the tang of topsoil and the softness of chalk; I imagine I see the glint of an eye deep in the cool black, the glance of a pale face. I don't hear anything.

―※―

The protest camp has moved since the incident with the security guards. It's come into the village, set up on the wasteland of scraped earth and concrete that used to be homes and gardens. Used to be my home and garden. It's weird to see it gone. The site looks smaller, re-populated with tents and shelters and coloured flags.

They're pleased to see me in camp, an ally, a victim, one of the locals. I tell them I wanted to come and see, now the house is gone. They're filled with righteous sympathy and make me a cup of tea. Elsie comes to say hello; she's not with the other kids, she's the youngest, she struggles to keep up. Her mum is still in prison with two others, I'm told, held on trumped-up charges and denied bail because of some previous record, but I'm not really listening. Elsie wants to play. Someone has drawn old-fashioned hopscotch squares in chalk on what used to be a garage floor and she wants to show me how to do it. She takes my hand to lead me there, small fingers, insistent. I go with her and watch her jump from one square to another, with no actual hopping or skipping, but I tell her she's doing well and that makes her happy. I keep hold of the tooth in my pocket the whole time.

※

There's a nasty car crash on the road out of the village, the spot where my mum always says, *home again*. One person dies, one person has life-changing injuries. I know both of them.

It's coming closer, the children tell me. "I don't know how to stop it," I say.

You do, they tell me.

※

The camp asks if I'd like to muck in when I visit again, so I help them with the lunchtime meal. Elsie wants to help me in turn, so one of the protesters gives me a bowl of flour and water to give to her to stir. They tell me she likes me. I tell them I don't know how to be with children. They tell me I'm doing OK.

Elsie and I work out which scraped concrete shape was my house. I tell her where the swing was, and Mum's tiny, raised pond that sometimes had frogs in it. I tell her where the garage was and where I fell over and broke my wrist. I walk her through where all the rooms used to be, but she's more interested in throwing stray bits of rubble onto the bare floor to see if they smash up, babbling on, northern vowels strong in her small, high voice.

On the mound on the hill the tree is still dead and the skylarks still sing. If I lie there for long enough the animals stop seeing me and they come out. I have seen a shrew scuttle through the grass; I have seen a black-tipped stoat play along the fallen tree trunk; I have seen a hare nose out from under a gorse bush really close by and lope lazily down the slope. I tell my ancestors about Elsie. I tell them about the new tree we're going to plant. The children listen.

The protest camp want to hold a ceremony for me on the ground where my house used to be. A way to say goodbye, they tell me. "Like a funeral," I say.

It's more like a party: food and music and more people than were ever in my house when it was standing. I don't really like it, but it's for me so I stay. Everyone brings a stone and we place them one by one in a mound in the middle of the concrete that actually used to be the space under the stairs where nobody ever went. Elsie puts a stone on with me, and then she and I sneak away from the people and I tell her stories about the children on the hill while she gets sleepy in my lap.

"Will you come and play with them?" I ask her.

"You too," she says.

"I'll be there," I promise.

When I get back to Grandad's there's an ambulance. Mum is there, not at work where she should be. She shouts at me, demands to know where I've been but doesn't wait for an answer. They think it's a heart attack. She's going with him to the hospital. Clive's wife, Kate, has come to take me to her house to wait. I don't say anything as the paramedics get Grandad into the back of the ambulance full of wires and bags and sterile packaging. He looks small lying down. He always looks big standing up. The tree looked smaller standing up, bigger lying down.

When they've gone Kate asks if I have a key to lock up and when I give it to her she asks what I've done to my hand. It's bleeding. I've been holding the tooth so tight it's bitten in.

Clive and Kate are harder to get away from than Mum

and Grandad. Kate seems to think I need to be kept busy, to keep my mind off things. "There's nothing we can do," she keeps telling me. Mum calls to say she's staying at the hospital. She asks if I'd like to go over; she tells me I should. I can hear what that means. "It's the tree," I say. She tells me to forget about the tree, the tree doesn't matter.

I don't go to the hospital. I pretend I'm going to bed and climb out of Clive and Kate's bathroom window.

The camp doesn't go to sleep; it quietens, but someone is always up. It's the first day of August today, Lammas, and dusk is late, lights only just starting to go on. I tell them I've lost a bracelet, that I think it's here. Elsie is in bed but she hears my voice and comes out to see me in her pyjamas. She wants to help look, even though she's half asleep. I take her hand and we say goodbye to the cairn where my house used to be, to the bones of the village the protestors are squatting in, the bit that has been hacked away, the disfigured shape of us.

Light is fading faster on the hill, the bones of the fallen tree strange-shaped in the gloaming. I still don't know if it's the tree or the tooth, but something taken has to be given back; something that matters the same amount. I put my hands flat on the rising mound on either side of the hole and try to hear the ancestors whisper. It doesn't matter if I can hear the words; I know what they mean.

The hole is big enough for a small child to crawl in.

Or out.

It's a tight squeeze for me.

I have to lie on my belly and crawl on my elbows. The last of the daylight doesn't go far ahead of me. The last glint of an eye shines deep in the cool black and then my body blocks it out. Earth and chalk are close on every side, touching, the tang of topsoil and the softness of chalk. I try not to be scared. I try to feel it throb up through my veins, cloak around me like a hug, like a welcome. I try to feel the chalk in my bones the same as the chalk around me, the same as the chalk in the tooth held tight in my hand. This is why it has to be me; not the kids in the camp, not Elsie with her rounded northern vowels. This is why it had to be all of the missing children, because the chemicals and minerals of the land are built into our bones, the chalk growing us like the old tree growing from our ancestors. The only way to right what was hacked away is to give myself back. The children have told me.

I push forward, dig my elbows into the dirt, into the dark, into the mound, tooth in my forwards hand like a token, like an offering, trying not to be scared but scared enough to be crying, quietly, in case I miss my ancestors when they whisper. The breeze on my legs has gone, the outside has gone, I am entirely within, everything narrowing as I go so I can no longer get up on my elbows, lying flat, dragging forwards with my fingers, pushing with my toes, chalk wrapping me, and then I hear something and I stop. A call. A long way away. I can't tell if it's ahead or behind. It could be Clive come looking. I told Elsie where I was going. I don't know if I'm far enough in, I don't know if he'll be able to see my feet and pull me out, so I go faster, less careful, dragging and pushing, worming deeper, tighter, earth and chalk, a sudden weight on my legs as the hole falls in behind, cold and heavy, hiding me so I can keep going, through the chalk, back to the chalk, bones and chalk and the children waiting. Grit is sharp in my eyes now, the taste of it in my mouth, the mineral of deep-soil, it gets in the way when I breathe, clags in my lungs, stops the air, another sudden cold weight on the whole length of my legs and I can hardly move, and now I panic, I can't see, I can't breathe, the mound pressing me down and I can't go backwards when I try, only forwards, I'm starting to kick now, starting to scrabble, breath snatching but there's no air, only soil, only chalk, and when fingers brush my outstretched hand and I want to scream there's no air to scream with, and for a heartbeat, just one heartbeat, I think it's Clive, I think it's Grandad, but the hand that grips mine is small and insistent, and will not let go.

ACKNOWLEDGEMENTS

I finish this book with sincere and endless thanks to the authors within, who dug deep and wrote with such raw bravery. I consider it a privilege to call myself Editor.

ABOUT THE AUTHORS

Elena Sichrovsky (she/they/it) is a queer disabled writer who explores the intersections of identity, trauma, and grief through the lens of body horror. Their fiction has been published in *Nightmare*, *Radon Journal*, *ergot*, and *Tenebrous Press*, among others. You can read more on elenasichrovsky.com or follow her on X or Bluesky @ESichr.

Nuzo Onoh is a Bram Stoker Lifetime Achievement Award®-winning Nigerian-British writer of chilling, speculative fiction from the African continent. Her latest book, *Where the Dead Brides Gather*, was published by Titan in 2024.

The *Oxford Companion to English Literature* describes **Ramsey Campbell** as "Britain's most respected living horror writer", and the *Washington Post* sums up his work as "one of the monumental accomplishments of modern popular fiction". He has received the Grand Master

Award of the World Horror Convention, the Lifetime Achievement Award of the Horror Writers Association, the Living Legend Award of the International Horror Guild and the World Fantasy Lifetime Achievement Award. In 2015 he was made an Honorary Fellow of Liverpool John Moores University for outstanding services to literature.

Caleb Weinhardt (he/him) is a queer and trans fiction writer. He grew up on a farm in the Midwest, but now lives near several Twilight filming locations with his dog, Winnie, and an apartment full of chicken-related decor. His work appears in or is forthcoming in *Tales to Terrify*, *Broken Antler Magazine Quarterly*, *Chthonic Matter Quarterly*, and others. Find him at calebweinhardt.com.

Premee Mohamed is a Nebula, World Fantasy, Ignyte, and Aurora award-winning Indo-Caribbean scientist and speculative fiction author based in Edmonton, Alberta. She has also been a finalist for the Hugo, Locus, British Fantasy, British Science Fiction, and Crawford awards. In 2024, she was the Edmonton Public Library writer-in-residence. She is the author of the 'Beneath the Rising' series of novels as well as several novellas. Her short fiction has appeared in many venues and she can be found on her website at premeemohamed.com.

Gabino Iglesias is a writer, journalist, professor, and literary critic living in Austin, TX. He is the author of the Bram Stoker® and Shirley Jackson Award-winning *The Devil Takes You Home*, as well as *Zero Saints* and *Coyote Songs*, and *House Of Bone and Rain*. His work has been nominated multiple times for the Bram Stoker Award® and the Locus Award and he won the Wonderland Book Award for Best Novel in 2019. His nonfiction has appeared in the *New York Times*, the *Los Angeles Times*, *Electric Literature*, and *LitReactor*. He also writes regular reviews for the *New York Times*, NPR, *Publishers Weekly*, the *San Francisco Chronicle*, *Criminal Element*, *Mystery Tribune*, *Vol. 1*, the *Los Angeles Review of Books*, and other venues.

Nadia El-Fassi is the pseudonym of Nadia Saward, who is a commissioning editor at Orbit Books UK. Her debut witchy fantasy romance novel was published by Bantam Dell and Del Rey in October 2024.

Hailey Piper is the Bram Stoker Award®-winning author of *Queen of Teeth*, *A Light Most Hateful*, *A Game in Yellow*, and other books of horror. She is also the author of over 100 short stories appearing in *Weird Tales*, *Pseudopod*, *The End of the World As We Know It*, and many other publications. Find her at haileypiper.com.

Usman T. Malik is a Bram Stoker®, British Fantasy, and Crawford Award-winning author of speculative fiction from Pakistan. He has also been nominated for the World

Fantasy Award, the Million Writers Award, and twice nominated for the Nebula. He is the co-founder of The Salam Award for Imaginative Fiction.

Erika T. Wurth's novel *White Horse* is a *New York Times* editors' pick, a *Good Morning America* buzz pick, and an Indie Next, Target Book of the Month, and Book of the Month Pick.

She is both a Kenyon and Sewanee fellow, has published in the *Kenyon Review*, *BuzzFeed*, and the *Writer's Chronicle*, and is a narrative artist for the Meow Wolf Denver installation. She is an urban Native of Apache/Chickasaw/Cherokee descent. She is represented by Rebecca Friedman for books, and Dana Spector for film. She lives in Denver with her partner, stepkids and two incredibly fluffy dogs.

Ai Jiang is a Chinese-Canadian writer, Ignyte, Bram Stoker®, and Nebula Award winner, and Hugo, Astounding, Locus, Aurora, and BFSA Award finalist from Changle, Fujian currently residing in Toronto, Ontario. She is the recipient of Odyssey Workshop's 2022 Fresh Voices Scholarship and the author of *A Palace Near the Wind*, *Linghun*, and *I AM AI*. Find her at aijiang.ca.

Adam Nevill is the British Fantasy Award-winning author of *The Ritual*, *No One Gets Out Alive* (both adapted by

Imaginarium for Netflix) and more. His alien horror novel *All The Fiends Of Hell* was published in 2024. Find out more about Adam's work at adamlgnevill.com.

V. Castro is a two-time Bram Stoker Award®-nominated Mexican-American writer from San Antonio, Texas now residing in the UK. She writes horror, erotic horror, and science fiction. Her books include *Immortal Pleasures*, *The Haunting of Alejandra*, *Alien: Vasquez*, *Mestiza Blood*, *The Queen of the Cicadas*, *Out of Aztlan*, *Las Posadas*, *Rebel Moon* (official Netflix film novelization) and *Goddess of Filth*. Her latest book is *The Pink Agave Motel* from Clash Books. Connect with Violet via Instagram and Twitter @vlatinalondon or vcastrostories.com. She can also be found on Bluesky, Goodreads, and Amazon. TikTok @vcastrobooks Pinterest @V.Castro.

Sarah Deacon has an MA in Creative Writing from Bath Spa University, for which her work was shortlisted for the Janklow & Nesbit Bath Spa Prize. She has won writing competitions for short stories including the Writers' & Artists' Yearbook Short Story Competition in 2012 and the Frome Alan Somerville Prize in 2019, 2020, and 2022. The opening of her novel *Shearwater* was Highly Commended at the Jericho Festival of Writing 2022. Sarah currently works in Bath & North East Somerset Libraries and is working on a novel. *Chalk Bones* is her first published story.

ABOUT THE EDITOR

Gemma Amor is a Bram Stoker® and British Fantasy Award-nominated author, voice actor, and illustrator based in Bristol, UK. She was named one of the 'Writers Shaping Horror's Next Golden Age' by *Esquire*, and features in Ellen Datlow's prestigious *Best Horror of the Year* anthologies, Vol. 15 and 17. She self-published her debut short story collection in 2018 and went on to release award-nominated, multi-adapted novella *Dear Laura* and a number of other books before signing her first traditional publishing deal for her novel *Full Immersion*, published by Angry Robot books in 2022. Her forthcoming folk horror novel *Itch!* is due from Hodder & Stoughton in 2025. Gemma is the co-creator of horror-comedy podcast *Calling Darkness*, starring Kate Siegel, and her stories feature many times on popular horror anthology shows *The NoSleep Podcast*, *Shadows at the Door*, *Creepy*, *PseudoPod* and *The Hidden Frequencies*. She also appears in a number of print anthologies and had made numerous podcast appearances to date. A short film she co-wrote called *Hidden Mother* (2021) was well received at film festivals and she is currently working on her first feature-length screenplay. Gemma illustrates her own works and provides original, hand-painted artwork for book covers on commission. She narrates audiobooks too, including *The Possession Of Natalie Glasgow* by Hailey Piper, in 2020, and *Full Immersion* in 2022. *Roots of My Fears* marks her second occasion as anthology editor.